Black is
Not a Color

ROZSA GASTON

ISBN 13: 978-1490340739
ISBN: 1490340734

Cover image by Razzia
Back cover photograph of Castle of Carcassonne, France
www.rozsagaston.com

CONTENTS

For my father,
Zoltán Iváni Nagy

CHAPTER ONE

ZSOLT THE LIGHTNING BOLT

I had a lot of conflicts and they all conflicted with each other. To begin with I wanted to look like Audrey Hepburn and I didn't. I wanted to act like Jackie Kennedy Onassis, but I couldn't. That's where my father came in. He was a connoisseur of precisely the brands of femininity I wished to cultivate within myself. He hadn't been in the picture for the first nine tenths of my life, but we were now approaching the final one eightieth of his, so I decided to be around, in the event we could do anything for each other. Turns out, we could.

Considering my father's high regard for Jackie Kennedy Onassis, it was clear he had a thing for hoity toity bitches, as did a lot of other men I'd come across. When he started referring to himself as Père Goriot, I realized my father thought I was a hoity toity bitch too. Secretly I'd always wanted to be one, though I was far from the type. It gave me a rush to think my father thought I was.

We sat in the window of *Kleine Konditorei,* a German coffee house on East 86th Street, sipping cappuccinos.

"Black is not a color, Ava," he said, not terribly sternly, wagging his right index finger in mock disapproval, as his eyes swept over my dress.

"What do you mean? It's a really dark color, isn't it?" I looked down at my jersey-knit black dress. I'd chosen it because I'd thought my father would admire me in it. What was his problem? The more I got to know him, the less I understood anything about him.

"Black is not a color, except in one case." He leaned toward me, his index finger now pointed up, about to make a scholarly point.

"What's that?" I asked, curious.

"When it's worn by a blonde." He sat back and laughed, his slanted blue-green eyes dancing.

"Ohhh."

His remark washed over me—spray from a cool fountain. My father was undeniably cool. That fact alone, made up for a lot of other things he wasn't. Moneyed, for example. Statused, for another.

"You mean black is not a color except when it's worn by a blonde?"

"Yes, darling." In his heavy Hungarian accent, it came out as "dah-ling." That accent Zsa Zsa Gabor had wasn't put on. That's the way Hungarians speak English. With flair.

"Well, thank you."

He winked at me over the rim of his coffee cup.

"Didn't someone else say that too? Renoir or someone?" I guessed.

"Manet," he corrected, referring to the French impressionist painter. "But he just said black is not a color."

"But it is, isn't it?"

"Not for him, it wasn't."

"I mean isn't it white, technically, that isn't a color?" It was either white or black, I couldn't remember which. But black was pretty dark not to be a color, no?

"It depends."

"What do you mean?"

"Are you an artist or a scientist?"

"I think you know, Papa." No one had ever mistaken me for a scientist. Especially not my father.

"Okay, artist. For you, black is a color and white is not. But for scientists, white is all colors combined and black is the absence of color."

"But you're an artist, not a scientist!" I exclaimed.

"So was Manet, but we agree—black is not a color."

"Unless worn by a blonde." Smoothing back a flyaway flaxen curl behind my ear, it suddenly occurred to me it was important to wear black well—with intention, with style. I straightened up in my seat. Did I not have a special responsibility to give black its due?

"And you wear it well," my father lifted his coffee cup toward me in salute.

"Ahhh—so you do like my dress." Inside, I exulted. Score one for American style with European flair.

"I like you in it."

"You're not supposed to say that, Papa!" I protested.

"Why not? It's not the dress that counts. It's the woman in it."

My first French boyfriend Jean-Michel had said practically the same thing about a woman in Paris we'd spotted on the street. I'd admired her scarf and he had corrected me, saying it wasn't the scarf that was admirable—it was the way the woman wore it. *Voilà.* How could I argue with my father? He wasn't a New Englander; he was European. Impossible not to notice a woman inside a black dress. Even if it was his daughter.

"So for the sake of speaking scientifically, black is not a color?" I refined.

"Who cares about speaking scientifically?" he parried back.

He had a point. My father didn't and I didn't either. We were all about culture; he had it and I wanted it. It was good to be back in New York where I had my father to translate to me what I'd experienced in Europe.

But my time with Pierre was something I had no intention of sharing with him. It needed a translation, but no way would my father be the one to do so. I thought back to the conversation Pierre and I had had a few days before Christmas, shortly after I'd left Paris the December before. It seemed like a lifetime ago.

"I've got to tell you something, Ava." His voice had been serious, concerned. He always sounded thoughtful, but this time it was as if something heavy weighed him down.

"What is it?"

Was he not going to be able to come as planned? That was too bad, but also not so bad, since I was staying with my mother and sister in my mother's small West Village apartment and I'd been wracking my brain trying to figure out where he could lodge if he visited me in Manhattan.

"My mother."

"Your mother?" I'd never heard Pierre mention his mother before. I knew nothing about her.

"She needs my help right now."

"She—she does?" Was she alone? Not in good health?

"She has a ... special situation."

"Oh." I paused then bit the bullet. "Could you tell me what it is?'

"I—it—"

"I want to know you better, Pierre." And I did. Truly. Whatever he had to tell me, I wouldn't be afraid. Or I might be, a teeny bit, but our relationship had been progressive and genuine. I wanted it to continue that way.

A long pause ensued. It was unlike Pierre, who was usually deliberate but rarely dramatic.

"Tell me what you feel comfortable with," I breathed into his silence. Apparently he had secrets. I did too. If we were going to deepen our friendship, it was time to tell each other a few. Before, rather than after we became more than friends, which would change the landscape altogether.

"She has *la scléroses en plaques*."

"She has what?" I searched my mental French dictionary but came up empty.

"I think you say MS."

"Multiple sclerosis?" Ouch.

"Let me check." He paused a moment. While he searched for the translation, I held my breath. Whatever it was, it would color our picture. One we had barely begun painting in. Was I ready for our pastel-shaded regard for each other to deepen into more vivid tones?

"Yes. That's it." His voice was guarded, careful. As if he was making every attempt to keep the emotion out of it.

"Ohhh." My eyes closed as my head went back, trying to absorb what he was telling me. MS was debilitating. Progressive. But people could live a long time with it; a long, laborious struggle. "Is she—is she?"

"She's doing well. But she needs help."

"I'm sorry. How long has she had it?"

"About fifteen years."

"That's very hard. Does she—does she struggle with it?"

"It struggles with her. But she manages."

"Who looks after her?"

"I live with her, Ava. When I'm not up in Paris at the Institute, "

So Pierre lived with a woman. No wonder he had so much patience.

"Is your father around?"

"They divorced when I was eleven."

We were both products of a broken home, but his story was different. My parents had split up over a language barrier compounded by a mutual disinterest in the realities of daily life. My mother spoke English, my father Hungarian. Neither one of them knew how to pay a utility bill nor cared. They were two peas in a pod, rare birds that had flown in from another planet. They hadn't been able to manage together longer than four years on this one.

"Was that after your mother got MS?"

"Yes."

"That must have been hard," I offered. How very hard I couldn't imagine.

"Let's talk about it when we see each other."

"When will we—see each other?"

"I can't come to New York right now, Ava."

"I understand."

"I'm working on coming late January, early February."

"It's a good time to travel," I neutrally commented. Air fares would be lower than usual.

"I won't say anything more until it looks like it's going to happen."

"Pierre—I know you have commitments."

"Do you also know how much I miss you?"

"I miss you too."

"Then give me some time. When things have—have stabilized I'll come."

"Take all the time you need," I said.

But it wasn't his timetable. It was out of his hands in the same way it was out of my ability to understand.

"I'll come as soon as I can."

"Don't feel that you need to, Pierre," I said, not meaning it.

"Don't tell me what to feel."

His words hit me in the bottom of my stomach. He cared.

"Okay."

"Think of me over Christmas."

"I will. I'll think of your mother too and say a prayer for her. What's her name?"

"Chantal."

"I love that name."

"I'll call you again soon."

I got off the phone, trying not to worry. If it was meant to work out between us it would. If it didn't, I would throw myself into my new life in New York. Whatever happened, I didn't want what had just begun between us to be cut short by circumstance. Yet circumstance counted for much in people's lives: my own parents' and Pierre's mother's, for instance.

"Mister! Mister" my father yelled, snapping his fingers and gesturing at the waiter.

My thoughts returned to the present as I looked at my father, mortified. Why did he always have to do that?

The waiter came over, an annoyed look on his face.

I sank back into my seat. Peeking around, I thanked God there was only a handful of customers in the coffee shop, none of them noticing us.

"Two wine spritzers. Rosé, Ava?"

"Yes." It killed me the way he couldn't say please or even request his order instead of demanding it. He was *ancien regime* all the way. Waiters were waiters. They weren't peers to be addressed politely. I'd been a waitress one too many times not to feel a twinge every time my father addressed one as a servant.

The waiter jerked his head, saying nothing as he took away our coffee cups.

"So who is the greatest American brunette of our age?" my father asked, out of nowhere.

He did that a lot. I didn't mind, because it meant something sparkling was coming along. Conversations with him were like frolicking with dolphins on the surface of a deep sea.

"Um—maybe Elizabeth Taylor?" I suggested, knowing she was on his all-time favorites list.

"No, not an actress. I mean a statesman, a real !#$*()*."

"A real what?" I couldn't understand a large chunk of what my father said, because he roamed over a wide range of European languages to express himself. Aside from French, I'd only had limited exposure to most of them.

"A treasure. A natural treasure."

"A natural treasure? But wouldn't you say Elizabeth Taylor *is* a natural treasure?" I was stuck on Elizabeth because she was one of my father's few American female cultural icons.

"*Nem.* No. *Kutyaszar!*" he spluttered, annoyed at not being understood. His invective was familiar, one that peppered his conversation frequently. It meant "dog shit" in Hungarian.

"Not 'natural.' National!" He spliced the air with his right arm, in an effort to get himself across, barely missing the flower vase at the end of the table.

I lunged forward, grabbing it before he made further contact.

"Oh—national. Hmm. Like Betsy Ross? Or Martha Washington?" I was sure my father had never heard of either of them.

"Noooo. Kennedy."

"Kennedy? You mean John F. Kennedy?" Hadn't "brunette" been in reference to a woman?

"Nooooo." My father looked deeply disgusted. "Jaaackie."

"Jackie O.?" She lived in the neighborhood, right on Fifth Avenue near the Metropolitan Museum, from what I'd heard.

"Yes. Jackie Ohhhhhh...." my father expounded, nodding approvingly. He smacked the table for emphasis.

The waiter looked over, frowning.

I could tell my father wasn't American, as if it wasn't obvious anyway, because when he referred to a Kennedy, the Kennedy he referenced was Jackie—not Jack.

"There is nobody greater than Jacqueline Kennedy. She is America's greatest contribution to the world. She is a true !!#@$*. An exquisite @#$& of a $%*%!"

"So you really like her, huh?" Whatever he was saying, it was deeply complimentary. Any average older American would be going on and on about how great Jack Kennedy was—America's fresh new contribution to the world stage in the second half of the twentieth century. But NOOOO. My father's idea of a great American national treasure was Jackie Kennedy, not Jack.

One of the really great things about Zsolt Fodor was that he didn't talk politics or religion. He talked about culture—movies, literature, style, celebrities, Viennese coffee houses, Paris, London, Berlin, art exhibits, artists, the art of the tango. There was no banality cluttering up the conversation. There wasn't a big contribution to the check at the end of one, either, but my father was a low-budget date, in the European coffee house sense. He could converse for hours over a single drink then continue the conversation for a few more back at his apartment over a good bottle of red wine. My favorite was Bull's Blood, Egri Bikavér in Hungarian, from Hungary's Eger region to the North East of Budapest. Robust yet refined, it was a lot like Zsolt Fodor—a rare bird.

৵

I'D GONE TO the U.N. staffing office within days of my return from Paris right before Christmas, armed with my resume and a copy of my college transcripts. But there, things didn't work out as planned, which had been the way much of my life had already gone. This didn't bother me too much since a few of those plans gone awry had resulted in some pretty spectacular re-routings. Who could argue with going to Yale instead of finishing music college to become a junior high school music teacher? Just the thought of teaching music to kids going through puberty would have destroyed my love of music. And the unexpected opportunity to work as an au pair in Paris had introduced me to a world far more glorious than the one I'd inhabited as a gas station attendant back in West Hartford, Connecticut. Not that there was anything wrong with West Hartford, but it wasn't exactly on the same page as Paris. Or even in the same book.

Some pretty amazing things had happened to me as a result of plans not working out. It almost made up for the fact that my childhood hadn't really worked out either. For that reason, I'd majored in history at Yale. Revisionist history, that is, although the "revisionist" part was written in invisible ink on my particular degree.

But the U.N. staffing office didn't care a fig whether I held a Yale Bachelor Degree or not. The fact that it was only a B.A. meant I was qualified to apply for a General Services job and that was all. Professional positions were reserved for holders of masters degrees or above or candidates appointed by their governments. Preferably the latter.

"If you like, you can take a typing and clerical test and we'll keep your application on file for next year's General Assembly." The Southeast Asian clerk sniffed. She looked pretty un-clerk-like in her Pucci-inspired dress and careful makeup.

"Does it—will it begin next month?" I asked hopefully.

"It begins at the start of September and lasts through the end of the year," the clerk explained.

The U.N. person back at Teddy's Bar in Paris had simply said the U.N. hired for their General Assembly every year. Who knew it began the start of the school year and not the calendar one? When I'd called the U.N.'s general information number from Paris to get more information about the process, no one had picked up, so I'd left a message. No one had gotten back to me so I'd gone ahead and booked my plane ticket anyway. It had been a big decision but something inside had told me my time in Paris was done. I'd broken up with Arnaud, I was fed up with being a pub pianist playing pop standards for drunken ex-pats, and with Christmas looming, I'd wanted to be back in the U.S., close to family.

Most people on the verge of thirty longed to get away from their parents, but that was because they'd spent their childhood with them. I'd long ago escaped from my grandparents who'd raised me to age fifteen. Then I'd spent two years in Maine with my aunt and uncle's family, a less than stellar year at music college, and at age nineteen I'd gone to Paris as an *au pair*. Now it was time to find my parents—for the first time. When I'd called my mother to say I was thinking of coming back for Christmas, she had offered to let me stay with her for the first time. It was a big step for her and for me.

Living abroad for large chunks of my twenties after growing up with my grandparents and aunt and uncle were beginning to point to a large gap in my formation—getting to know my parents. As much as I had liked to think it didn't matter if I got to know them or not, because after all, they hadn't bothered to get to know me as a child, when they'd simply disappeared from my life, I knew now that it did. There was something in my own self-actualization that wasn't going to happen until I got to know the people who created me. My mother's hesitant invitation was better than none, so I accepted, gladly.

"Is there any chance an opening could come up before September?" I asked.

"No," The clerk said succinctly, busying herself with the large stack of papers in front of her.

I stood to the side of the counter and thought for a moment. September was a long way away. But wasn't it said the early bird caught the worm? If mine was one of the first applications on file, wouldn't that count for something? A clear indication of interest? I stepped back to the counter and cleared my throat.

"So what would you like to do?" the clerk looked up, impatient. She looked prosperous, chic. Was this what U.N. general service workers looked like? I was impressed.

"I'll take the tests."

"Fine. Please go sit over there and we'll call you for your typing test first."

I took a seat, summoning up my New England practicality. I was here already so why not take the tests? What did I have to lose, except for my pride? I didn't have a masters degree, and even if I did, I didn't know anyone in government who might wish to appoint me to a professional position at the United Nations.

Glancing around, I surveyed the other job applicants in the room. In the next row, a slender, fashionably outfitted woman leafed through a copy of *Vogue*. About my age, her extremely bright, blonde hair announced a single process dye job. Apparently, she was not from Manhattan, where every woman who attempts to be blonde knows the only way to fake genuine blonde tresses was to color with a combination of high lights and low lights.

Catching me studying her, she looked my way.

"Hi," I said, with an automatically, friendly American response.

"Hi-eee" she said back, drawing it out into a dipthong. Foreign-born.

"Are you waiting to take the typing test?"

She nodded then smiled. "Yes."

"Where are you from?' Now that I was no longer in Paris, I was free to ask nosy, New York-style questions.

"Belgrade."

"Belgrade? You mean Yugoslavia?'

"Yes. Where are you from?"

"Here. I'm American."

"Sanja Darkoviç—" a voice called out.

The blonde woman rose. "Here."

"Come this way, please," the male Filipino clerk said with a gesture.

"Good luck," I called softly.

"Thanks," she breathed back. Her smile was charming, her teeth like perfect white seashells.

I studied the back of her burgundy knit dress as she disappeared behind the double doors of the U.N. staffing office. It fit her like a glove, almost like couture-wear. I wondered if women dressed like that in Belgrade. Ones like her did, apparently.

Forty-five minutes later I was out on the sidewalk, typing and clerical tests completed. As a pianist, my typing skills were pretty good. My fingers flew over the keyboard while my eyes stayed on the text. I'd guess I could tap out a good seventy words per minute. It had gone well, I thought. But now I'd have many months to wait. I could use those typing skills to find a temp job in the meantime.

My younger half sister worked as a temp and made decent money. I decided to ask her for the name of a few agencies and go register with them the following week.

"How was the test?" a voice came out of nowhere. The blonde woman appeared from the doorway I'd just exited. Her winter coat was striped plum and burgundy, with dark purple faux fur cuffs. She was now putting on a pair of even darker purple gloves to match.

"I love that coat," I blurted out, ignoring her question. "You didn't get that in New York, did you?"

It was refreshing to be back in the United States. I could be my enthusiastic, inquisitive self again. No one in Paris would ever ask such a personal question of someone they had just met. What a breath of fresh air it was to be back in the land of freewheeling, informal exchange.

"For sure, you're American," Sanja replied, coming up next to me.

"Why do you say that?"

"How can you love a coat?" She looked at me amusedly, one wondrously plucked and arched eyebrow raised.

"Okay, so I like it. Where'd you get it?" Again, I honed in on my point. I was back in Manhattan, recapturing my New York-style skills of high speed information-gathering.

"I had it made in Belgrade. From my own design."

"I love it, especially the cuffs," I enthused before remembering that coats were not meant to be loved. Spiky, feathery purple plumes were coming out of each cuff. In the brisk, December afternoon, they waved and floated like friendly antennae.

"Again, you 'love it.' Just like an American."

"In what sense?"

"Americans love to love everything."

"So what's wrong with that?" I'd just gotten back from living in Paris, where Parisians loved to disdain everything. It felt good to express enthusiasm again.

She laughed, letting loose a flurry of twittering birds. "Nothing. I love it too. It's a lot better than the way people talk about things where I come from."

"How do they talk about things back in Belgrade?"

"Dark, most of the time. And lots of ironic."

"Irony, you mean."

"Thank you. My English is not so good."

"How long have you been here?"

"About six months."

"Your English is amazing."

"I watched a lot of American T.V. shows when I was young."

"So why'd you leave Belgrade?' The troubles had not yet started, or at least not yet come to the attention of the world press. It would be another six months before Serbia became the official bad guy of the Balkan world.

"Like I said. Dark. Full of ironic."

"So now you're here in New York, where everyone wears black and acts ironic."

She shrugged. "It's not so dark here. It's hard, but not dark. Like the weather."

"You mean New York winters?"

"Yes."

"I know what you're saying. I just got back from Paris where it's much milder, but gray for months on end. I missed the bite here."

"The bite?"

"The ..." I hugged my coat closer and pretended to shiver. "The sharpness of winter here. It's different from Paris winters."

"I know."

"You do?"

"I spent a winter in Paris. It's gray from November to March." She made a face.

"Exactly."

"Do you want to go for a coffee?"

"I'd love to," I began to say, before catching myself. "I mean, sure, why not?'

"No, you don't. You mean you'd love to. Me too. There's a place near here on Second Avenue."

"Okay. You lead the way."

Thus I added the next rare bird to my collection; this one with purple feathers attached. Just like my father, she needed to be sorted and figured out. Who knew? Maybe in the process, I'd sort myself out too.

CHAPTER TWO

PÈRE GORIOT

*A*s rare birds go, my father was the rarest. I found almost everything about the man fascinating except that he had no money. The parts that weren't fascinating were embarrassing, but in a fascinating sort of way. When he spoke, he waved his hands in the air in wild gestures while describing something in not just half-broken, but fully-broken English. After his audience kenned that he was actually saying something interesting, he would take them on a wild ride of trying to decipher what his point was, while dodging a flying arm or elbow.

"Romaine Rolland did not just write *Jean Christophe*. He WAS Jean Christophe. His genius as a writer was in his vision as a !@#$)(*. The @#$%*%& of his work was the @@#$%@* of his _)*(^%$*. He was the ^*%#$* of his age—a direct)&^)(#$%^* to Henry Miller," he'd expound, stray fingers pointing up in the air or closing and opening in utterly non-understandable eloquence.

There were several obstacles to figuring out what my father was saying. Language was one of them, reference points another. I could barely understand what he was saying about ninety per cent of the time since I'd first met him at age sixteen. I chalked this up to my own lack of command of Hungarian—a language indecipherable to any but Hungarians and those who live near them—but it wasn't just that. It was hard to say whether the context or content of what he was on about most of the time was more inscrutable. Either way, I learned a lot once I waded through it all. Romaine Rolland? Jean Christophe? Somehow these names hadn't come up in my intellectual history classes in college. If I'd majored in literature they might have, but everyone there had said comparative lit was one of Yale's toughest undergrad majors. Figuring out quickly that I wasn't among the top tranche of brainiacs amongst my Yale peers, I'd opted for history—Yale College's most popular major, a safe choice.

The first time I accompanied my father to a Hungarian social gathering I realized I was not the only one who didn't understand most of what he was getting at. Most of the Hungarians present didn't appear to either. His fellow countrymen sat spellbound in front of him, absorbing in respectful or perhaps stunned silence, his magnificent oratorio accompanied by the pounding of the table before him, followed by dramatic hand and finger movements.

Afterward, people came up to me and said, "Your father is a great man," shaking their heads admiringly. I didn't dare ask why, because that would indicate a lack of confidence in the greatness of my own father, reflecting poorly upon my paterfamilial pride. I had no idea what was so great about what he was saying, but I did know that the way he made me feel when he was saying it was truly great when it wasn't embarrassing. It was like trying to catch a sunbeam.

"I am Père Goriot. At your service, *mademoiselle*," he greeted me the next time we met at his apartment.

"Hi, Papa. Drop the Père Goriot thing. It doesn't work for you," I snapped, as I pushed past him into his miniscule Upper East Side Yorkville apartment. Something on the stove smelled heavenly. I needed to find out what it was right away.

"Père Goriot has cooked for his daughter," he said, ignoring my request and gesturing to the big, white ceramic pot on his stove. It was one of those economy-sized New York apartments where the entrance opened directly into a pint-sized kitchen, through which the living room then bedroom beyond could be seen. My father was a neatnik, in classic German/Hungarian *hausfrau* style; this was fortunate, since there wasn't much space to hide clutter in his four hundred square feet of Manhattan real estate.

"Umm, is that chicken paprikash?" I asked, lifting the cover and sniffing the delicious aroma of chicken, paprika, onions, and *nockerln* or small Austrian noodles all simmering in cream sauce. This dish was an absolute no-no on my father's diet and an absolute yes-yes to enhance our evening together. I'd come straight from my office temping job and I was hungry. My father enjoyed cooking, although every cream-sauced and pork-larded dish he made had been strictly forbidden by his girlfriend Tünde, who had a long list of foods he wasn't supposed to eat because of his heart condition. My feeling was that taking away his pleasures in life would be like taking away his heart. At least having a heart condition indicated he had one. Plus, I was young and callow, not yet at a stage of life where I worried about food and drink choices, other than whether they were yummy or not.

I inhaled deeply.

"Give me your coat." My father hummed some old country tune I didn't recognize as he reached for a hanger and hung my coat carefully in the closet.

The Père Goriot allusion sort of frosted me. It didn't exactly place me in a favorable light. My father's humor was offbeat, to say the least. But it always had a point. Sometimes the point was sharp, but that was what made it interesting. It was similar to Hungarian cooking versus German or Austrian. All three areas used largely the same ingredients, but Hungarians seasoned with paprika—a sharp, spicy red pepper powder that added piquancy to a dish. Like fairy dust, it covered whatever it touched with a sprinkling of magic.

I pulled out the bottle of Bull's Blood red wine I'd brought and sat at my father's small, round living room table. It was decorated with a red and white Hungarian folk tablecloth one of his old school friends from Transylvania had sent him. After pouring us both a glass, I jotted down "Pear Gorio" in my datebook, to add to my journal. My father's cultural allusions were always worth remembering, even if they sometimes made me uncomfortable. Spending time with him was like getting a masters degree in European cultural history. The challenge was to catch what he was saying, no easy task, especially when he freely roamed amongst Hungarian, German, French, Italian and English idioms. I needed a translator for every other sentence. The obvious one would be my father's girlfriend Tünde, except that I was highly allergic to her.

Then I thought of Sanja. How would my father take to a Serb?

"Papa, I've made a new friend. Someone I met at the U.N. last month."

"Is he rich?"

I laughed. My father had never cared about anyone being rich, for which his older brother and my mother's entire family except for my mother had disdained him. Zsolt Fodor had somehow overlooked the practical side of life in his career as a poet/journalist.

"It's a she. And she's from Serbia."

"Is she beautiful?"

"Yes. Very stylish and very stylized.

"Not a natural beauty?"

"Yes, a natural one. But with lots of bells and whistles.

"Even better."

My father knew all about bells and whistles; his girl-friend Tünde had more than her share. When she applied makeup, which she did in public; an act not favorably regarded in New England where I grew up, it was best not to exchange kisses goodbye, unless ready to be branded with scarlet lipstick marks.

"So bring her over," he continued.

"What do you think about the Serbs?"

We were moving into an era of everyone loving to hate the Serbs. But I was the sort of person who loved to hate what everyone else loved. I sensed my father was like that too. In high school, when everyone was into dropping acid and smoking joints at lunchtime, or at least pretending to, I was in the library reading books by authors whose names I couldn't pronounce. I referred to Nietzsche as Nitch. Schopenhauer was forever associated with shopping in my mind, due to my miserable mispronunciation of his name. No one had minded amongst my Maine public high school peers.

"The Serbs are the gatekeepers to the West."

"They're what?"

"They kept the Turks from invading Austria. Hungary too, for awhile. The Serbs are natural warriors. They're fierce and noble people."

"And what about all their bad press. I mean, aren't they trying to strong arm the rest of Yugoslavia now? Take over?"

"Have you been to Yugoslavia yet?"

"You'd know if I had, Papa." How else would I have gotten there other than with a plane ticket from Zsolt the Lightning Bolt?

"You should go."

"I think it might be too late." Wasn't it breaking up into pieces as we spoke?

"It's the most beautiful country I've ever visited. But it's not really meant to be a country. It's lots of different groups of people that stayed together under Tito. Now he's gone. They're all going to go back to their separate ways, hating each other."

"So you've been there? Have you been to Belgrade?"

"Belgrade—no. But I've been up and down the Coast. Dalmatia, Croatia, Dubrovnik. It's *bella, magnifique.* they have everything—mountains, coastlines, harbors. It's breathtaking, like something out of a Fellini film."

Fellini was my father's favorite director, so that was saying something.

"So it's true the Serbs are trying to take over?"

"Ava, this is politics. The Serbs are the strongest now. Why shouldn't they try to take over? It's what everyone tries to do in a power vacuum. With Tito gone, the whole game collapsed. He was the only one who could keep them all in check."

"But why are the Serbs such bullies?"

"They're all bullies.When the Croats were more powerful, they were the bullies. In the War, the Ustaches killed the Serbs," he said, referring to the Croatian paramilitary fascists who came to power at the end of World War II as Nazi allies and were known to be even crueler. "No one ever forgets anything in those parts. Hungary too. The smaller the land, the bigger the grudges. Especially against neighbors. What's your friend's name?"

"Sanja."

"Saaaanja, Saaanja, Is she a brunette or blonde?"

"She's blonde. With some help, I mean."

"Some help?"

"Never mind. She's blonde, with brown eyes. Very funny. Very smart."

"When is she coming?"

"I'll invite her next time I come."

"Good." My father got up and went into the kitchen. A minute later, he was back with the pot of chicken paprikash.

Meanwhile, I picked up the heel of bread on the cutting board and cut off a few pieces. Dinner in my father's home was European-style. When I'd first begun visiting him in my mid-twenties after moving to New York, I'd been nervous, tentative. Still shaking off the manacles of sugar and junk food addiction, I'd shunned food-focused social events. Any occasion that involved sitting around eating for hours at a time had been a problem for me. If cookies, cakes or pastries were on the table, my focus would stray from company and conversation and anchor itself on the forbidden fruit in sight; except that it wasn't fruit I lusted after. One bite of something sweet, and I wouldn't be able to stop. It had been like trying to stay straight in a crack den. I couldn't handle, it, so I'd stayed away altogether.

But over time I'd begun to feel safe at my father's table. He wasn't a real sweets-oriented host. Instead, we'd sit before a wooden cutting board of slim Hungarian Pick salami, slicing thin pieces off as words such as *Schadenfreude, Weltanschuung, Weltschmerz* and existentialism all sluiced through the air from my father's mouth on their way to a mysterious destination I couldn't follow but wanted to. I'd cock my ears, shake awake the dull, slumbering halls of my intellect, and lean toward him, trying to grasp what he was saying. Frequently it didn't work, but when it did, I'd learn something new every time.

For example, who knew Père Goriot was a man somewhat like my father and I was a daughter somewhat like one of Père Goriot's? This bit of puzzling information sent me straight to a bookstore where I picked up Balzac's nineteenth-century novel and found out that Père Goriot had been the poor, devoted father of two upwardly mobile daughters who, as a result of his efforts to provide them with a good upbringing, had married well and were now embarrassed to be seen with him. The analogy almost fit, except the part about providing. My father had not been a provider. Being embarrassed to be seen with him? Frankly true, much of the time.

While we discoursed, or rather, my father held forth in his thick Hungarian accent, the tone was decidedly savory—not sweet. There was no junk food in my father's home, neither in his conversation nor in his kitchen. As a result, I didn't have to wrestle with the usual demons in his presence. There were other demons I wrestled with instead, the raging Scylla and Charybdis of bitterness and anger with him for not having been around for the entire first sixteen years of my life. Now that he was around, conversation was rich, but practical questions of financial support and responsibility were out. They simply didn't exist in my father's universe and it hadn't occurred to him to think about how I'd managed all those years and was managing now. It was up to me to figure out what to do when the bitter bile of anger rose in my throat, which it did frequently in the presence of both my parents.

Recently it had begun to occur to me that it was time to simply get over myself'; a thought that twisted my knickers into an even more uncomfortable fit, since it was clear that those responsible for past wrongs weren't in a position to rectify them anytime soon. So what was I going to do about it?

I took a deep sip of Bull's Blood and focused on my father's zesty conversation.

"Do you know why Jean Giono was a genius?"

I shook my head. Who was Jean Giono? And why hadn't my Yale degree in European intellectual history prepared me to even get through a single conversation with my own father, European culture buff extraordinaire?

A few hours later, I was somewhat enlightened that Jean Giono was a writer who had represented *la France profonde,* the sensibility of the French countryside; that deep, sacred place residing in the bosom of most French people, one that Marcel Pagnol depicted in his *Jean de Florette* and *Manon de la Source* films.

As I left my father's apartment that evening, conflicting thoughts chased each other around in the boiling cauldron of my mixed emotions toward the man who had sired me. One rode the crest of the wave, above all: it was good to have a man cook for me. Hanging tight to that sole, warming thought, I released all the others into the cold, biting air of the New York winter. My father knew how to warm my stomach; perhaps one day he would also warm my heart.

If only I would let him.

∽

"I'M COMING. TWO weeks from next Friday."

"You are? That's great!" I cried into the phone, almost beside myself. Pierre was coming to New York. My prayers had been answered.

"I— uh—listen, Ava, you may not have enough room for me at your place,"

"I uh—it's sort of small," and occupied by my mother and sister—not really my place at all, I thought.

"Not to worry. I've got a place to stay."

"Where's that?" *Thank you, God.*

If there was any way I could keep Pierre away from my mother's apartment, I would. She wasn't the social hostess type and I'd just managed to get myself over the threshold of her home. I wasn't taking any chances on inviting friends when I wasn't sure how firm my own invitation was.

"The mathematics house for visiting mathematicians at the CUNY. I stayed there the last time I was in New York."

The way he said "the CUNY" made my heart race.

"Where is it?"

"On the Upper West Side. Avenue Amsterdam and Ninety Fourth."

"Great!" That was ninety blocks north of my mother's place, but still on the West Side. The big challenge in Manhattan wasn't getting uptown from downtown or vice versa. It was getting across town from West Side to East Side and back. "How long are you staying?"

"I give a talk at the CUNY on Monday. I'll go back the following Friday."

"How did you arrange this?" I asked.

"The stars arranged it, " he joked.

"What's the topic of your talk?" I asked, hoping it might be something I could vaguely understand.

"I will talk about my progress toward defining M."

"You'll tell me in person and I won't understand."

"That's alright. Most of my colleagues in the field don't understand either."

"Do you understand?"

"Not yet. Not entirely."

"Is it exciting?" I caught myself, remembering the French understanding of the verb "to excite." It wasn't the same as the English one.

"Is coming to New York to visit you exciting? Yes. Yes it is."

Was Pierre using that word in the French sense? My tingling insides told me he was. Was I ready? I wasn't sure.

"You're coming to New York to present a paper," I corrected him. It was almost too scary to think he was coming just to see me.

"I'm coming to New York to see you, but IHES"—*Institut des Hautes Etudes Scientifiques*, where he was a professor—"is paying my way since I'm giving the talk for them."

"You're so clever, Pierre." I loved saying his name. It rolled off my tongue then disappeared in the clouds somewhere.

"I'm not so clever, Ava. I'm a simple man," he replied.

"You're not simple, but I have a confession."

"What's that?"

"I like simple." And I did.

I was the kind of person who went for simple things. I liked simple decisions, simple plans and simple, heartfelt, non-ambiguous statements, especially when they came from men. Otherwise, they were too confusing. I knew only too well after my time with Arnaud.

"You think you like simple, but you don't," Pierre replied calmly.

"What do you mean, I don't? I do. I really do," I protested.

"Then let me tell you simply, I can't afford to have this conversation on the phone, so let's have it in person next week."

I laughed straight from my belly. Actually it was my heart. It was so good to joke with Pierre. I couldn't joke with my father like that because we so rarely understood each other. Literally. Hungarian and English were worlds apart. I found him fascinating and often amusing but frequently, by the time I figured out what he had said, the moment for a spontaneous belly laugh had passed.

"You're right, Pierre. What's your flight number?"

"Never mind all that. What time do I pick you up Friday evening and where?"

I loved my French friend's style. He made everything easy, uncomplicated and simple. I hoped things would stay that way between us in the event we became more than friends.

"I'll meet you somewhere." No way was I taking a chance on introducing Pierre to my mother on her territory. Her place was off limits, a private haven for her alone. My mother was a classic New Yorker—she didn't have people over. What was the point of all those restaurants, bars and coffee shops anyway, if not to provide New Yorkers with a place to get together outside of their tiny apartments?

"Ohhh?"

"I'll explain it to you when I see you," I hedged.

"I hope it doesn't involve a man," he said.

"It doesn't." I laughed. But alarm bells were ringing. Did I need to explain why I couldn't receive him at my mother's place? It wouldn't be understandable to him. It hadn't been understandable to me either until my mother had actually offered to let me stay with her. It was best if I just stopped at that and thanked God that she had offered me shelter. It was a step in the right direction, an improvement over my childhood with my grandparents when she simply hadn't been around to offer anything.

"Where am I taking you for dinner then?" His adjustment was swift, gallant.

"I want to take you somewhere first for a drink," I said.

"Where's that?"

"The Royalton. It's near Times Square." I'd been there a few times with Sanja. It was a super sleek sort of place in a downtown, *belle monde* sort of way. Sanja and I had been intrigued to go ever since we'd noticed some superstar model-types striding up the steps of what looked like a bank vault or a Yale secret society. Enormous, chrome doors had swung inward and swallowed them up. Instantly, we wanted to know what was inside, so one evening on our way back from Campbell Apartment in Grand Central Station, another hot Manhattan watering spot, Sanja approached one of the black Nehru-jacket clad doormen and told him in charmingly accented English she would like to go in. She didn't *ask* the bouncer to let her in. She told him she would *like* to go in. That was the way to get things done in New York. Sanja somehow knew this better than I.

The blond bouncer gave us a onceover, swung one of the double doors open and *voilà*—we were amongst the *gliterati*.

Inside, huge coffee table books of Georgia O'Keefe's artwork lay slung around on low Moroccan-style lounge tables. Enormous goldfish bowls, with one lonely goldfish in each, lined the corridor in spotlit grottoes. The first time I'd used the restroom there, I hadn't been able to figure out how to turn on the faucets over the sink. A six foot tall Czech model-type (a dime a dozen at the Royalton) finally showed me how. I could hardly wait to take Pierre there and watch his eyes grow big.

Another point in common Pierre and I had was that we both retained the ability to be wowed by big, beautiful cities. He was from the provinces, I was from New England. We had both gone gaga over Paris. I couldn't wait to be his tour guide in Manhattan.

I even knew where the secret VIP room was at the Royalton. It wasn't actually roped off or available only to VIPs—it was just a tiny, fully upholstered cocktail lounge which most guests didn't know about, right off the main entrance on the other side of the grand hallway. Inside the tiny, secret cocktail lounge, I felt as if I was inside a cockle shell.

Perhaps Pierre was right. Maybe I didn't just like simple. I liked simply fabulous too. I was a Manhattan girl, after all, and before that I'd been a Parisian one. I'd begun as a Connecticut then Maine one, but it wasn't where one started off that mattered, it was where one ended up.

"The Royalton it is. For Royal Princess Ava."

I giggled. "See you next week, Pierre."

"See you Friday, *ma chère.*"

I put down the phone, shivering at his endearment. "My dear ..." It was a little thing, yet Pierre was an intentional sort of man. Unlike Arnaud, he wasn't a man to toss around compliments without meaning them. I burned to think of the merry game Arnaud had led me on. Yet I'd been a willing accomplice. Perhaps he hadn't realized that glib words without weight ended up bouncing off a duck's back. That's what they'd done after awhile, after it had become impossible to ignore his long absences, attention to other women, and complete lack of attentiveness to anything I really cared about or stood for; to begin with, my own songs.

I leafed through my music notebook and stared at the last song I'd written before leaving Paris. I was good at romances with exit plans. I'd never had any without. Pierre wasn't the kind of man with whom I usually got involved. He'd been perfect as a friend—measured, serious, unhurried. Was I ready for him to become something more? And what if there was no exit plan this time?

∽

"NOT JUST SHOES. Another thing, too."

"What? What's that?" I was all ears to hear what Sanja had to tell me about the two most important measuring points of a man's attractiveness. We were at Fino's on Second Avenue, around the corner from the U.N. staffing office, which we'd just come from, after taking French competency tests. French was the second working language of the United Nations. It was a good thing both Sanja and I had spent time in Paris. There was a reason the term *lingua franca* had been coined—French was still the international language of diplomacy.

"Guess," she teased, her smile belying the maddening mystery of her conversation.

"His—umm—eyes?" I ventured.

"No."

"His—uh—build?" I tried again, visualizing broad shoulders, slim hips, a foxy French-style boxer's build.

"No. Something that shows how he takes care of himself."

Whatever it was she was talking about, I wouldn't waste time referencing American men with my guess. Sanja was from Yugoslavia, a Balkan culture, where men probably paid more attention to how they looked, than men did in the United States.

"Um—you mean his aftershave?" The scent of Jean-Michel's Denim Aftershave wafted into my mind. My memory had been kind to my first French boyfriend. He'd been one of the strongest members of my supporting cast. Not a co-star. But tops in the B ranks.

"No. I'm talking about a body part, not something you put on."

I could think of a body part that might strongly sway me one way or another with a man, but Sanja was talking about something apparent upon first impression.

"Okay, hair," I finally guessed.

"No." She looked at me teasingly. Another one of those Sanja looks, the kind that made our friendship so much fun. Hanging around with her was like having ten close friends. She was all of them and more.

"What then?"

"Hands."

"Hands?"

"Yes. The way he takes care of his hands." She arched her brows. "You know?"

"You mean if his nails are dirty or something?"

"Yes. And his cuticles. Are they nice?"

I wracked my brain, searching for the well-kept cuticles section. It came up empty.

"Are his hands smooth?" she continued. "Does he have calluses? Is the skin rough? Does he buff his nails?"

"You mean not just cut them?" Was Sanja suddenly a professional manicurist?

"Yes. He should buff them too," she insisted.

Not wanting to sound doltish, I tried to recall what buffing meant. Was it something supposed to be done on a regular basis? Had I ever done it before?

"I see your point," I bluffed. "Do Yugoslavian men buff their nails?"

"Some of them. I wouldn't talk to any man who didn't." She shrugged dismissively. "Would you?" She looked me over critically.

"I—uh—have you ever dated an American guy?" I volleyed back, not wanting to lie but neither to give the wrong answer.

"Well—I had a friend when I came here last year." She took a sip of her spritzer, hiding her face.

"A friend?" The term could cover a lot of territory.

"He liked me." She looked away.

"Did you uh—were you ...?" I fished.

She looked back coyly.

"No."

I'd spent enough time with Sanja to know I'd never know the real answer to my question..

"Hands not up to snuff?"

"He was moving back to Mini-sota," she explained, carefully mispronouncing the name of the state.

"Not up to snuff, I'll bet," I said, thinking kindly of Minnesotan men I'd met, some of them handsome, none of them with buffed nails.

"The shoes were not good," she expounded.

"Did he wear hiking boots or something?"

"The clodhoppers."

"Ewww." I smoothed my eyebrows to hide the flush caused by the thought of the clogs I'd clomped around in during my first months in Paris at age nineteen. I'd paired them with Oshkosh overalls, a perfectly mainstream combination back in the State of Maine from whence I'd come. It was a miracle I hadn't been ticketed by the police for violating French fashion standards.

He didn't polish them," she elaborated.

"I don't think too many men polish their hiking boots," I volunteered, trying to defend my fellow countrymen.

She sniffed. "They weren't good."

"Do Yugoslavian men polish their shoes?"

"Always. The ones who are not peasants, I mean."

"I see. Well, we don't have the peasant system here. But we do have a lot of casual dressers."

"What about those men? Those ones are dressed very well. Look at his shoes over there." She nodded to indicate the woven leather loafers on the man at the next table.

I leaned toward her. "He's probably gay," I stage-whispered.

"He's what?" Sanja leaned in, almost bumping my head in the middle of the table.

"He might be gay," I quietly repeated.

"You mean he is fag?"

I hadn't heard that term in awhile.

"Don't use that word. It's not what we say here. We say 'gay.'

"You mean *pédé?*" she asked, using the French slang for *pédéraste,* a term from Greek meaning 'love of boys.' No wonder I was so drawn to Sanja. She was like a Frenchwoman except that she wanted to be friends with me, unlike any Frenchwoman I'd ever met.

"Yes. Like *pédé,*" I agreed, hoping she wouldn't drop the F-word again, at least not in public.

"There must be other ones who like women who dress well."

"There are, but they're all downtown. In finance," I explained.

"You mean the bankers?"

"Yes."

"But they're so boring." She rolled her eyes. "I prefer the artists. Where are the well-dressed artists?"

It was my turn to roll the eyes.

"That's sort of a contradiction in terms here," I said, thinking of my father's recollections of the café life he'd led in Budapest in his poet/journalist days. That had worked there then. But we were here now.

"You mean there are none?

"I mean there are some, but they're mostly *pédé*. It covers both categories—men in the arts and well-dressed men. Except for the bankers."

"So how do we find the bankers?"

"We go downtown."

"I don't go downtown." She shook her head slightly, giving her blonde curls enough of a shake to capture the attention of the man in Italian loafers at the next table. Perhaps my assessment had been wrong.

I sighed. Sanja already sounded like a Manhattan woman after only six months in New York, ruling out entire neighborhoods she didn't care to visit as well as types of men she didn't care to get to know.

"Why not?"

"Because it's too far away. And ugly."

"I know what you mean, but you've got to go where the action is, if you catch my drift."

She looked at me blankly.

"Where did you go to meet men in Belgrade?" I asked, curious.

"I didn't go anywhere," she sniffed. "They came to me."

"Nice." I could believe it. Sanja was not only beautiful and stylish, she had mystique in spades. From what I'd seen, men everywhere went crazy over that feminine mix, even in New York.

"It wasn't nice. I didn't like most of them so I went to Paris."

"I love Paris."

"Me too."

We both sat back and gave Paris its due.

"Why didn't you stay?' I finally asked.

"I couldn't. Why didn't you?"

"I couldn't either." I took a sip of my drink to maintain my mystery while I checked to see if the well-shod man at the next table was still looking our way. He was.

"So how do we meet the bankers?" she circled back to our main point.

"We research some places, then go downtown."

"We are not the supermodels," she stated accurately. For a foreigner, she had an acute insight into the way Manhattan worked.

"I have a theory about that," I told her.

"What is it?" she perked up, looking like the non-supermodel, super-attractive woman she was.

"Men don't actually ask out supermodels. They ask out women who look like they might date them."

"Like us?"

"Like us."

"I will only date the ones with good hands."

"And good shoes," I reminded her.

"Yes. They must have good shoes." Her severe expression told me this was a non-negotiable.

We looked around for more men wearing good shoes. Conversation with Sanja was like being on a conveyor belt that seemed to circle round but usually spiraled up to new and sparkling places I'd never been before. Only a month after meeting her, I was already addicted. I could only imagine what she might do to a man.

⌒◯

"SOUTHEAST," I HISSED.

Sanja looked in the opposite direction I'd referenced, due west. She didn't appear to be good at cardinal direction, but that was okay because she was so good at being fun, fashionable and fabulous. A sense of direction would have been overkill.

"The other way. By the door," I coached her.

A good looking banker type had walked in to the Gold Street bar we were sitting in. Sanja had picked me up after work, something we'd begun a Friday at five habit of, after I'd explained to her that my temp job was in the heart of the downtown financial district where most of the well-manicured, well-shod bankers were to be found. In an effort to meet the kind of man she hadn't yet uptown, she'd heroically conquered her resolve not to venture downtown.

"Ohh. Yesss," she sighed, her assessment matching mine.

"Nice, right? Probably Italian-American."

"He's not a Jewish?"

"Shhh. Maybe he is. A Jewish-Italian?" I whispered as I eyeballed the piece of confection heading toward us at the bar.

His eyes were lively, dancing behind Dutch architect glasses. Whatever he was, he didn't look like he was back office. A trader or private banker, I'd guess. We stared as the possibly Jewish private banker took the bar stool one down from where Sanja sat. We'd find out in a second, depending on what he ordered. He said something to the bartender we couldn't make out. In a minute the bartender set him up with a soft drink.

Sanja and I looked at each other and nodded. Nonalcoholic drink? Jewish, alright.

Was he waiting for someone to join him? A woman? I looked around. Wall Street was supposedly now being infiltrated by female professionals. Many of my female classmates from Yale had done a stint down here. One would never know it by looking around the bar. There were no women at all present, other than ourselves. I guessed they were at Century 21, shopping.

I looked at Sanja to see what she'd do next. She narrowed her eyes at me then picked up her purse and put it down on the empty barstool between the man and herself.

The man looked around.

"Oh excuse me, are you expecting someone?" she chirped in her adorably accented voice.

"No. Go ahead," the man replied, gesturing to the stool where Sanja's *faux* Louis Vuitton bag now lay. I say it was a *faux* because Sanja had mentioned buying it in Chinatown. If it had been a real Louis Vuitton she wouldn't have mentioned it, just quietly carted it around like some sort of religious relic attached to her body while women around her tried to determine if it was the real thing or not.

The man stared at Sanja's face for a second before looking away, which told me she had given him one of her beguiling "I'm from another world" smiles. In a minute, she began to rummage through her handbag for some-thing to capture his attention.

When he glanced at her again to see what she was doing, I saw he had a well-defined, curved mouth. He was looking more Jewish by the minute. Sucking in my breath, I rued the ridiculous, impractical principle that opposites attract. What was the point when opposites didn't under-stand each other? And never would.

"Where's my pen?" she muttered, almost under her breath, except not quite. She mentioned "pen" several more times, alerting the man to what the problem was.

"Need a pen? Here. Take mine," he offered gallantly. Reaching inside his suit jacket, he brought out a pen and handed it to her.

"Thank you. I don't know what happened to mine," she fluttered, pulling out a notebook and writing some-thing down in it. Probably her phone number, except that wasn't Sanja's style. She drew people to her; she didn't go to them. Nice.

The man went back to his soft drink then shot a look at the football game on the TV screen in the corner. That wouldn't do at all, per Sanja. She hated TV, especially sports events on TV. She didn't even know what American football was; one of the many reasons I found her so enchanting.

"Your pen is very nice," she whispered.

Why was she whispering? How was he supposed to hear her?

The man swung his head around and leaned toward her.

"What did you say?" His eyebrows went up as he asked, as if he were a scientist examining a creature from outer space. His eyes were warm and engaged; the eyes of a man examining an unfamiliar, attractive woman. Bingo.

"Your pen is so nice. Are you American?" Sanja asked.

There was a connection there. I knew, because I'd spent time in Paris. When Americans used pens, they whipped out disposable plastic ones; pens they'd picked up somewhere and would eventually lose somewhere else, but who cared? They'd just find another one. Pens were a dime a dozen, right?

Not everywhere, they weren't. In Paris, the kind of pen a person used indicated something about that person's status. As a result, anyone who was anyone, including those who were trying to be someone, which meant almost everyone, used elegant, expensive pens. If that was the case in Paris, I'd bet it might also be the case in Belgrade. In any case, Sanja's eyes were now lighting up.

"Uh—yes I am. You're not, are you?"

"No." Sanja laughed, a low, burbling warble that anchored the man's gaze, football game forgotten. "Is that a Cross pen?'

"Why? Are you planning to keep it?"

My friend giggled then recovered.

"No, my own one at home is much nicer."

Touché, Sanja. Why couldn't I ever think as fast on my feet? I made a note to use a line like that in the near future.

The man smiled.

"Mine too. I just take this one to work with me so if someone like you takes it, it doesn't matter so much."

"Shouldn't you get back to your game?" she asked, indicating the TV in the corner.

A deft play. First capture his attention then bat him away. Entice, then deny. Why couldn't I play games like that?

"I'm watching my game. Am I winning yet?" he asked, smiling wickedly.

It was the first time I'd seen Sanja blush. The blush ran up her face and hid somewhere beneath her unnaturally blonde hair, probably feeding into the wit section of her brain. It was too good to be true. The Jewish banker delivered all he'd promised with his entry. After meeting exclusively boring, culturally illiterate men in finance on our several previous downtown jaunts, we'd finally hit a homerun.

"You're doing well, but you've got strong competition," Sanja volleyed back.

"So I see."

I wondered when she'd ask him the question many women in New York would like to ask in the interest of saving time when meeting a possibly interesting stranger: "Do you have a lot of money?" But of course she wouldn't ask that. The cufflinks on his white shirt, along with his Cross pen already gave us our answer. Or did it? This was New York, after all. Anyone could pretend to be anything to anyone. That was the whole fun of being here. When my father went out with his Hungarian girlfriend, they looked like a million dollars. For an excursion to McDonalds for the hot apple pies he loved, he'd dress as if he was heading off on a mission of state.

Sanja giggled again. The murmur of it was pleasant, as if a faucet was on with cool, fresh water coming out.

"Are you—uh—a poet?" she asked, surprisingly.

My father was a poet. He'd never owned a Cross pen.

"A poet?" The man looked truly surprised. "No."

"What are you then?"

"I'm a kindergarten teacher," he deadpanned.

She laughed, her eyes resting on his black, onyx cufflinks.

"What about you?" he followed up.

"I'm a trapeze artist."

Brava, Sanja. Once again, I admired my friend's deft, feline mind.

"It's not even six o'clock and you're a trapeze artist?"

"Yes."

"You don't look like one."

"What do I look like then?"

He sat back on his barstool and studied her. It gave me an opportunity to study him—a very fine moment. The curve of his mouth almost broke my heart. I'd known a Jewish guy with a mouth like that once and he had.

Finally, he cleared his throat. "You look like a ..."

We both cocked our ears, hanging on whatever was to come.

"Like a what?" she asked, a tad vulnerably.

"Like a fireman."

"A what?" Sanja looked puzzled.

"A fireman."

Laughter seeped out of me on all sides. This was good. Very, very good. Too funny, really, and entirely unexpected on a late Friday afternoon. It boded well for the weekend.

"What do you mean, a fireman? I do not put out fires," she huffed indignantly then turned to me. "What does he mean?"

"You should ask him," I replied, batting the ball back into her court.

"Oh." Her face fell. She'd been teasing him too, but this round hadn't gone the way she'd hoped. "What do you mean?"

"I mean you look like you work with fires," he responded smoothly.

"Do you know what kind of poet you look like?"

"Umm... No. Should I?"

"A very bad one."

"That's it. I *am* a very bad poet. How did you know?"

At that, all three of us burst into laughter. Sanja made it through her slightly awkward moment and emerged victorious, or at least gleeful. The man looked interested and I was safely on the other side of Sanja, congratulating myself that my days of dating Jewish guys were over, along with my junk food addiction ones. They didn't belong in the same category except that they were both bad for me. Fortunately, Victor barely noticed me in Sanja's company, with her full-blown Serbian, falsely-blonde-but-even-better-than-real-blonde glory. I watched as she smoothed down her clingy black dress as Victor drank her in. Black had definitely sprung into color. This was going to be good.

AND SO SANJA began to see Victor. Men didn't get much more alpha male than Victor Friedman did and that was what Sanja appeared to like, to my great surprise. Forget the good shoes, buffed nails and well dressed artist-types. The kind of nails Victor majored in was the tough-as-nails variety. He was also smart as a whip; a quality that made Sanja's heart beat fast. I couldn't help but admire him from the far side of Sanja. The whole combination of dark, smart, Jewishy guy with lithe, sparkling, blonde non-Jewish girl was a dangerously attractive one, usually destined to end in disaster. Thank God Pierre was coming soon.

CHAPTER THREE

FRENCHMAN IN NEW YORK

"*W*hat it comes down to is that less is more," Pierre explained, trying to describe the concept he was presenting in his paper in a few days' time. His angular face came closer to mine as he brought his fingers to meet his thumb to form a small oval in a gesture I rarely saw American men make.

"I like that." It was antithetical to the way I lived, but intrinsically it appealed to me. Pierre personified it. No one else in the Royalton's lobby lounge appeared to buy into the concept of less is more, but that was part of why we were there.

"In what way do you understand it?" A scholar down to his fingertips, he insisted on examples from me to support my statement.

"As a pianist." I was no longer making a living playing piano, but I was still a pianist. Some nights I played pieces in my dreams—Bach inventions more often than anything else. I'd be well rested the mornings after I had such dreams.

"Give me an example."

"Erik Satie—*Gymnopédie.*"

"Good. What about fashion?"

Pierre asking about fashion? Apparently, the two women draped on the slouchy couch across from us, both wearing textured tights, were exerting a subconscious influence.

"Where do I begin? Coco Chanel?" *My grandmother?* "Whoever it was who said whatever you've put on to go out, take a look in the mirror before leaving and remove one item."

He chuckled. "I never heard that before, but it sounds right."

"You never heard that before because you're not a *fashionista.*" What would Sanja say about his shoes? I made a note to suggest getting side by side shoe shines when I took him for a tour of Grand Central station. Meanwhile I took in the shoes on the slouchier of the two women across from us. They were sky-high platform shoes that didn't appear to have any heels. The entire back section of the shoe she was now dangling from her foot was missing. How did she manage to walk any-where in New York? I guessed she hid a pair of flat bal-let slip-ons in the cavernous, buttery leather bag on the floor next to the couch, standing sentry to announce, " Just look at how big and beautiful I am. I belong to a very important person. Have you checked out her shoes yet?"

"Literature?"

"Some say the highest literary form is poetry because every word captures meaning distilled down to its essence."

I could hardly wait to ask my father what he thought about 'less is more.' I guessed he'd give me his thoughts on the more side rather than the less, being a larger than life sort of person. But the 'more' side of my family hadn't provided for me—the 'less' side had. My grandfather's kind, modest face came to me. He hadn't been a big conversationalist. He'd usually just say a few words such as "How're you set, Ava?" then pull out his checkbook to write a check for a modest, but respectable New England amount. My father had never done anything like that at all. He'd been too busy talking about Fellini, fashion, and the latest exhibit at the Met. Spending time with him was always an education but he hadn't provided me with the formal one I needed to earn a living. *Not his fault, Ava. History's. Really?* I wasn't sure.

"I think you're right. Art?"

"Art. Where do I begin?" I thought of the myriad examples of 'less is more' in art I admired. "There's so many examples ..."

Pierre nodded thoughtfully as my mind feasted on painting after painting I'd admired at the Metropolitan Museum. So many of the ones that had drawn me in had been examples of 'less is more.' I couldn't decide. Yet as I mused, a particular painting took shape in my mind—one I'd seen there in the Met's lesser known modern wing.

"Let's go to the Met. I'll show you one of my favorite paintings. It's all about less is more."

"The Met?"

"The Metropolitan Museum," I explained.

"*Bon.* Let's do it. When?" he asked.

As always, he was a man with a plan. It made my heart hum. But something held me back from bursting into full song. It wasn't Pierre, it was me. I hated it when men used that lame line on women. Yet here I was, secretly using it on the man sitting across from me. Would I get over it? Did one get over such feelings? I wanted to, very much. Yet.

"Tomorrow evening?" I asked.

"The museum is open in the evening?' He looked surprised.

"This is America, Pierre. Everything is open all the time. Plus it's New York. The City that never sleeps."

"When do you rest, then?"

"Good question. It's hard to rest here, so you have to work at it. I think I rest when my mind rests on something beautiful."

"Like the painting you want to show me at the Met?"

"Like everything about the Met. It's absolutely one of the most beautiful places in the world." Considering Pierre and I had met in Paris, that was saying a lot. Thankfully, Pierre was not a Parisian, so I wasn't stepping on his toes with such a sweeping statement.

"And what about 'less is more' appeals to you here?" He stretched out his arm and gestured at the large room around us.

On our low Casbah-style couch, we were positioned exactly as I'd envisioned the week before, except that Pierre wasn't a metrosexual by any standard and I wasn't a six foot tall blonde Amazon fashion model. We were well matched, both at the top of the B list.

I looked around, at a loss to find something that exemplified 'less is more.' Perhaps the one lonely goldfish in the bowl a few yards away? The Royalton's other patrons didn't really look like 'less is more' types. They looked like they were trying a teensy bit too hard. As did I. I shifted to conceal the glittery silver metal pattern shot through my black stockings. Would Pierre find it flashy? Who cared what he found it? I was undeniably flashy and he was here now because he liked me.

"Nothing comes to mind," I admitted honestly.

"See, Ava? You are not a lover of simple things. You love luxury too."

"I love simply luxurious things." Did that count?

"I see that."

"And you. A simple man, right?"

At that he smiled; his gesture simplicity itself.

Was that Pierre or was that just men in general? Not the gay ones, of course.

"But you know your tastes?"

"I know them." At that, he put one warm, bony hand on mine and folded his fingers around to my palm.

I could hardly breathe. Finally I whispered, "And what do you think? Do I?"

He shook his head gently, wryly. "You're moving in that direction."

"But not there yet?"

"Not there yet." He leaned in closer. "Which is what I like."

"What? That I'm immature?" My hackles prickled. I was inarguably immature, but that was for me to know and others not to notice, right? Plus, we were in Manhattan. Who would notice around here anyway? The entire island of Manhattan was filled with adult children, Peter Pan types. It was a well known fact.

"No. That you're dynamic, not static."

"You mean I'm on my way somewhere?" I asked. Hadn't he just described the American condition?

"Yes."

"So are a lot of people in New York."

"I like that."

"It's sort of the norm around here, actually."

"It's a great feature."

"One Europeans lack?" Oops, now I'd done it. Unwittingly I'd insulted him, something I was good at in my thoughtless, immature way.

He smiled faintly with an I-can-take-it-on-the-chin kind of smile. "One Europeans are not encouraged in," he replied.

"But Europeans know how to live," I argued on his behalf.

"So they do. But it's nice to be going places too," he pointed out.

"What about both?" I suggested.

"What do you think I'm doing here?"

"Studying M?"

"Studying you."

"Let's go study art at the Met." I took back my hand, although I didn't want to, but I needed to move, to go somewhere as opposed to be somewhere as he'd just described. Perhaps I was more American than I thought.

"Yes."

Our heads came so close together that our noses bumped.

I laughed but Pierre didn't. He was too busy kissing me.

❡

A BOY AND two girls lounged on a mountainside; a cloud-less, deep blue sky overhead. One girl lay on her side sleeping on the ground. The second stretched her arms over her head, her manner completely unselfconscious, as if no one was there. The boy looked out at the viewer, a scowl on his face, while a second male figure stood in the distant background looking to one side. Behind him, a male and female mountain climber ascended a ridge. None of the six figures looked at each other. A large expanse of empty space separated the three in the foreground from the three in the background.

"Less is more?" Pierre asked, studying the enormous canvas before us.

"Less is more," I agreed.

"Balthus," he breathed out.

"Yes," I exhaled too.

Mystical Balthus; a man who would have made me nervous at a cocktail party, but what a painter. Drinking in his iconic 1937 painting, "The Mountain," I relaxed into its mysterious atmosphere.

Pierre walked from one side of the large canvas to the other. Then back again, his hands clasped behind his back. Was M's definition in the painting somewhere, waiting to be discovered?

I paced in the opposite direction, my hands clasped identically behind my back. Counting seven steps across, I guessed the painting was about twelve feet wide: enormous and spacious.

"What do you see?" Pierre finally broke our companionable silence.

"I see a space for me in there." I pointed to the canvas.

"What else?"

I see sex, I didn't say. This wasn't the moment, plus it was too obvious, given this was a Balthus. Even the cats in Balthus paintings looked sexy. A waiting, still languor infused all of the twentieth century French painter's work.

"I see a big, empty sky."

"And?"

"Golden light on the craggy sides of the mountains in the background."

"I see you," Pierre remarked quietly.

"You do?"

"The girl stretching her arms. It's you."

"It is?" I took a closer look. He had a point. Her curly, prone to frizz hair looked a lot like mine had before I'd discovered hair-straightening products. "I— uh—hadn't noticed that."

"It was for me to notice."

I turned and smiled at him. Then he took my hand, just as he'd done at the Royalton the evening before. Nothing more, nothing less. His hand simply closed over mine and we stood there while the unassailable fact washed over me that Pierre Castel liked me. A lot.

His wasn't a lust-driven, hormonal desire, but a measured, mature one that didn't need to move in any particular direction. It just hung about, clear, calm and intentional.

We stood staring at the canvas, as our souls stared into each other. Something big could happen between us if I let it. Would I?

I was my father's daughter. My father was all action, flailing arm gestures, urgent expressiveness, readiness to pounce. My mother was the sphinx in the equation; quiet, self-possessed, kabuki-like in her inscrutableness. Unquestionably, she possessed something I never would—stillness. I could be still for awhile. Several seconds at least. Cats disliked me. But Pierre struck me as a dog person. I didn't want to hurt him, in the event things didn't work out. A cat person I could hurt. A dog person? Never. But that was what I needed. A dog person to offer devotion, faithfulness, and love. For the first time, it occurred to me not to worry overmuch about what I could offer in return. Perhaps whatever it was I offered had already been accepted, so why worry about it?

After a moment, we resumed our stroll through the museum. In another fifteen minutes we stumbled upon the American Wing.

"*Magnifique*," Pierre exclaimed, gesturing at the gorgeous expanse of Louis Comfort Tiffany stained glass and statuary dotting the sumptuous main hall of the American Wing.

He was right. It was glorious. Against the far wall, made entirely of glass, Manhattan's Central Park lay dark and slumbering, also glorious in its vast, inky blackness.

"I love the scent in here," I said, inhaling deeply. The air of the Metropolitan Museum was fragrant, dewy and warm. It was the perfect place to spend a wintry evening.

Pierre walked about, inspecting each statue, reading the inscriptions carefully. "These are all created by American artists?" he asked.

"Yes."

"Your country is filled with talent."

"It's a big place. But yes, it is," I said, thinking of the Georgia O'Keefe books we'd leafed through the evening before. Big, gorgeous flowers had beckoned us toward their secrets. I didn't care how fed up O'Keefe had been with the critics harping on how her flower canvases had been all about sex. They were right. O'Keefe's flowers were fabulously sexy, each in a different way.

And now the American wing of the Met fanned my native pride. It was my favorite room in the entire museum. The playfulness and liveliness of its statuary combined with the brilliant colors of Louis Comfort Tiffany's stained glass windows to flame my senses.

"What do you want to show me?" Pierre asked, slipping his hand again into mine. It was warm, medium-large, and lean. A very French male sort of hand. I was beginning to warm up to it, something I'd never done before. For the first time, I found the dimmer on my libido's on/off switch and dialed it up. Heretofore there had been two possibilities for when it came to men: attracted or not. Suddenly, what had not been, was. Astonishing.

"I want to show you the mezzanine."

"Why?"

"Live music—that's why."

"Why else?"

"Drinks, nibbles, conversation,"

"Let's go."

As we approached the exit of the large main room of the American Wing, my eye caught the figure of a man coming toward us. A woman with a cane walked slowly by his side. She looked frail, fragile. As I watched, the bounce of his gait seemed familiar. Then the curve of his strong, well-defined mouth came into focus.

Victor.

His face was turned toward the woman next to him. He looked as if he could barely slow down enough to match her pace.

"What? What is it?" Pierre asked, noticing my gaze.

"I—know that woman," I whispered, although it was the man I knew.

Pierre remained silent, waiting to see what I would do.

I stole another glance. The woman didn't look much older than Victor, but her hair was gray, with streaks of white in it. Deep furrows running from either side of her nose down to her mouth told me she knew pain. As she passed, she caught my gaze.

I quickly looked away, but not before I'd seen the yellowed whites off her gray-blue eyes. Their shape was beautiful, but they too held pain in them.

Fortunately, Victor didn't see me. It was better that way. As they passed, I heard him speak to her.

"Did I give you the..." the rest of his sentence was indistinguishable.

"I've got it in my bag," she replied, along with something more. I glanced at her again. His mother? Impossible. She was too young. I watched as Victor fished in her bag for something as they continued the murmured conversation of a long-married couple.

In a minute we were on the mezzanine, seated at a bistro table overlooking the Great Hall of the front entrance to the museum. Gorgeous, enormous white and yellow flowers sprang from huge urns. They looked like luscious nymphs. I thought of Sanja, of Georgia O'Keefe's flowers, of the way Pierre made me feel, then of the woman next to Victor in the hallway to the American Wing. Lovely, luscious, healthful life was so fleeting. I squeezed the moment and prayed it wouldn't break into pieces anytime soon. Then I looked down and realized I was squeezing Pierre's hand too. The dimmer on my light switch had dialed up yet another degree. Something was changing between us because I was letting it. I was letting go.

"So who was that woman back there?" he asked.

"That was—I—I don't actually know who she was, but I've seen her before," I fibbed. "Do you think that was her husband?" I blurted out before collecting myself.

"Of course."

"What makes you say that?"

"Did you see the way he reached into her purse? No one would do that unless he was her husband or child.

"Do you think he was her son?" I asked hopefully.

"Impossible. That woman wasn't old. She just has a condition."

"Like what?" I asked.

"Like what my mother has," Pierre said quietly.

"It is? You mean MS?"

"Yes."

Speechless, I shook my head. It was unfathomable to think what life did to some people. Which was better? To be a bastard and leave your wife with multiple sclerosis? Or to stay and be a bastard by cheating on her? But the 'bastard' appellation tasted unnatural in my mouth. Better not to judge a man until walking a mile in his shoes. And I never would walk in Victor's polished, Italian loafers. Wearing shoes like that couldn't make up for the journey he was on. Should I say anything to Sanja? Maybe, maybe not. One thing was sure. I felt bad for both the woman Victor was with and for Victor. Also for Sanja. Maybe she already knew. She wasn't born yesterday the way I was.

Unable to think of a single thing to say, I picked up my menu.

The mood was suddenly thick, as if a heavy fog had set in. In an attempt to dispel it, I ordered a flowery, light Sauvignon Blanc. Pierre did too, along with some Moroccan appetizers when the waiter appeared.

"Tell me about your mother," I finally said.

"My mother?"

"Yes. Chantal."

"She is beautiful."

"Do you look like her?"

"What do you think?"

I had to smile. I hoped not. Pierre's asymmetrical, lean face worked for a man, but wouldn't win prizes on a woman.

"I inherited the worst features of both my mother and father."

The laughter began deep in my stomach and rumbled all the way out. It was such an incredibly non-New York, modest thing to say.

"Who did you get the good character from then?"

"Thank you." He smiled. "My mother. I think."

"What's she like?"

She's—hmmm—how do I say? Loving, playful, but— ummm—*exigeant.*"

There was that French word again—"*exigeant.*" It meant exacting, demanding or not easily satisfied. *"Exigeant"* perfectly described the Parisian character. But Pierre was from the provinces. Maybe it was just a French characteristic.

"In what way?"

"She cares about things being right. Being just so."

She sounded like my grandmother, who had raised me.

"For example?" I would turn the tables on Pierre and force him to support his statements the way he did with me.

He sat back for a moment and closed his eyes, passing a hand over his face. When he removed it, he was smiling, lost in thought.

"She thinks there's a right way to do most things. And she wants things done well, with forethought and attention to detail."

There was that sense of intention again, the one I liked so much. So Pierre had gotten that from his mother. It certainly beat being a will o' the wisp in my book. With two parents like crickets singing in the meadow, I was a big fan of the ant team, who took in the harvest.

"Example?"

"The way she keeps the car."

"Neat?"

"Impeccable. She wants it neat as a pin or she refuses to get in."

"What do you mean?"

"I mean my father was fond of reading newspapers, journals, scholarly magazines and leaving them in the car. They'd come in plastic wrappers and he'd open them in the car and toss the wrappers on the floor of the passenger seat. Along with his work gloves, gardening tools, rope, old empty bottles and other stuff."

"Uh-oh. How did she handle it?"

"She would stand outside the car door and refuse to get in until he'd cleaned up the space around her seat."

"And would he?"

"Yes. Reluctantly, but he'd do it."

"Did he ever think to do it before she approached the car?"

He shook his head. "I don't think so. My father was a bit absentminded."

"And your mother is very much present."

"She notices details."

"And you notice her noticing details, right?"

"Yes." He looked wistful.

"You're her champion, aren't you?'

"Yes." He hung his head, his mouth curving into a private smile.

I could see him as a five-year old, rushing around like John the Baptist, straightening up and trying to make everything neat and perfect to clear the way for his mother's entrance.

"Are you close to your father?"

"Yes. In another sort of way." He looked out over the balcony railing, taking in the crowd in the Great Hall below. That was a good thing, different from my own story. I hadn't felt much of anything for either my mother or my father. My feelings had run to my grandparents, who'd been in the picture. There had just been a big black canvas where the picture of my parents should have gone. After I met them, the picture hadn't gotten much clearer. My mother's picture was still largely blank, and my father's was now filled in with vivid, abstract colors in an inscrutable pattern.

"Did you see much of him after they divorced?" I prodded gently.

"I see him, because he lives in the same town."

"Where's that?"

"Carcassonne. In the Southwest of France."

"Did he remarry?"

"No. He has a companion." He used the French word "*copine*," meaning female companion, so I knew his father hadn't switched teams, so to speak.

"Did your mother?"

"No."

"Who do you think was at fault?" I asked, quizzically.

"I think they both wanted to understand each other but the gap was too wide."

"That's what happened to my parents too," I confessed.

"Really? Was your mother *exigeant* as well?"

It was all I could do not to snort with laughter. "No! It was my grandmother who was." Exacting didn't even come close to describing the rigor of her personality, no words really could. "My mother rebelled against her *bon famille* background," I said, using the French term for 'good family. ' "She wanted adventure, something exotic. My father was it."

"Tell me about your father," Pierre said, his eyes lighting up.

"He's Hungarian. A refugee from the '56 Uprising."

"The spring that never came to Hungary?" Pierre asked, referring to the Prague Spring of 1968, an eight month period of political liberalization that was subsequently squashed by Czechoslovakia's Communist regime until the Iron Curtain finally fell in 1990.

"Yes. Or perhaps it's come now, but its early days yet."

"So your father was a political refugee?"

"Yes. He'd been a journalist in Budapest. Not a good profession to be in at the time. The Communists had sent him out to the countryside to deliver milk, so he wouldn't write anymore nasty articles about them. It wasn't his thing, so he walked across the border one night into Austria then found his way here."

"How did he end up in America?"

"He wanted to go to Paris, where his best friend had fled with his wife. But his older brother was here already, had diplomatic connections from working at the Hungarian Embassy in Austria, and sponsored him to come to the U.S."

"How has it gone for him here?"

"Not so easy."

"Was he able to practice his profession?"

"No. He's a poet as well as a journalist. He had a lot to say but my mother couldn't really understand most of it."

"And you?"

"I try." It occurred to me that I really did try. As opposed to the first few years after meeting him when I hadn't tried at all, just squirmed with mortification when he said something wildly dramatic that no one could make out. It might have had something to do with being at the impossible age of adolescence when the simple existence of parents was cause for embarrassment. Certainly it had plenty to do with my New England upbringing where men do not typically behave like drama queens when making a point.

"Hungarian is pretty impenetrable."

"Yes." Simply put, the Hungarian language related to nothing else, except perhaps Finnish.

"How long were your parents married?"

"Four years."

"It must have been hard on them both."

"My mother was caught up with his story at first. Then the reality of what she'd gotten into hit her and she wasn't prepared for the long haul."

"And did you go with your mother then?"

"No. I wasn't with them when they split up. I lived with my grandparents—my mother's parents."

"Why was that?"

"My mother had gone back to grad school when she realized my father wasn't able to support them. She got her masters in library sciences."

"Then what?"

"Then she met her second husband. And told my father it was over."

"That must have been rough on your father."

"It must have been rough on yours as well."

"How did you know it was my mother who ended things?"

"I'm the woman who would have stood outside the car door waiting until the passenger side was in order before I got in." In some ways I was like my grandmother. It had taken her leaving the planet for me to admit this to myself, but now that she was safely past the gates of immortality and no longer able to nag me, I could come clean and own up. I was a chip off the old block.

"Ah. The exacting Ava."

"I don't mean to be."

"But you are. Was it your father or your mother who gave you that gift?"

"My father." He was neat as a pin. His apartment in the German-Hungarian neighborhood of Yorkville, was spare but always clean. Unlike my mother's tchotchke-filled, dust-covered place in the West Village.

"The Hungarian."

"Yes." My grandmother had hated my father's guts, referring to him as "that dirty Bohemian." It would have surprised her to know how similar their rigorous house-keeping standards were.

"That's not surprising. He also gave you your musical talent, no?"

"He played violin in a gypsy band back in Budapest when he was a student."

"And do you like math?"

I cocked my head at him. "Yes. I love it. But I was always slow to grasp new concepts. Why do you ask?"

Pierre laughed. "You like math because it's in your blood. From your father's side."

"I've heard that." Hungary was known for producing top mathematicians.

"And music." He looked at me interestedly. "What songs are you writing these days?"

I shrugged. "None, Pierre. Now is not the moment."

"You decide when the moment is, Ava."

"No one decides the moment the muse hits." I looked out over the Great Hall, weighing the choices I'd made. No longer a performing artist with sand beneath my feet, I was now temping at a downtown financial firm while I waited out a response to my application to the U.N. General Assembly beginning in September. It was decent money, dull, plodding work on my way to yet another dull, safe civil service job with benefits. It wasn't bad to be able to enjoy some security. It kept me a safe distance from ending up like my parents, just barely hanging on.

"Wisely stated."

"And sadly true."

"Not too sad, Ava. Not for you."

"Why do you say that?"

"Because you are not a person born to sadness. You're born to joy, dancing, life, song."

"Another Hungarian attribute?" He might have a point. I didn't inhabit the serious, nose-to-the grindstone persona well. If I had, I would have followed the advice of my New England uncle and gone to law school, but I'd kicked up my heels and left academia behind in a cloud of dust the day I'd gotten my B.A. All I could think about was living a little. Joy, dancing, life, song. And men. Finding out about men.

I glanced at Pierre. Nobody would call him handsome. He was manly, genuine, smart, but with simple tastes—an anchor.

And as far as simplicity was concerned, I liked it to a point. Looking around me, I breathed in the elegance and opulence of the Met's mezzanine. To a very small degree, perhaps the point of a pin. Then I liked razzle dazzle. *Get real, Ava.*

"As long as I can pay my bills," I said crisply, picking up my glass and taking a sip as the floral bouquet suffused my senses. There was a part of me that danced the gay, mad dance my parents had in their brief time together. But that part would be firmly attached to reality. I had no intention of allowing my balloon to just float off into space somewhere.

Just as I had set my thoughts into cool, structured New England order, the string quartet in the center of the mezzanine struck up the throbbing, vibrant tones of Liszt's "Hungarian Rhapsody."

"Do you think someone is trying to tell you something, Ava?" Pierre's mouth curled up into an amused smile.

"What do you mean?" I asked, trying to keep my prim, proper New England thoughts in line. Meanwhile, the untrammeled wildness of Liszt's rhapsody washed over me, mocking my efforts to sit out on the sidelines. Who was I kidding? I had my mother's taste for adventure, my father's Hungarian blood. I was doomed.

"No one escapes being their parents' children. Not even those who didn't know their parents."

The thought of being anything like either of my parents revolted me. And yet, and yet...

I stared suspiciously at Pierre. Where was he going with this?

"Don't think about other people's tastes. Your mother's. Your father's. Think about your own. What's hitting you most now, at this moment?"

"The music. The scent of this wine," I replied. *Your eyes,* I didn't say. I liked the way they remained fixed on mine, unlike Arnaud's, which had constantly darted in other directions—especially when other attractive women had been present.

"Anything else?"

"You always ask that, Pierre." Our friendship hadn't missed a beat despite the months apart. We had picked up just where we'd left off, probing and carefully handling what we found in the other. We were like two archeologists digging into each other's psyches.

"The fact that I can enjoy both in a safe way."

"Why is that?"

"Because I have a job that isn't going to vanish and I'm enjoying all this with you."

"I'm not going to vanish either."

"Are you sure?" He'd taken me by surprise.

"I'm sure." His words weren't leading somewhere. They had just delivered a statement of commitment.

I weighed his words. He was right. He'd curled around my thoughts again and again ever since I'd returned to New York. And every time he'd twined around one of them, I'd taken pleasure and comfort in his memory. The fact that he was in my life to any extent allowed me to more deeply sniff the wine's bouquet and more fully enjoy the wildness of the Hungarian rhapsody now playing. He was the French equivalent of New England soil harboring and fertilizing the wild Bohemian flower I was. I'd found my way to him and he'd found his way to me. Now what was I going to do about it?

"Want to come up?"

I stared at him a long moment. The cab had pulled up in front of the CUNY Mathematics House on Amsterdam at West Ninety Fourth Street.

"I do, but I won't," I finally breathed out. Something restrained me from falling down lust's rabbit hole.

My high regard for our friendship, coupled with my low regard for my own ability to handle the wild ride lovers took each other on counseled me to proceed cautiously. I'd take that ride with my first two French boyfriends. But it had been easy. We hadn't had a meeting of minds and I hadn't been in love. It was so much easier to enjoy the ride on a speeding train when there was nothing to lose in case of derailment.

With Pierre it was different. There was something at stake. I wouldn't risk losing it until I knew my own feelings for him better.

"I told you you're not a simple woman," he said, taking a strand of my hair and tucking it behind my ear.

"Okay. You're right. I'd like to say yes, but I'm saying no."

He nodded then got out of the cab. As he shut the door, I kissed the tips of my index and middle fingers and held them out to him.

When the cab drove off, I didn't look back. I needed to think, to breathe, to let the fine diamond flecks of all we'd shared that evening sprinkle over me and settle into my soul. Surprised by my own lack of rashness, I leaned back into the seat, giving the driver my mother's West Village address. Something about Pierre was having its effect on me. Whatever it was, it was something I was unfamiliar with. Perhaps it was his self-control.

"Entice then deny" was my last thought before embracing my pillow that night. Had my actions been to protect us both or a feint? Even I myself didn't know.

CHAPTER FOUR

NEW YORK
THROUGH NEW EYES

The next day we went ice skating in Central Park. It was the beginning of February, but a mild winter. The sky was gloriously blue and the temperature low enough to rouge our cheeks but not so biting as to chill our fun.

"Are you free tonight?" Pierre asked.

"I could be," I said, gliding beside him, feeling like a fourteen year old except when he looked at me. Then I felt older. "Why?"

"They're having a super boat party at the place where I'm staying."

"What's a super boat party?"

"I don't know. I thought I'd ask you."

I thought. There were banners all over Times Square, decorating every sports bar saying "Go Giants." I was an American sports luddite, but even I knew that America's biggest football game was due to take place that evening.

"Do you mean a football game on TV sort of party?"

"Yes. I think that's it!" His eyes twinkled.

I groaned. No one hated football more than me. Except Sanja. Idly, I wondered what she had been up to that weekend.

"It's the Super Bowl," I corrected with a sigh.

"The Super Bowl? What's that?"

"It's like the European Cup—for Americans."

"*Genial!*" Pierre sang out. The word in French meant "great" or "awesome."

Finally, I'd found a character flaw in Pierre. It was reassuring. I guessed I could suffer through an evening of football with him and his math colleagues. But would they be all men?

"Will there be any women?"

"What do you mean? You're coming, right?"

"Yes, but any others?"

"The head of the department is bringing his wife."

I imagined someone in her fifties, perhaps from the Midwest.

"Are there any female math professors or students at the house?"

"None that I've met, but some of the boys will bring their girlfriends or wives. They said they'll make chili!" he rang out, enthusiastically.

"Wow, that's thrilling. And drink beer, I'll bet."

"Yes. Beer! They told me to get some. And chips. What are chips?'

Beer was my least favorite beverage of all times, except on a hot summer day. I couldn't think of too many activities less appealing than drinking beverages that produced bad breath and burps, and eating junk food while watching enormous men on TV try to hurt each other.

"Chips are potato chips—trashy American food that makes you fat."

"Great! I'm too skinny anyways. And you don't have to worry about that," Pierre said, joyfully putting a hand on either side of my waist and giving me a gentle squeeze.

I supposed I could make an exception to my usual high quality, small portion food choices for a single evening on Pierre's behalf. His enthusiasm was infectious. I wanted him to have a good time for the few days he was here.

"Okay, what time is this party?"

"Around six. They said the keek-off is at six-thirty."

"The kick-off, Pierre. When the guy kicks the ball to start the game."

Even Pierre's French accent couldn't glamorize the dull reality of spending an entire evening watching men watch bigger men assault each other around on TV while trying to move a small ball down a field.

"I'll go home first then come to your place."

"I'll come with you," Pierre offered.

"You don't have to do that."

"I want to."

I panicked. This was the tricky part. I wanted to present Pierre with a full package. But it wasn't just up to me. There was someone else involved too—my mother. She wasn't the meet and greet type, especially not in her own home. Miraculous enough that she was offering me a place to stay until I got on my feet and got my own, I didn't want to blow my welcome by inviting over friends. My mother's apartment had not been my childhood home, and I didn't kid myself that it was my home as an adult. It was her territory and hers alone and I knew her well enough to know she didn't like having visitors. Many New Yorkers didn't. My father was the exception.

"My mom's down with the flu right now, so I can't really bring you over," I improvised.

"That's okay." Pierre nodded understandingly. "But I need your help getting the chips and beer."

I didn't think you could buy beer on Sunday in New York. But there was some in my mother's refrigerator, put there by me for refreshment after long, sweaty runs along the West Side Highway. Another reason I needed to go downtown.

"I know. Let's go downtown together and you can wait for me downstairs for a minute while I change," I proposed. Never complain, never explain. It had served me as a motto in Paris and I prayed it would serve me back in New York.

"Sure," he agreed.

By four, the day had chilled so we got off the ice and headed toward Times Square. Pierre was the only person I'd ever met in my life who found riding the New York City subway enjoyable.

"This noise is amazing!" he yelled over the din of a train rushing past us as we stood on the platform waiting for our express train to take us one stop from 59th to 42nd street.

"Yes, if that's the word for it."

"The metro here is more exciting than in Paris."

"Is that what you call it?" I asked, careful not to bump into the large, sullen person standing directly in the middle of the doorway of the car we were getting into.

God forbid we might jostle the wrong person. Then Pierre could see how exciting it was to get knifed by someone off their medications. Or pushed off the plat-form onto the tracks. It had almost happened to me once. I didn't like to think about it.

"There are so many types of people," he pointed out. "It's so interesting to see all these different faces."

"Don't stare at anyone," I breathed to him in a whisper as I grabbed a strap. "You don't want anyone to ask what you're staring at."

"Oh sure, I know," he said as his eyes swept the car.

A South Indian family with a child in a stroller wrapped in plastic sat in one corner next to two studiedly hipster-types probably on their way to Williamsburg in Brooklyn. To our other side sat a large, black mother with three-inch long tiger-striped fingernails and enormous thick gold hoop earrings. Her children misbehaved around her, deftly avoiding her swats. A group of teenage girls sat opposite them, fiddling with their portable music players which leaked out loud rap music. It was all very familial in a tough, urban sort of way.

Then there was Pierre, all starry-eyed and enthusias-tic, drinking it all in, loving every detail. He was the only person in the subway car smiling, until I began to smile myself, catching his fever.

ALMOST OUT THE door after changing, grabbing the six-pack of Czech beer from the fridge and waving goodbye to my mother, the phone rang. I was next to it so I picked up.

"It's me. Are you alone?"

Sanja sounded upset.

"Yes. No. I mean—wait a minute, I'm going to the other room." I moved into the back bedroom where I slept.

"What's up?"

"I— I—something happened."

"What do you mean? Are you okay?" Something happened in New York could mean something serious. This was a country after all where people could buy guns and did.

"Yes. I'm fine. It's just that Victor—uh—cancelled our date tonight."

"That happens sometimes, no?" I asked, trying to keep my voice even. I hadn't decided what I was going to do about what I'd seen at the Met. I needed time before I just blurted out information that could hurt my friend.

"Yes, but usually it's because of work. It's Sunday, not a workday. I don't know what the reason is this time."

"But—so what? I mean, you see him all the time anyway, don't you?"

"I—uh—see him all the time during the week. Not so much on the weekends."

"Not so much or not at all?" I wouldn't say anything. I'd just lead her to the conclusion any sane, Manhattan female would arrive at who was dating a guy who disappeared on weekends.

"Not—well—not on weekends at all. Really."

'"Does that tell you anything?"

"I— uh—suggested we get together this weekend. Saturday night. But he said he had to take his daughter to some father-daughter dance. So I suggested Sunday."

"But he didn't, right?"

"No. So I asked him why he never saw me on weekends and he said that wasn't true."

"Except that it is."

"Well, no—he said Sunday then. But he just called and left a message saying something came up and he's got to cancel."

"So you'll see him tomorrow or Tuesday, right?"

"I don't feel good about this. Something is strange here."

You're not kidding, girlfriend. "I—uh—don't jump to conclusions, but I know what you mean."

"I just feel like something is off and if I ask him about it, it might end things between us."

"Are you ready for that?"

The sound of my friend's muffled sniffles on the other end gave me my answer.

"Can you come to a party with us tonight?" I prayed Pierre wouldn't mind. She needed distraction and a party would be just the thing.

"A party?"

"Yes. With some mathematicians."

"What does that mean?"

"It means a bunch of men."

"I hate men." Her voice broke up again.

"That's okay, there's something at the party you'll hate even more."

"What's that?"

"Football. On TV."

""Horrible. Forget it."

"Sanja, I really need you to come."

"Why?"

"Because I hate football too. And it will be almost all men there so I'll have no one to talk to unless you come."

A moment of silence ensued. I decided to make an executive decision.

"Okay, that's it. You're coming. It's at six at 237 West Ninety Fourth Street, corner of Amsterdam."

"But I hate football."

"See you there."

"I can't come."

"You have to. I need you." I needed her to meet Pierre so she could tell me what she thought afterward—even though I already knew what I thought. It was a go. All systems clear.

"You do?"

"Yes."

"What should I wear?"

"Football fashion," I giggled then hung up.

It would be fun to see what my fashionable Serbian friend's interpretation of that directive might be. In a minute, I was on the sidewalk where I joined Pierre. Hand in hand, we strolled west to look for a place to buy chips before we headed back uptown.

"Who's that ?" Sanja whispered, as we stood in the doorway of the kitchen.

"I don't know," I answered, as I eyeballed the dark, copper-skinned beauty stirring something in an enormous pot on the stove.

Tentatively, we tiptoed into the kitchen, pretending to need something in the refrigerator. Pierre and his colleagues were in the darkened living room, watching the game. Seconds after kickoff we already couldn't follow what was happening on the TV screen, so Sanja and I had slipped away to explore the rest of the large, high-ceilinged guest apartment for the City University of New York's graduate math department.

The young woman at the stove turned her head and smiled at us. "Hi," she said with an unidentifiable accent.

The steam and heat in the kitchen had made her skin all dewy and flushed, increasing her sexiness exponentially straight into the stratosphere. Did the guys in the other room have any idea she was in here?

"Hi. I'm Ava, Pierre's friend."

"Sabina."

Even her name was smoking red hot.

"Are you—uh—a mathematician?"

Her smile grew wider, until a dimple appeared at one corner of her Snow White rosebud red mouth.

"No. I'm Tucker's wife."

My jaw dropped. Tucker Corbin was the Chair of the CUNY mathematics department. The big enchilada. Pierre had met him in Paris one summer, a few years earlier, when Tucker and his team had spent the summer there on an exchange with *Institut des Hautes Etudes.* Pierre had said they'd spent most of the summer playing tennis in Luxembourg Gardens and throwing parties. But Pierre hadn't mentioned anything about Tucker's wife. A remarkable oversight, since any heterosexual male on the planet would have noticed her instantly.

As if on cue, Professor Corbin walked into the kitchen, snuck up on his wife at the stove and snaked an arm around her tiny waist, squeezing her against him. The effect accentuated the ample curve of her so so sexy rear end.

Sanja and I gaped as he leaned in and planted a wet one on the back of her neck. They looked like they'd been married all of ten minutes. It was time to retreat before they decided to try for a baby right there in front of us. The sight of Tucker Corbin, with his jowls, leathery, tennis-tanned skin and slight pot belly cuddling up to his pulchritudinous wife wouldn't have been pleasant. I prayed any child they might have would look like her.

Sanja kicked me with one foot. We withdrew from the kitchen and moved down the long hallway in the opposite direction from the living room, where a bunch of doors, some shut, some open, indicated we were in a three or four-bedroomed apartment. It dawned on me we were in one of those sought after Upper West Side pre-war apartments that almost never went on the market.

"Ugh. That was disgusting," Sanja opened.

"That was almost unbelievable. How old do you think she is?"

"Younger than us."

Sanja was a year younger than me. Sabina looked to be about eighteen, meaning she was probably around twenty-three.

"Why do you think she hooked up with him?'

I shrugged. "Where do you think she's from?"

"Brazil."

"Really? Why? Her accent?"

"Her shape."

"Her shape?" There was a Brazilian shape? "I thought they came in all shapes and sizes down there."

"Did you see her backside?" Sanja patted her own rather trim one.

"Uh—yeah, it was hard not to notice."

"That's a Brazilian backside."

"That's a lot of territory."

"Brazil's a large country."

"And a shapely one."

I thought about my own Hungarian backside. Sabina's curves hovered somewhere between my own and say a black female Olympic athlete's.

"Did Pierre mention her to you?'

"Not at all. Can you imagine her sleeping with Tucker?" I shot out, unable to resist a bit of gossipy observation.

"You mean the old guy with the dingle dangle?" Sanja put a hand up to either side of her face and pulled down her cheeks to create jowls.

I shuddered. "It's hard to imagine. Almost gross." Compared to Tucker Corbin's paunchy, comfortably middle-aged body, Pierre looked like a greyhound. Suddenly I wondered what my friend's long, lean torso would look like unsheathed. Would there be hair on his chest? I guessed yes. Which one of these was the bedroom he was staying in?

I glanced into the nearest one. The wood paneling was rich, the furnishings austere—a bed, night table, bureau and Shaker-style chair on a bare wood floor. This was upper-crust, New England style decor, straight out of a J. Peterman's catalogue.

My grandfather's room had looked a bit like this one. He'd been relocated to the far bedroom on the second story of his own home after my grandmother had tired of his snoring and moved him out of their master bedroom suite shortly after their only child together, my mother, had come along. It had been a second marriage for both. Both had been widowed.

I wondered what Sabina's story was. She was too young to be widowed and she sure didn't look desperate. What might have driven her to marry Tucker Corbin?

Behind us, the door clicked shut.

"Pierre!"

He stood inside the door, leaning against it looking from me to Sanja, an amused expression on his face.

"I'm sorry. We were just uh—"

"Looking around?" he asked.

"We were bored," Sanja broke in.

"The game's going great. Seven to six. You should come out and see," he entreated, giving me a warm look.

"We met Tucker's wife in the kitchen. She's cooking chili or something. Have you met her?"

"That's not chili. That's oxtail stew," Pierre corrected.

"How do you know?" I asked.

"Tucker told me. It's his wife's special recipe from back home."

Both Sanja and I sprang to attention.

"Where's that?"

"She's from Brazil."

"From Rio?" I asked, naming the only city in Brazil I knew besides São Paulo. Sanja's toe gently pressed the top of mine to claim victory.

"No. Tucker said she's from a very small place in the interior. West of São Paulo."

"How did he meet her?"

"It's quite a story."

"Sit," Sanja directed him to the spindle-backed chair.

He did, swinging one long, lean leg over the other knee, looking like a Cheshire cat with a secret.

"So tell."

"Why are you so interested?'

"We're into international relations."

"This is definitely one of them."

"I noticed," I said, wondering what Tucker was now doing to Sabina back in the kitchen. Did she mind being mauled by an old man while she cooked? I hoped for her sake, Tucker knew how to fly her rocket ship.

"So how did they meet?" Sanja pressed.

Pierre scraped his chair forward, leaning toward us. In response, Sanja and I both moved closer, our heads down, hands on thighs.

Pierre chuckled.

"Spit it out," I prompted, burning with curiosity at this point.

"You both look like linebackers. That's the way they stand," he began.

"Get to the point. How did they meet?" Sanja re-routed him.

"Well—remember I told you Tucker and his team from CUNY spent the summer in Paris a few years back?" he asked, looking at me.

"Yes. I remember."

"He rented a house near *Hautes Etudes* and we went over there a lot for all sorts of gatherings."

"So?"

"So he had a housekeeper who came with the house. She was assigned by the school to look after Tucker and his team and help him out with his parties and —I think you call them— Happy Hours."

"Right?"

"So he had a big party right before the August *vacances*. And for that one, the housekeeper brought her cousin to help."

"Sabina?"

"Yes. She'd come to Paris to work as an *au pair* and it was her off day, so she was free."

"So?"

"So you know the rest of the story. Tucker took one look at her and lost his head."

"Wasn't he married back then? I mean didn't he have a daughter or something?"

"He'd brought his adult daughter with him to Paris but she was off with friends touring Europe. "

"Why didn't his wife come?'

"I think it was the end phase of their marriage. A few years earlier he'd started the middle age male *crise*."

"The what?" I asked. He'd used the French word for crisis.

"Yes —of course. The *crise* de dopey male maturity," Sanja stated succinctly. "Like menopause for women."

"Huh," I breathed.

"So he was there alone, supposedly with his daughter to keep an eye on him, except she'd gone off traveling. He took one look at Sabina and spent the rest of the summer trying to seduce her."

"And did finally."

"The second he won her favors, he moved her into his house."

"To seal the deal?"

"To seal the deal. And make himself feel like he was twenty five again."

"Why did she let him?"

"She was in France on a tourist visa. About to run out."

"So why didn't she go back?'

Pierre leaned closer to me.

"She was from someplace deep in the jungle. She'd just spent six months in Paris. Do you think she was in a rush to go back?"

So that's what kind of supernatural creature gets created in Brazil's deep interior jungles? No wonder it was said that Brazilians are among the world's most beautiful people.

"Why hadn't she met a Frenchman?"

"Apparently, she had. The father of the family she was babysitting for. She was trying to get away from them when Tucker met her. But they'd sponsored her for her visa to France, so she was in a—say—delicate position when she bumped into Tucker.

"Up shit creek without a paddle is what they'd say back in Maine," I remarked.

Both Pierre and Sanja looked at me curiously.

"So how did Tucker get her back to New York with him?"

"He basically kidnapped her, but she was happy to go. He flew her back with him and since he was already living in this apartment since his wife had kicked him out the year before, he set up house here with her.

"Wasn't his wife furious?"

"More like fed up and ready to move on. She'd already filed for divorce, since the year before he'd shacked up with a female grad student. That story had been all over campus before Tucker came to Paris. In fact, he'd been sent to Paris to give the scandal a chance to die down."

"What happened?'

"The grad student got her Ph.D and moved on to a great job in California. She left Tucker behind in the dust, so he was licking his wounds by the time he met Sabina."

"She knew how to patch up the big bad tiger's boo-boos, huh?" I asked.

"Yes. Sabina has natural instincts. She knows how to land on her feet."

"Comes from growing up in the jungle, I'd bet." A bit like growing up in Maine. One lived close to nature, so one learned a few things. I hoped I had.

"Tucker says she has native intelligence like no one he's ever met before," Pierre agreed. "She told him flat out he had three months to decide what he was doing before her tourist visa to the States ran out. In less time than that, he finalized his divorce and married her."

"What happens when she points her assets in another direction, without him?" I asked, wondering if I was coming off a tad too cynically. Still, it was hard not to be cynical, seeing Tucker's weather beaten, middle-aged body pressing into a copper-toned version of Snow White.

Pierre laughed. "She's Tucker's wife now. Why would she go anywhere? They've got a place downtown, he's putting her through college, and they'll probably have a baby as soon as she finishes her studies. Everyone's happy."

"Tucker's not just happy. He looked like he was crazy in love back in the kitchen just now."

"He's thinking he's a lucky guy."

"She's very nice too," I added, the first positive comment I'd made in the entire conversation.

"She's nice, she's smart and she's beautiful. How many years longer does Tucker think she's going to waste her time with him?" Sanja added, rather practically.

"I think he's not really thinking about that right now," Pierre said.

"It's the man *crise*," I agreed.

"His hormones are out of whack so he can't think right now. He can only enjoy," he explained, looking like a doctor describing his patient's diagnosis.

"I'm sure she's doing the thinking while he's doing the enjoying. She has to stay with him for three years or else it'll look like a green card marriage. That's about the time it will take her to get her degree. Then she'll have her own *crise*."

Pierre shrugged. "I think you say "What goes 'round, comes 'round', *non?*"

"There's no reason why a nice, smart girl from the jungle shouldn't enjoy her life in New York, is there?" I mused.

""Just like another nice, smart girl from Maine?" Pierre put in.

I nodded wryly, charmed to think Pierre had remembered all my details, even where I came from. The only difference between Sabina and I was that I'd had more luck than her in life and my introduction to New York came armed with a college degree. That and the fact that she was about five hundred times more beautiful than I was. There were advantages to being at the top of the B list; I wasn't competing with the A one.

I raised my glass. "So here's to Sabina's *crise* one day. May Tucker set her up to have a good one."

We clinked glasses and toasted Sabina. Then Sanja got up and led the way back to the kitchen where we laughed and joked and drank and got to know Sabina better until she was no longer just the beautiful Brazilian, but a fully-colored-in person from some backwater having her moment in New York. Just as we were. Just like my father.

∽

PIERRE PRESENTED HIS paper the next afternoon at CUNY while I went to work. Then he had dinner with Tucker Corbin, so we met for drinks afterward. I suggested the Royalton again since it was only three blocks from the restaurant near CUNY where Pierre was with Tucker, and fifty blocks south of Pierre's apartment, meaning there would be no temptation to go back to his place based on logistical ease. In New York, the outcome of many relationships rested upon logistical issues—ease of travel time to get to the other party, and occasionally precipitate decisions to stay overnight based on difficulty or danger traveling home alone on a subway after midnight. It was no wonder relationships in the City were so tenuous. People were dealing with a lot more than just whether they were interested in the other party. Safety and accessibility issues colored the picture too. Ever heard of someone in the Bronx dating someone in Staten Island? It didn't happen often.

At the entrance to the Royalton, I scanned the room for Pierre. No sign of him. Slowly, I traveled the length of the long, narrow lobby lounge then back again. It was Monday evening, so the clientele looked slightly less glamazonish, more touristic. Back at the main entrance, I wondered if I should check the tiny, private bar Sanja and I had discovered on the other side of the main lounge. I thought of it as the VIP area, even though anyone could have a drink there, as long as they knew where it was. Most didn't. Pierre and I hadn't sat in there the Friday before because I had thought it was too intimate a spot for us to catch up with each other after almost a year. I was beginning to think otherwise.

Wandering over to the hidden entrance to the private lounge, I blinked. The pink-gold lighting illuminated the bar area only, casting the rest of the room in shadows. Intentional. Plus the lights were angled so as to spotlight whoever was walking into the tiny lounge, making entrants feel like VIPs. I couldn't make out a thing other than the vague outline of a man in a hat sitting on the far side of the curved, plush banquette seat in the tiny cockleshell-shaped room. He looked long, lean, elegant, a tad bit dangerous. It crossed my mind that I'd never seen Pierre look dangerous.

Impatient, I turned to return to the entrance.

"Ava." A hand came from behind and rested on my shoulder.

"Pierre! Where were you?" I stared at him.

The charcoal grey fedora hat he wore transformed him. Suddenly he was sexy, stylish. What had happened to my geeky, mathematician friend? A tremor ran up my neck.

"In the lounge. The private one. You just left it."

"That was you?" The dangerous-looking figure in the lounge had been Pierre? *Hello, Ava. Wake up.*

"You looked like you were looking for me. I got here about five minutes ago, thought we might sit somewhere quieter this time."

"I didn't recognize you in that hat. Where did you get it?"

"Do you like it?"

"I love it! I mean—I like the way you look in it," I corrected myself. Sanja was always making fun of Americans for saying they loved everything. Was it a crime to be enthusiastic? At least we weren't all dying of European *ennui.*

"You stared right at me. I thought you didn't like what you saw, so you left," he joked.

"I couldn't see a thing. The lights blinded me," I stammered. *And you looked so different, so intriguing.*

He steered me back to the lounge where we sank into the curved salmon-colored banquette sofa. He took off his hat and placed it on the plush, tufted upholstery beside him. I eyeballed the fedora with wonder. How could a simple hat transform Pierre into someone else? Or transform my feelings about him into something more? It was magical. No wonder fashion stayed in fashion.

"How did you find your way to this room?" I asked. "No one knows about it."

"I didn't. I asked the hostess for a quiet corner. She led me here."

"Sanja and I love this room. It's like a jewel box."

With his French accent and wearing that hat, no wonder the hostess had seated him in the VIP section. I was taking a closer look at my safe French friend, starting that moment. Apparently I'd missed something.

"It's like the colors of your complexion," Pierre observed.

"It is?" I blushed. He had a point. The salmon pink interior combined with the pink-gold lighting, made me even more gold and pink than usual. And I usually was rather gold and pinkish.

We both looked younger, rosier, more alive. Except that Pierre looked something else too—there was something sensual and dangerous to him tonight that hadn't been there before. Was it the lighting or was it me waking up from a long winter's nap? The sleep of getting over Arnaud. Hibernation on the heels of love's disappointment. Healing rest had done its work and I'd woken up. Refreshed and ready for action.

"So now I'm done. Finally," he announced, his face relaxed.

"Congratulations. Did you convince them that less is more?"

"No one is ever convinced of anything in mathematics, Ava."

"What do you mean?"

"Things are either proven or they aren't."

"It sounds so satisfying. Sort of like an alternative universe where everything is clear. And if it's not clear, it's simply because it's not clear yet."

"It's satisfying to a point. But real life is better." He looked at me.

"In all its shades of gray?"

"In all its shades of gray." With his right index finger, he reached out and ran a long, slow line down my arm, from the shoulder to the inside of my wrist. This was a new, bolder Pierre. The one I'd caught a glimpse of without recognizing the Pierre I thought I already knew.

I trembled, my senses alit, wondering what he'd do, where he'd wander to next. For once, I had no idea. Neither did I know how I'd respond.

It was February but I was wearing a sleeveless grey winter silk top. This was due to the incredible overheating Manhattan was well known for. I'd never lived anywhere in the City where I hadn't had to throw open windows in the middle of winter to escape the overheated stuffiness of my living space. Restaurants and public places were the same way. It gave New Yorkers an opportunity to buy resort wear without actually needing to travel to resorts.

I shivered. Then with the little finger of my right hand, I reached over and stroked his. Both of us were rapidly moving into new territory. And we hadn't even had a drink yet.

A veiled look came over his face that I hadn't seen before. A new Pierre was revealing himself to me, one I hadn't yet met. Was I ready to meet him? We had four more days until he returned to France. It was time to answer that question.

"What else do you want to do while you're here?" I asked, somewhat dangerously.

The arm thrown onto the top of the banquette behind me came down behind my neck and pulled me toward him.

"Let's play a game."

"A game? What game?' I loved to play games. Had he known? I'd tried so hard not to play any with him. But this game was his suggestion.

"A hat game. It's a game I play sometimes when I get stuck with a problem.

"A hat game? Isn't that some sort of hockey move?"

"No, Ava. This is my own move. Want to play?" He lifted his hat from the banquette seat beside him and turned it over.

"Okay. What do we do?"

He took out a small, memo pad from his inside pocket and tore off four pages, handing them to me.

"Write something down you'd like us to do together before I leave. One idea on each page. Then crumple up each page and put them in the hat. I'll do the same and we'll have eight choices."

"Then we'll draw?"

"Then you'll tell me how many times we draw, a number between two and eight. We'll draw that number of times and we'll pick the idea that comes up most frequently."

"What if something comes up again and again?" Something was coming up in my head again and again with regard to Pierre, but it wasn't on the tourist circuit.

"We'll definitely do it before I leave on Friday. Maybe we'll do it more than once."

I choked.

"Sounds like a plan," I murmured, rejoicing in Pierre's plan-making capabilities. This game sounded like fun. At least it was simple enough for me to easily understand. I wasn't good at complicated games, like the ones I'd played with Arnaud and so frequently lost.

"Got a pen?"

"No."

"Here." Pierre handed me an American-style disposable, plastic pen. Sanja would not have approved, but I did. It wasn't the pen that interested me, it was beginning to be the man. And what about the hat, anyway? Not bad. Sanja hadn't weighed in on hats on men yet. I'd ask her next time we met.

I thought hard as the waitress swept away with our drinks order. There was so much to do in New York City.

But it was February, slightly limiting our outdoor choices. What might Pierre enjoy? I scribbled an obvious one in my neighborhood. "Check out the view from the revolving lounge on the top floor of the Marriott Marquis Hotel in Times Square." Then another idea came to mind. "Visit Lincoln Center."

But it might rain or even snow over the next few evenings. Days, I had to work, so we were really talking about what we'd do from 5:30 P.M. on. A revolutionary thought came to me. I could cook dinner for Pierre. Not at my place. But in the kitchen at the CUNY Mathematics House. If it wasn't a possibility, then we could just toss that one out and go for dinner in his neighborhood on the Upper West Side. Somewhat disingenuously, I scribbled "cook dinner at Pierre's place." It would warm Pierre's heart and I was sure there'd be a way I could get out of it. In Manhattan there was always a way to get out of cooking. Take-out, for example.

One piece of paper remained. I looked over at Pierre, who seemed deep in thought. His pages were all tossed into the hat, except for the final one, which he was working on now. Carefully, he shielded the scrap of paper from me so I couldn't see what he was writing.

A very naughty, very clear thought streaked into my head. It was the same thought that had been hanging around ever since Pierre had arrived. But this time, its tempo had picked up, as if on wings.

There was no way I would write it down. But the thought was most definitely there. Wasn't that sort of the subtext for everything else we'd been doing the past four days? Weren't we dancing around each other with this particular possibility infusing the air, scenting everything we did together? Especially after being just a trifle inauthentic with my proposal to cook dinner, it was time to get real.

I wrote down "something else," to cover that possibility, crumpled the paper and tossed it in Pierre's hat.

Done.

Our drinks arrived.

"Here's to your paper," I said, lifting my glass.

"Here's to picking the right piece of paper together," he replied, clinking mine.

The cocktail waitress was now looking over at us. Another couple came into the bar and sat at the counter. The woman eyeballed Pierre's upside down fedora with interest.

"Shake it," Pierre instructed, handing me his hat.

I shook the hat back and forth then up and down. For good measure, I put my hand in and mixed up all the crumpled up bits of paper. There was no way either of us could tell who had put in which scrap.

"You mix too," I told him.

He reached in and mixed the papers further. Good.

"So how many times do we draw?" he asked.

"Umm—four." It was a good number. I liked the symmetry of it.

"Ladies first, then."

I put my hand in and drew out the first scrap of paper I came in contact with.

Unfolding it, I blushed. On it was written "another idea." In Pierre's handwriting.

Huh. I looked at his eyes, but they were veiled.

"Score one for 'another idea.'" He stroked a tally mark on his cocktail napkin.

"Now your turn," I directed.

He put his hand in the hat and withdrew a piece of paper. Opening it, he read, "Hot drinks in front of the fire at Math House."

"Sounds nice." Whew. Maybe I'd be off the hook about cooking dinner after all.

"Your turn."

I stuck my hand in, again taking the first piece of paper I came in contact with.

"Something else" was written on the unfolded paper. This time, in my handwriting.

I blushed and busied myself shaking the hat.

"You seem determined to try something else," Pierre remarked.

I coughed delicately. Perhaps not determined, but moving in that direction.

One more time. I held up the hat for Pierre and when he put his hand in, I gave it an extra shake. The piece of paper he was holding onto fell back into the hat, but he reached in and grabbed it again. The man knew which scrap of paper he wanted.

"Something else," came up again. This time, my handwriting.

"I guess I'm not the only one," I commented, looking into his eyes and trying not to think too much about how uncanny it was that we'd both written down more or less the same thing then chosen it three out of four times. It was a sign. And if it was a sign of the something else I'd been thinking about being the same as the one he'd been thinking about, we were about to change the course of our relationship.

Pierre raised his glass. "Ready?"

"Ready for what?"

"For something else?"

"I'm not sure," I said truthfully.

"Let's drink to divine uncertainty then."

We touched glasses and drank. I liked that. Whenever I thought about sex, I mean seriously thought about it, I thought about the divine too. Were other people like that? Was it because I thought sex was divine or because God had fortunately installed me with a braking system whenever I was ready to go off the tracks? It was a good feature to have and God knows I hadn't installed it myself. It was one of those divine gifts my creator gave me; that and the secret, ludicrous longing I had for John Boy Walton types.

"Pierre?"

"What?"

"Where did you get that hat?"

"Sabina gave it to Tucker. I admired it and Tucker took it off his head and gave it to me on the spot. Said he hates wearing hats."

"I hope you don't."

"That depends."

"On what?"

"Do you like me in it?"

"I love the way you look in it." Oops, maybe I needed to hold back on casual "love" statements, especially with a man as serious as Pierre. "I mean, I like the way you look in it."

"Good. I like wearing hats then."

"I like you."

"I know you do."

"You're silly."

"Sometimes."

And so it went into the double digit hours of the night until I went home and fell asleep thinking about another idea of what to do with Pierre over the next three days. Something else was going to happen between us soon. Very soon.

CHAPTER FIVE

SOMETHING ELSE

*T*he next day it snowed, as if on cue. Pierre picked me up under the clock in Grand Central Station, a convenient meeting point between my downtown office and the CUNY graduate center.

"Shall we walk a ways?" he asked.

"Sure," I agreed. At half past five, the snow had stopped, and there was still a trace of light in the sky. A winter wonderland hid New York's grime and erased the scowls of rosy-cheeked pedestrians on the street.

With my deep winter, snuggly sheepskin boots on, I was prepared for a hike in the snow. Chances were good we'd end up walking most of the way back to Math House, where Pierre was staying on the Upper West Side. New York City was predictably primitive in a snowstorm. All transportation systems either shut down (mass transportation) or vanished (taxis.) If we wanted to get anywhere, we walked; a system which kept New Yorkers reasonably fit.

At Park Avenue and Forty Fifth, a snowball fight was in progress between two young banker-types. Their serious looking leather briefcases lay propped against a statue of a young boy reading a book on the steps of the imposing skyscraper that housed the mid-town offices of one of Switzerland's largest private banks. A group of female office workers stood nearby, stamping their feet and egging their male colleagues on.

"You know how to have fun here," Pierre remarked, taking in the gaiety.

New Yorkers had surrendered to the snow; a carnival atmosphere was on.

"That's one of America's biggest export items."

"What do you mean?"

"Fun. Entertainment."

"This is the best kind," he remarked, picking up a mound of snow and carefully packing it into a snowball. He lobbed it, not too hard, at one of the banker-types, hitting him on the shoulder.

The banker turned, looked surprised, then leaned over, scooped up a snowball and smashed one back at Pierre, hitting him on the thigh.

Pierre turned and lobbed one at me.

"Hey!" I said as I sidestepped him.

"Come on, Ava!"

I scooped some snow from the ledge and packed it into a nice, firm ball. Then I held onto it as I waited for one of the bankers to engage Pierre's attention. As he responded to a hit from the left, I smashed one into his shoulder from the other side.

Frolicking like five-year-olds at recess, for the next ten minutes we lobbed snowballs at each other as well as complete strangers.

"My feet are turning blue," a woman finally shouted out, tossing a briefcase back to one of the snowball lobbers, who caught it then dusted the snow off his wool coat.

We broke it off, laughing, smiling and bidding each other goodnight.

At Third Avenue and Forty Eighth Street, someone in a car was attempting to leave a parking spot, but spinning its wheels in vain, blocked by snow. Two men on the sidewalk yelled encouragement then went round to the trunk where they struggled to push the car out of the snowdrift.

Pierre spotted them and jumped in. After two tries, the driver accelerated like crazy and the car's tires bumped over the snow and out onto the street.

"Thank you, sir," the driver yelled to Pierre, rolling down his window. His turban and beard indicated he was probably a Sikh from India or Pakistan.

"This is what I like about your country," Pierre gasped out breathlessly as we continued northward on Third Avenue.

"What's that?" I asked, congratulating myself on Pierre's snow-covered shoulder, where I'd scored more than one direct hit.

"You don't stand on ceremony. People talk to people they don't know. Everyone is connecting."

He had a point. Americans were rather well known for not standing on ceremony.

"Don't people help each other out in a snowstorm in France?"

"It doesn't snow like this where I come from. And in Paris, it usually melts or turns into rain."

I thought back to my time in Paris. From November to March, Paris was one long season of gray, peppered with frequent rain, occasional sleet and perhaps one or two mild snowstorms at most. Parisian winters lacked the harsh, crackling coldness of New York ones. There was something to be said for a crisp, cold New York winter's evening after a snowstorm. Everything lay muted and frozen while New Yorkers scrambled and skidded their way home, reaching out to help each other along the way.

At Fifty Ninth and Fifth Avenue, we crossed and walked along Central Park South. The Park lay sleeping and fairy-like under its white gown.

"When we get to the West Side, let's stop for hot chocolate," Pierre said.

"It's on our list," I reminded him.

"Right," Pierre agreed, grabbing my gloved hand in his and hastening us along.

Endorphins raced inside me as the crisp, cold air snapped at my face. Anticipation hugged me, cloaking me in growing awareness of what the evening before us might offer.

In a minute we were at Columbus Circle, where we turned right and headed up Central Park West.

"Come on, let's jog." I nudged Pierre. "Show me what you've got." The cold, crackling air made me want to race. What Pierre didn't know but I did was that the chances of us getting a cab in this weather were about nil. It was time to rev up our engines.

"*Allons-y!* let's go" Pierre shouted out into the night air. We slow motion raced each other up Central Park West, clumsily and slowly lifting our legs to wade through the snow, which was up to about three inches on the sidewalk. Fortunately there were plenty of cleared spots where we could pick up our pace, thanks to the many doormen out sweeping their building entrances, clearing a path for residents.

After ten blocks, at the corner of Seventy-Fifth, we finally slowed down, out of breath. Pierre picked me up and whirled me around. As he set me down, I smiled.

His face came down to mine, his lips closing on mine. We kissed for a long time, while people passed on the street, hurrying home amidst the sound of scraping shovels and doormen calling to each other in different languages. My long winter's sleep was over. Suddenly, I was fully awake to the fact that Pierre was an altogether different man from the one I'd taken him for.

"So where do we stop for hot chocolate?" Pierre asked when we finally broke apart.

"Come on. Let's go over to Columbus." I took his hand and turned down West 75th Street, hiding my expression after our kiss. It had been a new sort of kiss from him, probing for the answer to the question that now lay on the table.

At Columbus we looked northward where I spotted the huge looming red brick edifice of the Museum of Natural History. As we hastened toward it, a vague memory of a cozy, dark café that I had visited years earlier when I'd looked for piano gigs on the Upper West Side came to mind. The Evelyn Lounge. Perfect for hot chocolate and something more.

"Let's cross. There's a café over there that's nice."

"Why not?" Pierre said, moving to the traffic side of me as we crossed Columbus Avenue. There wasn't much chance of getting hit, considering what vehicles there were on the road were moving at turtle pace.

The snow-covered sidewalk on the west side of Columbus Avenue was busy with people hurrying home, going about their errands.

"I think you'll like this place. It's sort of famous."

"For what?"

For romance, I thought but didn't say. The Evelyn Lounge was known as one of the City's most happening pick up spots. "For atmosphere," I said instead.

"What kind of atmosphere?"

"The kind you'll like." I tugged his hand and we ran the final block until we reached Seventy Seventh Street and the entrance to the Evelyn Lounge. We hurried up the stairs and in the door where we handed our burly coats to a model-type coat check girl then moved into the cavernous upstairs lounge. Clusters of low slung couches dotted the room and a fire blazed merrily in a fireplace on the far wall.

Pierre moved toward it.

"You can't sit there. That's reserved for parties of four or more," the hostess behind us said.

Pierre motioned to me to wait for him. He turned back to the hostess then whispered something to her. Judging by the expression on her face, I could see his French accent was having its effect.

In a minute he came back then led the way to a slouchy sofa to one side of the fireplace. A roaring fire crackled before us.

"This is great, Ava. The first part of our game coming true."

"We're supposed to be in front of the fireplace at your place, no?"

"Tucker told me the fireplace isn't working over there. So this is our substitute plan."

"Great!" It was the home away from home plan—typical for Manhattan dwellers who lived in thimble-sized apartments and relied on neighborhood cafés, coffee houses and bars to do their entertaining in. In our case, something more targeted than entertaining was on the agenda.

An "I'm really an actress" sort of waitress approached and asked what we wanted.

"Two hot chocolates, please."

She looked disdainful.

"Do you want the house hot chocolate?"

"What's that?"

"Peppermint schnapps and hot chocolate. Something else too, I can't remember."

"Is it good?" Pierre asked.

"It's our most requested drink today."

"Two then."

She sauntered off, flicking her hair back, perhaps hoping a film director or casting agent might be in the room somewhere, warming up on the long trudge home.

In a minute, she was back, with two steaming hot beer steins topped with whipped cream. The smell of peppermint-scented alcohol cleared my nostrils and sharpened my senses.

"Here's to 'something else,'" Pierre said, raising his glass.

I said nothing but raised my glass too and clinked. The red hot jolt of peppermint schnapps instantly lit a fire in the pit of my stomach, matching the dancing flames before us.

Within seconds I was warm, tingling and lit up with anticipation.

Pierre moved closer to me, his hand coming down from the back of the couch to close around the back of my neck.

The secret spot.

No one had touched that spot in a long time.

Pierre's fingers stroked gently, circling.

I relaxed back into his hand, trusting. Slowly, I felt myself let go. For the next quarter hour we quietly explored each other's secret erogeneous spots: the crook of Pierre's arm, the back of my neck; spots we exposed everyday for anyone to see but which had been waiting to flame into life by the right touch from the right person.

Finally, Pierre was the right person. It was still him, but it was no longer our old dynamic. My affection for him was now flaming into something with another name.

An hour later, we were back at Math House, quietly letting ourselves into the apartment which stood silent, empty, waiting. We hung our wet coats on the coat stand then silently I followed him down the hall past the closed doors until we reached his bedroom. Inside we shut the door and to my surprise, I saw that Pierre had replaced the spindle-backed chair with a rocking chair from the living room. Without a word, he lit a candle, put on some Brazilian-sounding music and pulled me into the rocking chair onto his lap.

We rocked and listened and got to know each other better. Meanwhile the whistle and wheeze of steam heat flowing through the apartment's old pipes provided a background hum to our sighs.

I slid my fingers through Pierre's full, dark brown hair. It was bushy, almost wiry. Gathering it in a clump in back, I pulled. His head leaned back, his eyes looking up at mine. They gleamed in the candlelight. This was a new Pierre, the man in the fedora at the Royalton, not my faithful, conversational friend.

I leaned over him, pulling away when his mouth sought mine. Then finally, I relented. Together we rocked, silent, locked together, the beating of his heart almost audible, like the beat of a samba band.

Pierre had tremendous patience. Or was it restraint? He waited for me to signal when to proceed, when to stop. It worked for me the way it always had. I needed to be in the drivers' seat— until the point when I wasn't. But until that point, there was only one way I felt comfortable proceeding; I needed to stop and start, taking all the time in the world. Finally, my turn to direct was over and it was his.

In one fluid motion, Pierre stood up from the rocking chair and lifted me onto the bed. Then he was on top of me, his weight on one leg alongside mine, his other leg flown over both of mine, pinning me on my back.

I watched as the shadows from the candle danced on the wall. The room's simple, New England spareness perfectly complemented the rich, opulence of the new sensations we were giving each other.

With sure fingers, I unbuttoned Pierre's soft, brushed flannel plaid shirt. Underneath, wiry hair sprang out blanketing my chest in a tickly forest. Soon my hands were on his stomach, feeling the smoothness and tautness of his skin below his chest hair.

With a deft move, Pierre slid his hand under my back and lifted me off the bed so I could get more comfortable. He did likewise and when the intoxicating feel of his skin on mine combined with the earthy, dizzying scent of him, soon we were entwined like a tree and vine.

That was Tuesday night. We spent the next two nights in the same manner, getting to know each other and marveling in what we hadn't known about each other for the more than two months we'd been friends. There was something to be said for moving from friends to becoming lovers—something I'd never done before in my puerile instinct to lump men I knew into categories—dangerous or safe; lover material with a short expiration date or friend material with no expiration date. Now that Pierre occupied both categories had I shortened the expiration date of our friendship? I hoped not.

༄

ON FRIDAY, PIERRE flew back to Paris. I returned to my mother's place to carefully blank looks from my mother and equally curious ones from my sister.

Sanja was another story. Over coffee the following week she grilled me.

"Your friend Pierre is nice. He is more serious than most Frenchmen. He won't cheat as quickly."

"Who says he'll cheat?" I asked indignantly.

"All men cheat sooner or later. He'll be later."

"Come on, Sanja. All men don't cheat, do they? " Victor flashed through my mind, slowly walking toward us at the Met, his face half sulky, half sad. Maybe they did.

"He's French. What do you think?"

"I think he's a very decent and honest guy. He's not the type to cheat."

"Cheating isn't about being decent and honest. It's about the other section."

"What other section?"

"The dodgy one."

Her adjective took me straight back to Paris and conversations at outdoor cafés with my English *au pair* friend, Elizabeth.

"He's the dodgy type," she'd say, passing judgment on a complete stranger walking by.

"How can you tell?"

"Look at the way he looked at himself in that mirror."

Parisians were always checking themselves out in enormous mirrors affixed to corner buildings at major intersections. It was considered a public service to look good on the streets there. Men preened as much as women did, constantly checking their teeth, the twist of their scarves, the tilt of their hats.

"So?"

"He checked his teeth, but didn't look into his own eyes."

"Maybe he's embarrassed to be looking at himself in public."

"Are you kidding? Men pee in public here. He's not embarrassed. He's hiding something." Elizabeth and I had been *au pairs* in Paris in the last days of the *pissoirs*, public urinals on the grand avenues of Paris, such as the Champs Élysées. Men's shoes and the lower parts of their trousers were fully exposed as they relieved themselves inside the *pissoir* stalls. The first time I'd seen one being used, I turned scarlet with embarrassment to think of what the man was doing inside it in almost full public view. Then I'd realized I was in France. Things were different over there.

"So what's in the dodgy section?" Sanja asked, bringing me back to where we sat at a counter in the window of Bloomingdale's ground floor café, sipping cappuccinos.

"That's where we get ideas to do things we aren't supposed to want to do."

"Like what?"

"I mean stuff like—uh—" she looked around, scanning the throngs walking past us on the sidewalk. "Okay—see that delivery boy?"

"Where?"

"The skinny one over there with that stupid cap on his head and the pants falling off."

"Yeah."

"Okay, so the dodgy section of your brain might want to sleep with him."

"Ewwww." Disgusting. Gross. Yuck. I took another glance. He did have sort of sexy shoulders.

"Yeah, I agree, but don't tell me you've never had a thought like that about some guy you've seen on the street."

"Well ..." Okay, busted. But I'd never done anything about any of those dark, little fantasies. Almost never.

"Okay, so don't you think sometimes the dodgy section takes over from the Boy Scout section?"

"It's not supposed to. Those are fantasies, Sanja. You don't act on fantasies, you just think about them."

"Tell me you've never acted upon a fantasy."

I remained spectacularly silent, sipping my cappuccino and slitting my eyes at her. Who did she think she was?

"So what do you think men do in places like France or Italy, where acting on fantasies is practically a code of machismo?"

"But they don't all act like that, do they?"

"Maybe not. But remember—not only are they men; they're Latin men. What exactly do you think stops them from behaving in a way that's already expected of them?"

"That's sick, Sanja. People aren't animals. They're— they have consciences."

"Of course they have consciences. That's the section that bothers them after they've acted like animals."

"Look—I don't think all men everywhere act like that." I thought about Pierre. Why were we assigning all these potentialities to him so soon? He was a brand new entrant to my love life. Couldn't he enjoy a brief moment of glory before my girlfriends besmirched his reputation?

"Of course not, Ava. The ones you like probably act just like you, right?"

That would not necessarily be such a good thing. But at least they would have consciences, no? Not that my own had always prevented me from acting upon instinct. Especially when it came to desire.

A sermon my minister had once given came out of nowhere and slapped me in the face like a live fishtail. He'd been preaching on the seven deadly sins and I'd pretty much snoozed through successive Sundays on the first five topics of pride, avarice, envy, anger, and sloth. The final two he'd combined into one sermon; that one woke me up.

Lust and gluttony had riveted my attention. Two of favorite obsessions—food and sex—were of inexhaustible interest to me. He'd made the point that lust and gluttony in particular were sins to overcome as they both occurred at the confluence of necessity with desire. In other words, people couldn't just cut either lust or gluttony out of their lives or else the human species would become extinct. I'd wondered why God would have played such a trick on us as to give us urges that needed to be satisfied to fulfill His mandate of being fruitful and multiplying but then to give us opportunities to exercise those urges in ways that went way beyond the basic mandate. WAYYYYYY beyond.

I'd wrestled with the gluttony issue in my late teens and early twenties. More or less, I'd emerged victorious: having squelched, subjugated and finally vanquished my unnatural desire to simply continue eating foods that were delicious, fattening and sugary until they were—well—all gone.

It hadn't been easy. Spending time in France and learning to eat the way the French did—small amounts of exquisitely delicious, artistically presented food had delivered me from sugar and fat addiction. Something else must have too—probably the discovery of two other food and drink groups I liked even better than sugar and fat—protein and alcohol. The discovery of oysters, smoked salmon, runny smelly cheeses, and liver paté—all with the right wine pairings—had ultimately given me something even more satisfying to chew on than creamy Bretons and pain aux chocolats. Mmmmm...

The lust thing was something I still wrestled with. The problem was that I tended to admire one type of man and lust after another. Did anyone else have this problem? Or to rephrase—did everyone else have this problem?

"Sanja, do you ever feel like you admire one type of man, but you want to sleep with another type?"

"You mean the human condition?" she asked smoothly, as if she'd said, "You mean the January clearance sales?"

"Yes. I mean—no, I hope. Why does that happen? Isn't that sort of crazy? I mean why would God do that to us?"

"Ever read the Greek myths?'

"I love the Greek myths. I grew up on them." Artemis had been my favorite. She had been so immune to men.

As a young girl, she'd been the only Greek goddess I'd fully understood. Plus she went hunting at night.

"Remember how the gods would play little jokes all the time?'

"Yes, I think so." Hadn't Hera turned one of Zeus' girlfriends into a cow?

"So that's what God likes to do sometimes. Play little jokes on us."

"But that's sort of—unfair, right?"

"Like having a period every month even though you're only going to get pregnant once or twice your entire life, if at all?"

"Uh—yeah. I see what you mean." Whoever came up with that system was having a joke on women, alright.

"On a scale of one to ten how much do you think nuns want to get their periods every month?"

"Not much. Maybe a one?"

"Maybe a zero. God plays His little jokes the way everyone else does."

"So what's His joke on men?"

"That they need women to survive."

"You mean, they need women to reproduce?"

"Yes. And to do everything else. Get dressed, eat, go to work, pay bills, function in the real world."

"What about gay guys?"

"The gay guys play with each other like men. Then when they settle down, they find a gay guy to turn into a wife."

"Well, that's still another man. I mean "wife" is just semantics. You mean partner."

"I mean men depend more heavily on women than women depend on men. Gay guys love women. Even if they don't love to sleep with them."

I'd been a singer pianist. Gay men had been the core of my fan base in New York. "That's true," I admitted. As if to underscore what I already knew, my eyes lit upon the handbags and accessories section next to where we sat at Bloomingdale's front entrance. All products made for women. Many of them designed by gay guys. Women and gay guys needed each other, even if it wasn't for sex.

"But are you sure men depend on women more than the opposite?"

"Okay, let's say there's an older couple and the man dies. Does the woman remarry right away?"

"Umm, usually not." Maybe never.

"So when it's the wife who dies, how long does the man wait to get married again?"

"Umm—maybe a year?"

"Maybe a minute." Sanja rolled her eyeballs. "Men can't function without a woman managing their lives."

"I thought that difference was because there's less single men available at an older age than single women. Plus older men marry younger women all the time."

"It's not that. Older women could remarry too—if they've got money, they can find a partner. It's not that they can't find anyone, it's that they're free from serving and slaving for the first time in their lives and they're happy to stay that way for as long as possible. Who wants to marry another old man, then spend the final years of their lives nursing him until he dies? Plus they get bad breath when they get old."

Plus they snore, I didn't add. My grandfather's bedroom had been at the other end of the house from my grandmother's. He'd been relocated there largely due to his snoring habit.

My father's Hungarian girlfriend, Tünde, popped into my mind's eye. Petite, blonde, heavily made up and fashionably outfitted, she wasn't one to mince words. "Why would I marry at my age? I did that once and never again. Who wants to cook and clean up after an old man? I like to work and I like to keep my own money. When I come home, I turn on the TV, I relax, I plan my next vacation. If I get lonely, I call your father."

My father and Tünde had dated for more than twenty years. She wasn't going anywhere, most certainly not up a church aisle ever again.

"Okay, so say men need women more than women need them. How does this have anything to do with cheating?"

"Men need reassurance from women again and again."

"Reassurance about what?"

"That they're necessary. That someone needs them."

"Don't women need that too?"

"Women have children hounding them all the time, needing them nonstop up the wazoo. Then their husbands. They don't need to run around town to reassure themselves of how important they are. They already have proof of it everywhere."

"What about when they get older?

"Their grandchildren. Their jobs or their volunteer organizations. Their dogs or cats."

"Men have all those things too."

"That's precisely my point. They have them, but they get their validation from women. Not so much those other things."

Was it true? And if it was, didn't that add up to a lot of power for women? Even if some men here and there did cheat?

"So what should a woman do if a man cheats?"

"Get him to stop cheating."

"How?"

"To begin with, keep an eye on him."

"You mean, don't lead separate lives?"

"Something like that. Don't take separate vacations. Don't go to the country house when he's in the city. Don't let him go off on business trips alone. Go with him."

Pierre was now in Paris. I was in New York. Paris was a city filled with slim, fashionable, impeccably poised women. The only advantage I had was that I was American and Pierre loved America. Fun. Spontaneity. Entertainment. That was us. That wasn't Paris.

Paris had been fun for me, because it had been full of sights to see, behaviors to learn, fabulous food and wine, and lots of smells—some good, some bad. As for Parisians, I could see how Paris could be a tough gig—a place where social jockeying and keeping up appearances would be a full-time occupation, one not involving lots of laughs.

"What should I do about Pierre then?" I asked.

"Get him back here. Or go there."

"Easier said than done." Both suggestions were tall orders.

"I know," Sanja said non-judgmentally. We finished our cappuccinos in companionable silence, having covered the waterfront on men, cheating, lust, attraction, monthly cycles, Greek mythology, God's sense of humor, gay guys, widows and widowers, and how to get men to stop cheating. It was just another one of Sanja's and my fascinating spiral conversations—taking us somewhere fun and playful where we could wrestle with truth but not feel too bad if the match ended in a draw.

CHAPTER SIX

DANCE OF THE MOTH

A few weeks later, I arrived home to find a message waiting for me on the answering machine. Someone with a thick accent had called. A woman. "This message is for Ava Fodor. It's about your father," she'd said then left a number I didn't recognize.

A shiver ran up my arm. The woman's curt tone told me something had happened; something too important to reveal in a phone message. All of a sudden I wasn't ready for something to happen to him. When something happens to an eighty-year old man, it's usually not good. All I could hope for was that it wasn't very, very bad. I dialed the number while huge sections of my conscience, most probably pricked by the Holy Spirit, suggested to me that I hadn't been altogether fair to the man who was my father. Was I going to get a second chance? I'd find out within seconds.

"Hello?" A strange voice answered.

"Hello, did someone call me from this number?"

"This is a pay phone at Doctor's Hospital. Who do you want?" The female voice was curt, but not harsh. It didn't sound like the one that had left the message.

"Oh," My God. "Is—do you know if Zsolt Fodor is there? He's my father."

"Who? What kind of name is that?"

"I—umm—is there a man there with an older, blonde woman with an accent?"

"There's a lady who came in with an old man awhile ago, who's very upset. He's in intensive care right now."

"Can you find out if her name is Tünde Szabo?"

"I'm not a secretary."

"I'm sorry. Please. I'm sorry to bother you..."

"Wait a minute."

Several long seconds went by then the sound of the receiver being jostled and handed to someone.

"Hallo?" A harsh female voice came on.

Tünde alright. Hungarian accents were unmistakable, unlike any other.

"Tünde —is that you? It's Ava."

"Ahhhhhh. Ava-aa-aa. Your father.... ahhhhhhhh...."

Please God, let him not be dead.

"Is my father okay?"

"He had a heart attack. *Istenem. Istenem.*" I recognized that word in Hungarian. It meant "My God," or "Oh God."

"Is he alive?" What a question. I trembled.

"He's here. With tubes and things all over him. Beeps and flashes. Terrible. Terrible. *Istenem.* When can you come?"

Thank God, Thank God. I wasn't ready for him to die—for all the wrong reasons. I barely understood him. Over the years I'd had a hard time appreciating him. But when we could make a connection, it was an interesting one. His commentary on cultural topics never failed to rivet my attention. I wanted more before our moment was over.

"I—you're at Doctor's Hospital?"

"Yessssss," she wailed. My father's girlfriend was the polar opposite of anyone on my mother's white Anglo-Saxon Protestant side of the family. She made Anna Magnani in an Italian movie look like a New England ice princess. At least my father was being properly mourned. Although he wasn't dead yet.

"Okay, I'm coming as soon as I can. Can I talk to a doctor or a nurse for a minute?"

"Come now, Ava. Come! your father is—ahhhhhh-hhh!" Tünde wasn't one to downplay drama. The phone jostled again and I waited a few more minutes until someone else got on the line. This time a nurse told me that my father had suffered a moderately severe heart attack, was now stabilized and asleep and was not in imminent danger. Was I his next of kin? If so, I should come as soon as possible, as the woman who'd accompanied him had informed her that she was not his wife and couldn't sign any papers on his behalf.

One hour later, I was at Doctor's Hospital, a small private hospital across from Carl Schurz Park next to the East River on the Upper East Side. As hospitals go, it was a nice one.

"What floor is intensive care on?"

"Who are you looking for?"

"Zsolt Fodor. My father. He had a heart attack."

The receptionist skimmed her list.

"How do you spell that?"

"Fodor. F—O—D—O—R." Very simple, really.

"And the first name?"

"Zsolt. Z—S—O—L—T." Simple again. Simply unbelievable.

"What was that?" The receptionist looked alarmed, as if I might be a crackpot, reeling off the name of a comic book superhero.

"Z—S—O—L—T." Even by New York standards, it was a pretty unusual name.

"C?"

"Z. As in zebra." As in off the charts weird. Just like my father. Yet a completely typical male name in Hungary.

The receptionist looked baffled.

"Do you see Fodor on your list?'

"Ummm, there's a Jolt Fodor."

"That's him."

"I'll need some I.D."

By the time a visitor made it through security, their family member could be dead, I thought. Especially with a Hungarian name.

In another minute I was on the intensive care floor. Nurses chatted at the nursing station, not looking terribly intense. It took several minutes before anyone acknowledged me.

"I'm looking for my father, Zsolt Fodor."

"Are you his daughter?" They eyeballed me with shadowed eyes. I could tell my father's girlfriend had already made an impression.

"Yes."

"This way, dear. Come with me." An older, Irish-looking nurse stepped forward.

At the entrance to his room, I paused. Tünde and I didn't do well together in close quarters. I wanted to see my father alone, not with his girlfriend's body thrown across him, sobbing, wailing, accusing me of neglect. What did she know about neglect? Had her father forgotten to call her for the first sixteen years of her life?

Actually, I had no idea what Tünde's story was, but I could guess it hadn't been easy. No one coming out of Hungary who'd lived through the Second World War had had an easy time. People had either been persecuted then gassed or they'd been passive and arguably complicit in not doing anything about half a million Jews disappearing in the waning months of the war in the dark spring of 1945. I'd guess shadows of guilt followed them wherever they ended up. When Tünde said, as she frequently did, that it was better to be dead than to have lived through those days, I hadn't understood what she'd meant, but I'd marked her words. Maybe one day I would understand. I hoped not.

The Irish nurse stopped outside an open door and motioned to me to enter.

Hesitantly, I went in. My father lay sleeping under tubes and wires, just as Tünde had described. I crept closer, looking down at him.

"Why don't you wash your hands, dear?" the nurse whispered.

I complied, then returned to the bed, staring down at my father's sleeping face.

He looked surprisingly youthful, his golden skin relatively wrinkle-free for an eighty-year old man. He'd had me, his only child, at an advanced age, probably another reason he hadn't thought to raise me. Aside from my grandmother running him off, he'd known nothing about raising children and it's hard to teach old dogs new tricks.

"Is he going to be alright?" I asked.

"He's stabilized now," she said, sidestepping my question. "You can visit with him for a few minutes then come out to the nurses' station and find me."

"Could you do me a favor?"

"Yes?"

Is his girlfriend still here? Mrs. Szabo?"

The nurse frowned. "Do you mean the woman who came in with him?"

"Yes."

"I believe she went down to the cafeteria." She looked disapproving. Tünde had probably let loose on her in her inimitable Hungarian way.

"If she returns, could you just keep her out at the nurses' station until I come out? I want to visit alone for a few minutes." I looked at my father and again felt surprise and a little guilt at how peaceful he looked in repose. He certainly didn't look like the raging maniac I thought of him as most of the time.

"I understand. I'll tell her." I'm sure she did. No one who'd been at the receiving end of Tünde 's hysteria could fail to understand the desire to keep her at a distance. It was a wonder my father had survived twenty plus years of her ministrations.

Pulling up a chair, I sat down and took his hand. It was warm, surprisingly smooth in mine. A large, broad-boned hand. No wonder I hadn't come out looking like my film idol, Audrey Hepburn.

Zsolt Fodor looked undeniably handsome in repose. His broad, high-cheekboned face had two vertical furrows running down either side of his mouth from mid-cheekbone to jaw. With a jolt, I realized I'd have those too some day. They didn't make him look grumpy or disappointed in life, as did the ones older people sometimes had that extended down from the sides of the nose to the mouth, effecting a permanently soured look. My father's lines looked rather noble, as if he'd won them in a sword fight or fencing tournament. He'd certainly won them in the fight of his adult life, surviving life in New York City as a fifty-plus-year old political refugee speaking no English and hated by his American wife's family.

So I had a few charges against him. Neglect to raise me. Neglect to shelter me. Neglect to support me. Nevertheless, now that my father's mortal coil was coming undone, what was the point of serving an eye for an eye, a tooth for a tooth? I knew I was supposed to do unto him what I would have wanted done unto myself, but this was more complicated. It always was, when it came to your own parents.

What I really wanted to do was get to know him more, without my big, galumphing unanswered needs getting in the way: without drama, without anger, without expectations. I was a genius at getting in the way every time I tried to hear what he had to say. Big, howling winds of recrimination would rise up and roar in my ears drowning out his exegesis of Fellini's final film or why Anna Magnani was sexier than Sophia Loren. Still, I did want to know what he thought Anna had that Sophia didn't. He must have been one inspired café conversationalist back in Budapest.

"It's not what happens to you, it's how you handle it," my college roommate had always said. She was right. I'd been perfectly justified to hold a grudge against my father my entire life. He deserved it. But the clock was running out and my unanswered needs from him weren't about to be answered anytime soon. Better to move on and enjoy the party his company always guaranteed. It was something, after all, for however long it lasted. The ball lay in my court.

I sat and toyed with my father's hand. Half of my DNA was from him. The more interesting half, frankly. The New England, Puritan, hardworking Girl Scout half had gotten me through Yale, but it had been the fiery, adventurous, acquisitive Hungarian half that had gotten me into Yale in the first place, and to Paris before that and wandering around the Guatemalan countryside before that. The whole crazy musician side of me was pure Hungarian. My father dancing the tango with an exotic stranger in a Budapest café was something I couldn't fail to recognize. It was me, in drag.

Time was running out. I wanted to get to know this man. Yet where was I supposed to go with my anger, my rage, my basic bloody needs?

Jesus on His cross came to mind. *Toss them at the foot of my Cross, Ava. That's what it's there for.* Maybe He had a point. God knew I wasn't going to get rid of my baggage any other way.

I squeezed my father's hand, sending a *zsolt* of electricity through it (pun intended).

Amazingly enough, my father squeezed back.

Then he woke up and said my name like no one else said it. "Aaaeeevaaaaaaaaa." Like a prayer. Like a song. Like the way a father says his daughter's name. Maybe it was time to cut him a break. I tossed a few pieces of baggage in the Cross's direction. Just as I began to feel lighter, Tünde 's voice rang out from the hall.

"Zso-o-o-olti-i-i-i-i-i-," she bawled, using the diminutive for my father's name. The virago was nigh. I turned my head to the door, carefully controlling my expression not to turn into the prune-shaped disapproving New Englander I always became around my father's girlfriend.

"He's awake," I said.

Tünde made my father look like Calvin Coolidge on Xanax. There was no room to breathe, sit or express oneself anywhere she was present. All I could do was defend myself from whatever she was screaming at me about or accusing me of. And that was just the way she made pleasant conversation.

"Zsoli! You're back. Zsolikoooo....." a stream of Hungarian endearments mixed in with a few swear words followed. Hungarians knew how to swear like fish knew how to swim. Tünde brushed past me and threw herself across my father's body on the bed. I checked quickly to ensure she hadn't disconnected any tubing or wires, then slipped out to confer with the nurse I'd spoken with earlier.

"Your father will most likely be transferred to the regular ward tomorrow. Then we'll see how he's doing and maybe he'll be able to go home in a few days. Do you live with him?"

"No. He lives by himself."

The nurse frowned.

"I see. And the woman who came in with him?"

"That's his girlfriend. She has her own place, downtown."

"He'll need some level of care after he's discharged. Are you able to look after him?"

"I'm—umm—I work full-time downtown, near Wall Street."

"Oh." The nurse's frown deepened. "Then what about his girlfriend? Can she look after him?"

"She does. All the time. They talk about twenty times a day if she's not actually with him."

"Good. Well, we'll have the hospital social worker speak to you before your father's discharged."

"You will?" What was that about?

"She'll give you some idea of options down the road."

"Down the road?" What was she saying?

"Your father has a heart condition. You're aware of that?"

"Yes." I was, more or less, although mostly I knew he needed to be careful of his diet from listening to Tünde lecture, hound and nag him about the heavy Hungarian sauces and fried *wienerschnitzel* he loved to cook and eat. My father was a good cook, unlike any females on my mother's side dating back to the pilgrims and beyond. The long line of WASPY females I came from on the distaff side were all dedicated to avoiding cooking like the plague. It interfered with entertaining guests, serving drinks with Ritz crackers with cheese, and managing staff, never mind children. By the time I entered my grandparents' household, the staff had been reduced to a single weekly housekeeper and one Jamaican nursemaid I hung out with until I entered nursery school at the Episcopalian church my grandparents were members of but rarely attended.

For the reduced staff reason, among a host of others, my grandmother became exceedingly cranky on the subject of cooking. Why was she doing it anyway, night after night? For once, I could see her point, entirely. Despite her complaints, she knew how to cook a mean steak, pork chops or lamb chops or just about any other piece of red meat. Where she came up short was in the salad department, offering such delicacies as canned fruit in red Jello with a dollop of mayonnaise on top, served on a wedge of iceberg lettuce. I thought salad was something that came out of a can until I left for Paris at age nineteen. *Lardon frisée?* not in the household I grew up in.

Do you know if your father has paperwork in place in the event of becoming incapacitated? A DNR order?" The Irish nurse asked cryptically. I wasn't good with acronyms, having overdosed on them in France, where just about everything official in Paris came in the form of an acronym—one I didn't understand.

"A what?"

"A do-not-resuscitate order," the nurse explained briskly.

"I—I don't know. I'll ask him." That wouldn't be easy. My father was terrified of official forms, anything that required his signature on some sort of legal document. When I'd been at Yale, I'd needed his signature on independent status forms the financial aid office had required. None had been forthcoming.

My father, for reasons hidden in history's mists, was scared to death of being deported for failure to pay child support or any other reason my grandparents on my mother's side might trump up against him. I didn't think they would have. But my father did, and I hadn't been able to appreciate my father's sense of terror at being asked to affix his name to any legal document.

The standoff was finally resolved when my older Hungarian-American cousin, a lawyer, signed the papers himself with some sort of explanation as to why my father couldn't do it.

I went back down the hallway to my father's room, where Tünde had recovered herself. She sat in the chair

I had just vacated, applying scarlet lipstick with a vanity mirror, one leg swinging energetically over the other. Hungarians are by and large an energetic race. Perhaps it's the paprika in their diet, or maybe it's in the blood. I didn't grow up eating paprika, and I was one of those types of people who never stops moving unless I'm asleep. As I said before, cats dislike me, since I'm tossing them off my lap to get up the moment they've settled there.

My father's blue-green, slanted eyes leapt as I entered.

"Évikaaa," he murmured weakly, his arm stretching toward me. I moved up to his bed, at a safe distance from Tünde, on the other side.

"Papa, how are you?"

"You look so lovely, Ava. Like Penelope when O–dee–say came home." Odysseus. Leave it to my father to come up with a classical allusion.

"Hah," Tünde broke in. "What have you been doing to your skin, Ava? It's all broken out. You don't pick at it, do you? Let me see." She got up and began to come around to my side of the bed.

My father's girlfriend was a skin care specialist. She worked at Mario Badescu, a top Manhattan salon where celebrities and wealthy women had their skin maintained. Tünde's clients included some well-known Hollywood actresses, all of whose names she had sworn she couldn't disclose to me, then had. No blemish went unexamined by her, especially ones on my face.

All of a sudden I was back to being a thirteen-year-old. It wasn't a great feeling.

"Nothing, Tünde, I'm fine." I backed away from her, turning toward my father and meeting his tired but amused expression with one of my own. When it came to

Tünde, my father and I were close allies. Neither of us could escape her, and both knew she was a necessary and important fixture in my father's life.

"No you're not. You've been picking at your skin. How many times have I told you not to do that?'"

"I don't. It breaks out all on its own, every month like clockwork, okay?" *Chill out, lady.*

"Don't worry about Ava's skin, Tündike. She looks beautiful."

"Hah. Where did you get that jacket?" she followed up, eyeballing my Betsy Johnson jacket. I could tell she liked it. It didn't matter. She'd find something savage to say about it within seconds.

"I got it at the Betsy Johnson after-Christmas sale." I'd bought it just before Pierre showed up in early February. It was fabulous, and I knew it. Nothing Tünde said could diminish my joy in my faux black velveteen riding jacket with light pink piping.

"How much did you pay for it?"

Back in West Hartford, Connecticut, where I was raised, people didn't ask how much other people's clothing cost directly to their faces. Ta-a-a-a-cky. New York was a whole other ballgame and Tünde was a total New Yorker.

"I uh—got it on sale. Marked down."

"How much?" She grabbed one side of my jacket, running her finger up and down the light pink piping. It even had feathers. It was fabulous, really. I knew my father would love it, which had been why I'd worn it, grabbing it from my mother's coat stand as I rushed out the door.

"It was really reasonable," I parried, toying with her. Suddenly, I'd turned into my New England-born and raised mother. My mother was a master at not revealing details. She knew how to hedge questions with the best Kabuki masters.

"What do you mean by reasonable?"

"I mean it was cheap." Wild horses wouldn't drag out of me the price I'd paid.

"How cheap?"

What was this? The Spanish Inquisition? No matter how hard I tried, I never failed to lose my cool with Tünde. She drove me up the wall and down over the other side.

"Cheap!"

"Like what?"

"Like I don't remember!" Now I was shouting.

"Of course you remember. How could you not remember what you paid for it?"

Because I don't spend all my time thinking about money, okay? I wanted to scream, but even mentioning "money" was a big no-no in New England circles. Instead I named a low amount, significantly discounted from the price I'd actually paid.

"You paid wha-a-a-a-t?"

"I just told you," I answered dryly, wondering how I'd gotten into the same predicament again that I always did with Tünde; at loggerheads, this time with my father's weakened form between us.

"I could have gotten that for half that price," Tünde chortled predictably. Some things never changed. Her final slash in any verbal swordplay we engaged in, for example.

"I don't think so," I countered, trying to look threatening.

"You should have gone to Century 21. They have Betsy Johnsons there for half the price you pay for stuff in her shop."

"I like going to her shop," I said to Tünde 's retreating form as she huffed out of the room. And I did. I especially liked going there at the end of January when everything was drastically reduced. It had ambience, style, a sort of sassy sexiness that I admired. When I wore Betsy Johnson clothes, people took notice, even if they didn't know what they were noticing. They showcased the women in the clothes, not the clothes themselves. That was the way clothes were meant to be worn. I'd learned that in Paris, but it applied everywhere. When my father said black is not a color unless it's worn by a blonde, he wasn't just talking about the color black or women who were blonde. He was talking about the animus inside the packaging—the spirit inside the body, the woman inside the dress.

Zsolt Fodor was all about soul. If he'd been a bit more about how to feed, clothe and shelter the soul over the course of my childhood I might have been more receptive to all his crazy, intriguing talk. As it was, I was sort of begrudgingly receptive. I was coming around, more or less.

I looked down at him, the animus coming back into his eyes. Our time was short. I either got to know him now, minus the bitter agenda, or my chance would be over. *What's it going to be, Ava?*

"Surrender." Clear as a bell, the word popped into my mind. Nothing more. I turned it over, contemplated it, kicked it around. It made no sense.

Yet.

THE NEXT FEW months went by in a haze. My father was discharged from the hospital into my care. At the exit interview, the social worker tossed a curve ball.

"You're aware that your father has some beginning signs of dementia?"

"I—of—no, I mean no I didn't know that." I had no idea. None. My father got agitated at times, but I'd thought that was because either 1) he was who he was, meaning a raging, maniacal penniless poet living in a very expensive city or 2) he was frustrated with not being able to express himself clearly in English.

"It will worsen over time."

"How much time?'

"No one can say. But he'll need to be followed by his doctors very closely."

"Does he—will he need extra—care down the road?"

The social worker paused and studied me thoughtfully. She looked tired, but kind. "Yes, dear. He will. You should begin looking at options for him when that time comes."

"What options?"

"You may wish to explore assisted living for him. It could be very difficult to care for him at a certain point."

"I can't do that. He's got—I mean he doesn't have any money. And I don't—I mean, I can't—"

"Your father has Medicaid. He'd qualify for one of the Medicaid spots in one of the assisted living facilities in his neighborhood," she spelled out, to my vast relief.

"I—uh—don't think he'd ever agree to leave his apartment."

"It's something to think about, Ms. Fodor. Just keep it in mind for down the road, if you aren't able to look after him yourself."

"Thank you," I said, dazedly. Getting up, I signed the discharge papers and went back to collect my father and bring him back to his apartment. For once, I was grateful that Tünde was there, although she was clear about the limits of what she intended and didn't intend to do.

"I cannot nursemaid your father, Ava. I have done enough. Your father doesn't listen to me. He eats what he wants to eat, he doesn't follow my advice. I wash my hands of him," she told me in ringing tones, not exactly dulcet, as I stood outside his room, ready to take him home. As much as her words were harsh, her actions spoke louder. She would wash her hands of him then turn around and run the same hands all over him, fussing, fixing, slapping and massaging the poor guy into pulp. His girlfriend of twenty six years would be there for him in a big way, just not in an official one.

As the sole official exit vehicle for my father from the hospital, I was in no way prepared for this role. Not only was I working full-time downtown as an office temp while waiting to hear back from the U.N., but I was the person who once upon a time had gone through hell in college when my father had refused to sign any and all official paperwork stating I was of independent status, thereby holding up my financial aid for weeks and barring me from eating in the college dining halls. It was a perfect opportunity to return an eye for an eye, a tooth for a tooth. I wanted to, desperately.

But it wasn't right. Some Body or something far better than myself counseled me inside that this wasn't the way to serve my very own father—the one who liked to refer to himself as Père Goriot. By association, I was one of Goriot's spoiled, callous daughters. In Balzac's novel, neither of the old man's socially ambitious daughter's had attended their father's funeral. He'd died a pauper, the daughters both sending empty carriages from their husband's households so the neighbors would see and think they were inside. That wouldn't be me. My grandmother had always said I was too selfish not to get what I wanted. she was right. This time what I wanted was to make some sense out of the time I had left to spend with my father. He was a man who had infuriated and disappointed me, but he fascinated me too.

I was no Florence Nightingale, so the whole nursing him back to health thing was a little lame on my part. I followed the example of the downtown financial firm I worked for as a temp and took the route of least responsibility: outsourcing. My first move was to invite over Sanja, since she knew how to cook soups and I didn't. She'd have patience with him when I didn't. By the end of the first week, I was already tapped out. That Friday I called her at lunchtime from work to see what she was up to for the weekend.

"I'm going to a gallery opening this evening, do you want to come?" Sanja asked, sounding excited. She had stopped seeing Victor and was now embarked on a whirlwind of social activities to leave his memory behind in the dust.

"I can't. I've got to look after my father," I said, wondering how Pierre handled looking after his mother. I was sure it was different from my conflicted attitude.

"Didn't you say he lives on the Upper East Side?"

"Yes. He's in Yorkville." I referred to the neighborhood around Eighty Sixth Street which was a subset of the area east of Central Park from Fifty Ninth Street all the way to Ninety Sixth Street known as the Upper East Side. Yorkville had been a largely German neighborhood dotted with a few Hungarian butcher shops, cafés and restaurants although now the yuppies were moving in. "On East Eighty Fifth Street."

"The gallery is on Seventy Ninth. I'll come with you, then we'll go together."

"I—ummm—I don't know how long it will take," I parried. Was I ready for Sanja to meet my father? Was I ready for anyone to meet my father? He was a one-of-a-kind sort of guy. Plus now he wasn't in the best of health, and he needed stuff done that I didn't really feel comfortable doing. I didn't want Sanja to see. Not so much my father's weakened form as my pathetic nursing abilities, exacerbated by a bad attitude. Why was I looking after this guy anyway? What had he done for me lately? What had he done for me ever? The same old issues were still around, no matter how many times I kicked them back to the foot of the Cross. I needed big help on this one—the supernatural kind.

"Come on. I want to meet him. You've told me so much about him."

Had I? In between discussing men, money, and securing U.N. jobs, I might have mentioned him a few times. Apparently whatever I'd said had made a strong impression. God knows I'd mentioned Sanja to my father. He was dying to meet her.

"Listen, he's not feeling well. He may not be up for a visit," I fudged, knowing full well my father would forget all about his heart condition the second he laid eyes on her. Once they began talking, it would all be over. We wouldn't get out of there until two bottles of good red wine were emptied and a little dancing had ensued. Come to think of it, it sounded like a pretty good evening.

The thought of it made me giggle until the follow up thought of Tünde's inevitable call intruded. She'd interrogate my father as to what we were doing; what he was eating and drinking, then ask to speak to me, whereupon she'd scream at me for trying to kill my father by having too much fun. Was it such a bad way to go? And was it heinous of me to be thinking down these lines? I was a party hound at heart, just like my Papa.

"Then it's decided. I just made cabbage soup so I"ll bring some with me. Where is he on Eighty Fifth Street?"

"323, between First and Second," I said caving in to her insistence. "I told him I'd be there around six." Homemade cabbage soup would appeal to him. Sanja made great soup and stews. I didn't know how to make any kind of soup and wasn't planning to learn anytime soon. What were Korean delis for anyway?

"Okay, I'll meet you in front of his building."

"I'll be upstairs already. Just buzz #2B and come up. He's on the second floor." Sanja-time was different from anyone else's time. She would typically float in to any scheduled rendezvous anywhere from thirty minutes to an hour and a half late. She made the French look punctual. I'd learned the hard way not to wait for her on a street corner. Better to pick a good singles scene spot to settle down at the bar with a volume of *Remembrance of Things Past* in case she was delayed even more than she usually was. There was always some sort of story attached to why she was delayed, but having witnessed Sanja getting ready to go out, I knew the biggest delay factor was Sanja herself. The ritual of getting ready to go out was a high art form with her. She'd chat while putting on mascara, put on a kettle of tea while choosing her outfit, drink it while deciding on another outfit, then spend a final thirty minutes deciding on which cape, hat or coat to wear while checking on how her soup stock was coming along.

But this time signals got crossed. Instead of Sanja arriving her usual one hour late, she was actually there in front of my father's stoop waiting for me with a big bundle as I hurried down East Eighty Fifth Street.

"You're early!" I called out, meaning "on time," something I'd never witnessed her to be before.

"Didn't you say five?'

Phew. So she'd just gotten the time wrong and was there her usual one hour late. Some things I depended on; Sanja's evanescent floatiness was one of them. I'd be disappointed if she started acting like a normal Manhattan person with professional standards. It would diminish her magic.

"Don't worry, let's go up," I said, kissing her once on each cold but warm cheek then leading the way into my father's brownstone walk-up building.

Adrenalin coursed through my veins. Hungary was about to meet Serbia. They'd both probably fall all over each other. It was New England Girl who wouldn't know how to act, prudishly standing in a corner, wondering what all the *sturm und drang* was about. It's not that I didn't like emotion. It's just that people from New England aren't encouraged to express any. I decided to focus on drinking too much in order to give myself something to do while my otherworldly friend and crazy father went bananas over each other.

"Aaaaaeeeeva," my father greeted me, pulling me inside into a bear hug, which was another one of those non-New Englandy things he did which made me feel uncomfortable yet warmed at the same time. I hadn't had a lot of practice with bear hugs in my childhood. No one did that sort of thing back in my hometown of West Hartford, Connecticut. Even less so in Maine, where I'd spent summers until I'd moved up there year-round for my last two years of high school. People in Maine showed intense emotion by standing in front of each other, heads down, looking at the ground in opposite directions and making terse comments about the weather.

"Looks like rain."

"Ayup. So they say."

"Ayup."

"Papa, I want you to meet Sanja Darkovic. She's also applying for a job at the U.N."

"Sanja, Sa-a-a-a-nja, you broke my heart," my father sang out weakly, as my Serbian friend fixed her warm, brown eyes on him and giggled.

He bent over her hand and kissed it. Suddenly we weren't in New York anymore. We were at the U.N., or in Paris or Budapest. I'd never heard him sing that song before and had no idea where it came from. As usual, I wanted to know more.

Sanja giggled again—sincerely, delightedly, unlike my nervous and embarrassed one.

"This is my father, Zsolt Fodor. I mean—Dr. Zsolt Fodor." I always forgot the doctor designation, since it seemed sort of silly, considering he wasn't a medical doctor nor was he a university professor. For once, I remembered that it mattered to him.

Sanja's eyes widened.

"Doctor Fodor?" Her voice emphasized "doctor" in a way that made my father's eyes light up. I could see a mutual charm campaign was underway. "I'm so happy to meet you. Ava has told me so much about you."

My father helped Sanja take off her coat and led us to the small round table in the center of his tiny living room.

As we walked in to the cozy, cheerful room I felt proud of him. One thing that could be said for my father was that he had sharp domestic skills. I didn't know it at the time, but this was a Hungarian attribute. His apartment was clean and neat as a pin, the small table nicely decked out with a red and white Hungarian woven tablecloth, the seltzer-making device, two glasses, a pitcher of water and bottle of wine on it, as well as a small bowl of olives and a tiny platter with a single salami and a sharp knife on it. He was one competent *hausfrau*.

Sanja sat down and looked around her while my father went through one of his favorite rituals—making wine spritzers. As he fiddled with the seltzer-making device, he hummed an obscure Hungarian tune, one I'd heard before. It was funny how some people become friends instantly. Sanja and my father fit like a Florentine leather glove to a hand. She had a magic about her that drew people in. My father and I were both putty in her long-fingered, graceful hands.

"Ava told me you write poetry," Sanja said, practically purring.

My father looked gratified. Another thing about Hungarians that isn't common to New Englanders is that they show their emotions. New Englanders can't even find their emotions, never mind show them. But with my father, everything he felt, at least from what I could see, showed up on his face, making our language barrier less daunting.

"Ahhhh, did Ava tell you about my books?"

"Books? You've written more than one book?" She acted as if he'd just mentioned he was on the New York Times Bestsellers List. "Ava told me about your book of poems. Have you written more? Could I see them?'

My father's smile broadened with each of Sanja's effusions. She was doing more to restore my father's health than a team of doctors could under any circumstances.

"Of course, my dear. But first we eat and drink." He took a tiny, sharp knife and began to peel off the cover to the bottle of red wine he held. A big no-no in Tünde 's book.

I slammed it shut.

My father loved to eat, drink, and talk all evening long. So did I, come to think of it. So did a lot of people, so what was the harm in it? I prayed Tünde had a heavy T.V. viewing schedule that evening so she would forget to call. I didn't want to have to recount to her every bite and sip my father had indulged in during our visit, just to have her scream at me about everything we were doing wrong on the road to killing him.

We toasted.

"*Prosit,* " my father said, using the German word for "cheers" that Hungarians typically did.

"*Egészségedre,*" Sanja said back, toasting him in Hungarian.

My father beamed.

I vaguely recognized the word, but didn't try to repeat it. There were at least three too many syllables for me to screw up, and I knew if you pronounced it wrong it came out in Hungarian as "I'll beat your mother like a dead horse," or something to that effect. Tünde had let me know what I'd mistakenly said the last time I'd tried it out in her presence.

"*Santé,*" I offered in French instead, keeping our toast in the urbane, European atmosphere my father and Sanja swam in. I knew so little of where either the two of them were coming from, but of one thing I was sure—I was in the company of two maestros.

We ate some salami, drank some Bull's Blood spritzers—that's Hungarian red wine, and in a minute my father got up and went into his bedroom. A minute later he returned with two books in hand.

"*Pilletánc?*" What does that mean? Sanja asked, staring at the cover of the slim book he handed her. Hungarian words have accents, umlauts and double dots over almost every other vowel. They add spice and glamour.

"The dance of the moth," my father explained.

"Ahhh," Sanja nodded approvingly. "Is that the name of one of your poems?"

"Yes."

I'd always wondered why my father had written about a dancing moth. Why not a dancing butterfly?

"Would you read it?" She fluttered her eyelashes at him.

My father looked as pleased as punch. He turned to the *Pilletánc* page and began reading. Mercifully, it was a short poem of seven stanzas.

"Wow, that was beautiful," Sanja sighed, when he was done. "What does it mean?"

I nudged her ankle under the table. Was she kidding?

She turned to me, her face all dreamy-eyed and dewy as if she'd just heard from the Oracle of Delphi.

"Did you understand it?" I asked incredulously. As far as I knew she didn't speak anymore Hungarian than I did.

"Not a word," she replied pleasantly.

"Then what do you mean "it was beautiful?"

"The way your father spoke. I can tell already."

What was this amazing effect my father had on people when he read his work aloud? And why did it have no effect on me?

"What does the whole moth dance thing mean again, Papa?" I'd already heard his explanation of this particular poem a few times and it had never made sense to me. I shook my philistine New England head, hoping to clear out the cobwebs and gain a little European *ancien régime* clarity. Pouring some more red wine into my glass, I reasoned if I drank some more, I might get it this time.

My father sat back and sighed in preparation for his translation task—a labor of love, especially with Sanja sitting there staring at him adoringly. My father liked to be adored the way Picasso liked to paint.

"There's a moth who likes to dance. All the *@#$* think he's a great dancer. When he dances, his $^&* wave like a &^*. The *&9 encourage him to @$%* his %*$@.

Tünde had already explained the poem to me in two lines, so I knew where this was going. My problem was, I just didn't know where we were once we got there.

Sanja nodded at every one of my father's dramatic pauses, as if understanding every word.

"He wants them to see how well he dances, so he moves closer to the light. "Finally, he dances too close to the light bulb and gets @$*%'d. Then he dies," my father explained.

"That's so beautiful," Sanja sighed.

"That's so stupid," I thought. There it was—the New England side of me rearing it's churlish head again. My objections to the moth getting zapped lay on multiple fronts. Why was it so beautiful to die from doing something so stupid? Why was the moth dancing instead of gathering food or doing something practical like paying a utility bill or whatever the equivalent was in Moth World? Why was I so attracted to people who thought stories like this were beautiful?

I inwardly shook my head as I studied Sanja and my father gazing at each other, in mutual admiration of the noble, dead moth.

"You've got to be kidding," I thought to myself. It was one of those moments when I realized how truly American I was. The whole romantic sensibility behind the dumb, dead moth story left me cold. Yet the two Europeans at the table, both from countries with romantically tragic histories, soaked up the poem like sponges soaking up wine. One had even written it.

Yet who were we kidding here? Neither one of these two were moth-types. They were both sophisticated, big-city types, about as moth-like as Madonna was an introvert. But they were both appreciating this story because it was about a moth—not a butterfly. What did it mean?

Then it hit me. My father was writing about the little people—for the little people. Not for the society types in Budapest. For his own Transylvanian countrymen. He was a man of the people. Except that he had liked to hang out in Budapest cafés. And now he lived in Manhattan. Somehow I didn't think he was the only walking contradiction around.

Suddenly, I felt the beauty of the moth's big moment, the reason for his sacrifice, the delicate dance of romance with death. I got it for the first time. What had changed?

It was because I was there with Sanja and my father—two people I really liked. Just the brief moment I allowed myself to realize I really liked my father was a watershed moment for me. I think it was because Sanja was there too and somehow it became okay for me to just relax, toss the excess baggage overboard and surrender to the moment, shared with two people I found undeniably attractive.

The only person who had ever translated the dance of the moth poem for me had been Tünde. No wonder I hadn't been able to hear its message. It was like having a poem translated by a professional hatchet handler. Not that Tünde wasn't smart. She just wasn't subtle the way Sanja was. And, for the first time I realized, the way my father was. He was a poet, yet all this time I hadn't had the ears to hear his poetry. But with Sanja present, for the first time I did.

"Ava, can you come here? For a visit?" Pierre asked. It was June, four long months after we'd last seen each other.

"I can't. My father's sick now. I need to take care of him. Plus my job," I sighed. It was true. There was no way, no possible way, I could hop on a plane and fly to France to see Pierre. Not with my father in such a frail state. He vacillated between weak moments then angry ones. Since coming home from the hospital in March, I'd noticed a change in him. Over the past three months his rages had become more frequent, his anger at times inexplicable.

My mother had begun to join me at least once weekly to visit him. On her last visit, she'd bent down to tie his shoe and my father had kicked her. I'd been horrified. Yet my mother had taken it calmly, whispering to me later that it was part of what was happening to him; he wasn't to blame.

I was impressed. My mother's career as a librarian had re-routed to social work in her mid-thirties. As a social worker, her specialty had been visiting homebound senior citizens. Apparently she'd learned some skills: patience and forgiveness amongst them.

"Then for the *vacances,* Ava. Let's spend them together," he pressed. In April, when Pierre had planned to visit again, his mother had fallen. He'd had to cancel his trip. Suddenly it was already June and what had begun so promisingly between us seemed destined to fade. There was no way either of us could move in the other's direction.

"Pierre, I can't. I'm temping until I hear back from the U.N. And I don't get paid holidays. And August will be busy for me because all the regular workers at my company will be taking vacation and they'll need temps to fill their spots."

"So I'll come to you."

"I'd like that."

"*Bon.* I'll arrange it and call you."

Before Pierre called again, my father ended up back at Doctor's Hospital, this time with a milder heart attack. The social worker informed me he would need full-time care arranged for him this time, before he could be released. The only way I could spring him was to begin the process of applying for a spot for him at a nearby nursing home. It was complicated, due to the fact that he would be admitted as a Medicaid patient. There were forms to fill out, interviews and a tour, and some surprising details involved in the process.

"You'll need to pay for your father's final arrangements and bring us the contract."

"Excuse me?"

The clerk stared at me. "You have to make final arrangements for your father before we can admit him."

What do you mean, final arrangements?"

"What do you think I mean?"

"You mean—his—his death?"

"Your father is eighty, right? You want him admitted here as a Medicaid patient. What do you think I mean?"

"How do I do that?" I'd never arranged anyone's funeral before. What did you do? And what did it cost? I shuddered to think that thought had crossed my mind so soon after the thought of my father's death. I was beginning to think like Tünde or perhaps I was simply becoming a New Yorker.

"You find a funeral home in the neighborhood. Here—we have a list you can take." The clerk shuffled in a drawer and produced a slim photocopied booklet.

"How do I—How do I..."

"Pay for it? I'll give you a tip," the clerk lowered his voice. "You need to spend down your father's assets, you know."

"Do what? I was good at spending up. What did spending down mean?"

"For your father to qualify for Medicaid guidelines, he can't have any assets. He doesn't have any, correct?" He stared at me significantly. Like he was trying to tell me something.

"He—uh—as far as I know, he doesn't."

"Good. Well when you do know definitely, make sure he doesn't," he said, lowering his voice.

"What happens if he does?" I whispered.

"This place will take them and you'll never see a dime again," he whispered, leaning across his desk to ensure no one was listening. "Got it?"

"Got it," I replied.

Outside, it occurred to me the clerk had done me a favor. I had no idea what my father had in his bank account, but it was time to find out. Although Tünde was a battle axe, she was an honest one. She'd told me months earlier to get power of attorney and take possession of my father's bank account. I'd recoiled at the idea, thinking it sounded like stealing. But who else was supposed to be in charge of my father's paltry assets? I was the appointed, the anointed one. I couldn't wriggle out of being my father's only child and closest living relative, no matter how uncomfortable I was with the responsibility it entailed. There was no one else to do the job.

"Mom, did you know Papa can't have any assets to get into this place?"

"Well, he doesn't, does he?" She looked mildly surprised.

"I don't actually know."

"You need to find out."

"I feel like I'm sneaking around, getting my hands on his bank account, clearing it out," I said.

"You're not. You'll be doing what you need to do as next-of-kin." It was reassuring to hear her advise me. She so rarely did.

"Can't you do it?" I asked? I felt like Jesus in the Garden of Gethsemane asking his Papa to take back the whole idea of the Crucifixion.

"No, I can't. You're the only one who can, as far as I know. You need to get power of attorney."

"I feel strange doing all this."

"If you want me to, I'll come with you. I've gone through this with my clients. It's something older person who become incapacitated have to do."

"Is he—has he—become incapacitated?"

My mother just looked at me.

"Okay, I'll do it tomorrow."

"I'll come with you."

Once again, my feelings for my mother took a right turn. She was coming through, offering support when I needed it. Because she was doing the right thing, she gave me strength to do the right thing too. It was an adjustment, whether from not being entirely used to doing the right thing as opposed to the expedient one, or not being used to recognizing my mother as a family member who offered support.

In the next ten days, power of attorney was granted, funeral arrangements made and paid for, and the small sum of money left in my father's bank account wasn't enough to worry about until the time came for his transfer to the nursing home. How to put off that day from coming wasn't clear to me, so I prayed God would fill in the gaps. On a scale of one to ten, my nursing skills were somewhere between zero and one, so it was a big job. The Big Guy would have to help me handle it, because there was no way I could alone.

Then it hit me that He already was helping. He'd put help and support in the form of my mother, who was reaching out with practical suggestions and the gift of her time; neither of which she had offered before.

Something didn't add up. It was me. Whatever I'd decided about my mother had to come undone. She was changing before my eyes and I had no words to make up the new narrative.

CHAPTER SEVEN

DOWNWARD SLOPE

"*B*ut my wife's father is a doctor. He is a very important mister. He is powerful man," my father raged, gesturing wildly; most probably scaring the two elderly ladies who sat nearby. My mother and I were at De Witt Nursing Home on East Seventy Ninth Street, for an interview and initial visit. Perhaps it had not been a good idea to bring my father with us, but I needed to keep an eye on him now, and Tunde had said she was out with her girlfriends for the day.

My father's laughing references to being Père Goriot were suddenly no longer a joke. Whether I wanted to be cast in the role or not, I was, at that moment, one of Père Goriot's unappreciative daughters, highy embarrassed by the words now spilling out of his mouth. In the throes of a moment, the creeping dementia had overtaken him. It would pass. My father's perception of himself was something I was powerless to change. All I could do was control my reaction to it, I told myself. But inside, I wanted to kick him and tell him to shut up.

"Can you believe he said that?" I whispered to my mother, furious on her behalf. He'd just implied he'd married my mother partly because her father had been a doctor. Clearly it had factored into my father's decision-making somewhere.

"I didn't hear what he said," she replied calmly, pouring a sugar packet into a mug of tea for my father.

I was doubly enraged. My mother was a master at deliberate deafness when unpleasant things were spoken. She'd picked that up from her father, my grandfather, the doctor who had been hard of hearing for as long as I'd been alive, due to my grandmother's incessant and endless picking apart of both his character and actions.

I wanted my mother to hear what my father had said and get angry about it. Yet she wouldn't cooperate. Pretty soon I'd go into a demented rage too if someone didn't offer me the satisfaction my anger at my father's words demanded.

He was saying things my grandmother had suspected him of long ago. That he'd gotten my mother pregnant in short order so as to be able to stay in the United States, where he hoped to be supported by his father-in-law, the doctor.

"Over my dead body," my grandmother had said. She had loved to use that phrase. Usually she'd used it in connection with me, so it had been a relief to hear her say it in reference to someone else.

Now my father was proving her right. I couldn't believe it. What's more, my mother didn't even seem to mind. Incredible.

"Here, Zsolt." Calmly, she handed him the mug of tea.

Instantly, he quieted down, sipping the tea like a kitten taking milk from its mother. My mother's sphinx-like stillness held some sort of power over him, certainly the power to calm him. I silently thanked God Tünde hadn't been able to join us on this visit. She had a way of escalating drama instead of quieting it down, the way my mother did.

"E-li-za-beth," my father said, lovingly drawing out each vowel. There were a lot of them in my mother's name just like many of the words in my father's native tongue. God knows she understood much of my father's Hungarian without speaking a word.

"Drink your tea," my mother answered calmly.

"I see nothing, I say nothing," my father said. I watched in confusion as he dreamily stared into her eyes.

My mother smiled in response. What was going on? My father had tried to kick her just one minute earlier.

"Erzsebet," my father said using the Hungarian name for Elizabeth while patting her hand.

My mother patted his hand back. Prepared, she'd avoided his kick, since he'd already pulled that stunt months earlier. Both times, she'd handled it calmly, like a saint. Something about her was changing before my eyes. It was my perception of her. Another feeling now battled with rage inside me.

Shame. I didn't understand the slightest thing about either my mother or my father nor about the feelings they had for each other. It was clear they could appreciate each other in ways and for reasons I couldn't appreciate either of them. Perhaps it was time to stop condemning them for being people other than the ones I wanted them to be.

"What did you say?" I asked my father.

Without looking at me, still he stared into my mother's eyes. "I see nothing, I say nothing," he repeated.

"What is he talking about?" I demanded. As usual, he was saying something metaphorical and I was out in the cold as to its meaning.

Being grown up wasn't as easy as it looked. I was beginning to see it took a good deal of forbearance, a quality I'd never really understood. But looking at my mother now, patiently taking my father's tea mug from him and setting it down, then picking up his hand again, I was impressed. What was going on between these two?

My mother looked over at me, mute, but her eyes sparkled. 'I see nothing, I say nothing' fit her like a glove. How well my father knew her.

"Does anyone want to tell me what's going on here?" I asked, one last time.

Instead of answering, the two lovebirds from Strange Planet went back to staring at each other. Adoringly, no less. It occurred to me my mother must have made a terrific New York City social worker. If there had been a Most Discreet Social Worker of the Year award, she would have won it, annually.

Leaving them to their moment, I got up and wandered over to the door to the outdoor terrace. It was locked.

The day was beautiful, but access to the flower-filled terrace was denied. I looked around to see if I could find someone to unlock it for me.

My father had raged when we'd told him we were going to find a comfortable apartment for him here. No wonder. It wouldn't be an apartment, it would be a room with a roommate. Someone he wouldn't know, most likely from a completely different cultural and educational background. My father would no longer be free to go outside, roam around, go to his favorite café on the corner or buy a newspaper from the Punjabi Indian man who ran the newsstand on Second Avenue and Eighty Sixth. No wonder he didn't want to go to the nursing home.

"It's a prison," Tünde had wailed.

"It's a place where he'll be safe," I'd reasoned with her.

"He wants to stay in his own home," she'd shouted back.

"I know he does. But he needs someone there to make sure he doesn't hurt himself," I'd yelled back.

"So stay with him! You're his daughter," she'd screamed. As I said, Tünde had a special way to escalate things. Fast.

"I work, okay? I have a full-time job. I won't be there most of the time if I stay with him. What about you? Why don't you stay with him?"

"I'm not looking after an old man! I told your father that years ago. I made my own money and now I want to enjoy it. He's your father!" In the same moment, she turned to my father and ran her hands all over his neck.

"Zsolti-i-i-" she crooned, practically molesting him.

To say the least, her attitude was confusing. What wasn't confusing was the massive cannonball of unfair guilt she aimed at me. Why should I look after a man who had never looked after me? Still, who else was there to do it? His girlfriend of twenty-six years had defined her boundaries clearly. She did a lot for my father. At a minimum, she kept him on the phone at least six times daily, chewing him out over whatever he had last eaten or drunk. It was clear she cared, but the extent to which she was going to be there for him was also clear—not totally.

Tünde had a point. She was his girlfriend, not his wife. Zsolt Fodor had no wife. He had one immediate relative—his daughter. Me. The appointed, anointed, unwilling one.

Back at my father's place, I got him to lie down, no easy task; then I called Tünde and shoved the phone receiver into his hand. She'd keep him busy while I ran downstairs to the corner and used a phone card to call Pierre. It didn't matter that we hadn't seen each other for months. I needed to talk to him desperately.

"I don't know how you do it," I cried into the phone.

"Do what?"

"Take care of your mother."

"It's easy. I love her."

"That's where we're different," I said. I felt something for my father, but was it love? I admired him at moments when I was taking a break from being disappointed with him. And there were times when I found him fascinating when I wasn't finding him embarrassing.

"Ava, I know that. And it's okay."

"It's not okay, Pierre. I want to be like you, to feel the same way you do for your mother. But I can't. There's nothing there."

"There's no childhood memories, I know. But there *is* something there."

"There's no stories." Well maybe there were a few. It's just that they took place when I was an adult, not a child.

"Maybe no stories from long ago, but a few from not so long ago, no?"

"A few, I guess." I thought of all those crazy evenings my father and I had spent in the company of Sanja. There were most definitely a few. All of which I enjoyed more when I thought of myself as one of my girlfriends instead of who I was—my father's daughter; the one he'd handed over to his in-laws at the age of fourteen months, then never visited for the next fifteen years. To be fair, they had run him off.

Yet.

"Ava, you don't have to be a saint. You just have to have a relationship with your father." Why did Pierre have to be so smart? I wished madly he was there at the moment. In New York, next to me on the sidewalk, hugging me hard.

"I have to put him into a nursing home. He hates the idea and he'll hate me when the time comes."

"He won't hate you, Ava. Trust me. He'll be angry but he won't hate you. He can't, because he loves you. You're his daughter."

"How can he love me? He didn't even bother to raise me!" I yelled into the phone. All these bloody platitudes irritated me. What was the weight of love if it didn't involve being around?

"Circumstances got in the way. They do sometimes, don't they?"

I thought about it. Circumstances were getting in the way of Pierre and me right now. It was frustrating. How could love grow with no shared experiences to knit two people together?

"Okay, so you've got a point. But I don't feel the same way about him that you do about your mother."

"That's okay."

"No it's not okay!" I screamed Why was I screaming at Pierre? Someone needed to understand that it wasn't okay that there had been a big black hole where the section for my parents was supposed to be when I was a child. How was I supposed to know what love was when the love section of my childhood had been left vacant all those years?

"Then make it okay! he yelled back. I'd never heard Pierre yell before. Stunned, I paused.

"I don't know how to," I whispered, taking it down a notch.

"I have an idea for you," he answered, slightly less steamed.

"What?"

"Shared meals. Shared conversation."

"Huh?"

"That's all you can do for now. So do it."

"That's what I have been doing," I said crankily. I couldn't understand half of what my father said. Then when he said stuff like "I hear nothing," clear as a bell, I still couldn't understand. What was the point?

"So keep doing it. Don't you see you're making those stories between you right now?"

"It doesn't matter now. It mattered when I was a child!" I yelled. But as the words spilled from me, something told me I was wrong. I'd needed him when I was a child, but he hadn't been there. Now he needed me as an adult, and I was here. Was the point to pay him back, tit for tat? Or was the point that it wasn't a good thing to not be there for someone who needs you?

It was unfair. Yet this was my moment to make the world a slightly less unfair place. But at my expense. Could

I afford it? What if I walked away? Could I then afford the hole in the place of where my heart should have been?

"Ava, it does matter now. He won't be around forever. Or maybe you won't be. So make those stories together now."

"Pierre?"

"What?"

"I hate you." I meant something more in the opposite direction, although I didn't know exactly what. Love was out because I didn't even know what it was.

"Because?"

"Because you're wise."

"Thank you. I hate you too." Pierre was good at matching my pace.

"Why?"

"Because you're a half-Hungarian hot-head."

"Thank you."

"I love you too."

"Don't talk about love if we can't be together," I exploded, heating up again. "It's like my father saying he loves me. What does it mean if we didn't spend any time together?"

"Spend the time together now," Pierre yelled back. "Because he means it when he says he loves you. Make it mean something to you too."

I hung up on him. Pierre drove me up the wall. He was like a cowboy trying to tame a wild horse. Yet I knew he was drawn to me, kicking and screaming for justice and not finding it anywhere. Maybe it was the way Pierre's mother felt the moment she found out she had multiple sclerosis. Then again, every time her body refused to do something it had done before. Not fair. Ridiculously, unbelievably unfair.

I spent the rest of the evening kicking myself. Because Pierre was right. Who knew the price of being a hero was to accept sacrifice at huge injustice? It wasn't all glamour. In fact, being a hero wasn't glamorous at all. It just meant doing the right thing. I wasn't up for the job.

❧

TAKING A PAGE from Pierre, I started hanging out with my father. Instead of looking at it as a nursing job, I thought of it as an entertainment one. I'd been a singer-pianist, so I knew that business. Every time we got together, I told myself it was a party. It takes two to tango, so we did.

On an early August evening, I even cooked for him. I know you think I'm lying, but I'm not. On a recent visit to the U.N. Staffing Office, I'd picked up a U.N. Cookbook, hoping it would bring me luck in my job quest. I'd found a recipe for Nicaraguan chicken and made it one night at my father's apartment, in his cozy kitchen, while he hummed tunes in the next room and went through his papers. He was always looking over his papers. It might have been part of the advancing dementia, but who knew? Most of them were in Hungarian, so I couldn't make heads nor tails of them. Even if they'd been in English, I wouldn't have been able to understand what he was hashing over. It was best to stick to food, drink and conversation, just as Pierre had advised.

I couldn't compete with my father's chicken papri-kash, one of Hungary's most delicious traditional dishes, so I was happy to have the Nicaraguan chicken recipe to screw up. With almond-stuffed olives, capers, red and green peppers instead of the sweet Hungarian yellow ones he was so familiar with, he would have no preconceived notions about what it should taste like.

"*Finom*," my father declared after the meal.

My ten-word Hungarian vocabulary included "*finom.*" It meant "phenomenal" or "delicious." The Nicaraguan chicken had been a hit.

Exhausted from my culinary efforts and still a big city take-out girl after all, the next evening I brought back sushi for my father to try for the very first time.

"How do I eat this?" he asked suspiciously, picking up his fork and knife.

"Put down the fork and knife. You pick it up like this and put the whole thing in your mouth. Just let it melt in your mouth." I demonstrated, picking it up with the chop-sticks the take-out sushi place had included.

"I put the whole piece in my mouth? I have a big mouth, but are you sure?"

"Yes, Papa," I giggled. "That's how they do it in Japan." I'd taught English in Tokyo, the summer between sopho-more and junior years at Yale. I'd picked up a nice bun-dle, working for a joint venture engineering firm teaching their executive employees conversational English. I'd met the head of the company in a nightclub, where after four hours of dancing, drinking and schmoozing during which time he'd complained bitterly that he was trying to groom his successor, but none of his knuckleheaded managers could speak English competently, which they would need to do to run the company—a joint venture with a U.S. firm headquartered in Texas.

If ever an opportunity had been handed to me, this was one. On the spot, taking full advantage of our somewhat inebriated state, I talked him into giving me an exclusive contract to teach his top management-level employees during one-hour weekly lessons. My father had been responsible for providing the Pan Am employee pass plane ticket that got me to Tokyo. That had been the summer I'd come up with the entire $2,500 the Yale financial aid office had deemed should be my contribution toward my financial aid package that year. The experience had been so successful, that after I'd graduated and gallivanted around Europe a bit, I'd gone back to resume my position at the Niigata-Masoneilan Engineering Company in Toranemon, Tokyo's downtown business district.

"The ladies cover their mouths with their hands when they eat. Like this," I demonstrated, cupping my right hand over my mouth, slightly in front of my face. I always felt like I was about seven years old when I used this particular Japanese feminine gesture. It only looked cute on Japanese females. On Western women, it looked ridiculous, as if we were trying to channel our inner five-year-old selves.

My father looked at me and laughed. He brought his hand up to cover his mouth too.

"No, Papa! You don't do that, only the ladies. Giggling, I grabbed his arm, pulling it down. "Men are supposed to be macho in Japan. They belch, they burp, they eat with their cheeks puffed out. It's allowed."

"It's not gentlemanly." My father looked shocked.

"You're not kidding." There were a number of things Japanese men did with their bodies in public that made me want to cringe—on the other hand, Japan was a highly civil, non-violent sort of place where the incidence of domestic violence, rape or murder was practically non-existent. Spending time there had been like having a free pass to Disneyland, cast in the role of a fairy princess. I couldn't complain. But eventually it had gotten too easy. Having been brought up in the school of hard knocks, I wasn't fully comfortable just sitting around getting paid for being cute, young, blonde, and American. I needed to get out of there after a few years, to sharpen my edge before I lost it.

"You know, this fish is good!" my father said, after a minute of thoughtful chewing.

"It ought to be, considering how much it cost." Sounding like Tünde again, I caught myself. Was it living in New York that did that to a soul? After awhile, it was all about "how much was it?" or "You paid too much!" or "Let me tell you where you can get a bargain." I was no longer a restrained New Englander, abhoring talk of money, especially—God forbid—actual amounts. In New York it was all about the money, the more detail the better.

"It's like butter."

"That's because of the way they cut it. Sushi chefs train for years to learn how to cut different types of fish for sushi or sashimi." I was impressed. How many eighty-year olds were open to new types of food? Not many. But if there was anyone open to new experiences, it was Zsolt Fodor— Zsolt the bolt of electricity that was my father, housed in an old man's body.

We ate, drank, and talked our way through the next hour, trying the different types of sushi and sashimi I'd brought over. Discovering sushi had aided me in my recovery from junk food addiction. The first summer I'd spent in Japan, I'd found it tasteless. But on my second trip there, my palate had been cleaner, and six months into my stay, I'd found I was eating less and less sweet crackers and packaged sweets at Tokyo convenience stores, and instead heading for the savory soup and take-out sushi offerings. It was hard to overeat on sushi. My body was content when I'd eaten enough. It wasn't like the strange aftereffects of eating sugars and processed carbs, which I'd crave more of long after I'd finished off a bag of chips or a box of cookies. Tokyo food offerings had the same effect on me that Parisian ones had—first I'd exhausted the sweets, then when I'd finally begun to eat like a native, a small miracle had taken place: I'd stopped being a slave to foods that were bad for me and started enjoying foods that were healthy, as well as delicious. My slavish food addictions no longer held me in a stranglehold. It had been life-altering for me.

The phone rang. It was my mother.

"There's a message for you on the answering machine," she said, in a voice similar to Minnie Mouse. No one would have been a greater hit in Tokyo than my mother, had she gone there as a young woman. She had every attribute the Japanese admired in females—mystery, a teeny tiny pookey wookey voice, cuteness in spades, a quiet, demure style and most of all—Kabuki Princess coolness.

My father's face lit up as he kenned it was my mother on the phone. The mystery of their romance would forever beguile me. What was it with these characters? Somehow they'd kept their love alive by living on opposite ends of Manhattan island for the past twenty six years. There was something to be said for one of Katherine Hepburn's more memorable quotes: men and women should live next door and visit frequently. Yet my father and mother hadn't visited at all since they'd divorced. They'd simply kept lit the candle of their good memories together and snuffed out the bad ones. It was something I couldn't get my arms around; perhaps my arms weren't big enough.

"What? Who from?" Had Pierre called? We hadn't spoken for weeks. He'd been on his summer holiday and since I'd been clear I couldn't see any way to us spending them together, we'd been out of touch.

"I think it's from the U.N. You might want to call in and listen."

Sure enough, the U.N. staffing department had called about an appointment to that fall's General Assembly. The Nicaraguan chicken had been lucky, after all. I was in.

"Papa—they called. I'm going to work for the U.N.!"

"My darling, that is good news. No more working for the money house."

"No, Papa. I'm not a real money house kind of woman."

"You are an international woman."

"Thanks to you, I am."

"It's in your blood."

"Your plane tickets didn't hurt either." He may not have given me protection, guidance or financial support, but the plane tickets he'd begun providing at age eighteen had given me something else altogether—a free ticket to the world. Anywhere Pan Am flew, I could go. With Flight One circumnavigating the globe clockwise and Flight Two counterclockwise, that covered a lot of territory. Already

I'd flown to Tokyo via Frankfurt, Tehran, New Delhi, Hong Kong, Bangkok. It was the long way to go, but it had been worth it to stop over in New Delhi, Hong Kong and Bangkok along the way. I'd skipped Teheran since they were having a revolution there. It had sure beat not having anywhere to go over Christmas break during college years.

"What do you mean?"

"I mean, you made me who I am." Words I'd never put voice to spilled out. It was a miracle I was now feeling them. Ever since my delivery from junk food addiction, I knew miracles could occur. That and getting into Yale.

"Who are you?" My father looked at me expectantly. It was the kind of question my grandfather would never have asked. The fact that my father was open to whatever answer I gave him correlated with the kind of guy who could be open to the experience of trying sushi for the first time at age eighty. That was my kind of guy. Once again, the ground I'd walked on for years, stomping my parents into the dirt for all the wrongs they'd done me, shifted beneath my feet. A general reassessment was due.

"I'm a U.N. sort of person. An international hybrid," I answered gaily, happy to have this kind of free-flowing conversation with my very own free-flowing flesh and blood. Most flesh and blood relatives I'd grown up with hadn't flown very freely. My grandmother's martial form rose before me and I shivered. No free thinking had flowed in her neck of the woods, deeply mired in antebellum Southern thinking as she was. *No woman should take the place of a man in a college classroom. One day a man will have to support his family. A woman's job is to support him in doing it, not to take it away from him.*

"You are part doctor's daughter and part tango dancer."

"Thank you, Papa. You put it so neatly." And he did. When I'd first met him at age sixteen, I would have bristled to hear him call me a tango dancer. But that was long ago, before I knew what the tango was. Before Paris, before Tokyo, before New York. Now it was fourteen years later, and I didn't exactly know how to dance the tango, but I knew what he was getting at and it was the same thing out of life I longed to get at too. He was right. I was part tango dancer. I'd had to leave behind New England and my grandparents way of life.

They hadn't been wrong. It's just that there was more out there I needed to discover. My father's blood had called to me and I had answered the call of the wild.

That night, falling asleep on his couch, I thought of Pierre. The news of my U.N. appointment would cement the distance between us. He was there, I was here. But because Pierre, with his dependable, not very flamboyant, steady style, was there in my life somewhere—even if he was far from me—I felt as if I had something to anchor and steady me. Even more, I would have a dull, plodding administrative job with an organization that boasted one of the most fiercely protective civil service unions in the world. All these factors spoke to me, a former singer/pianist, with job security like quicksand. Sanja had told me all about it from information she'd gathered from U.N. workers she'd gotten to know over the past six months of working on gaining a position there. I hoped she'd gotten a call too.

My thoughts skipped over the people now in my life—Sanja, Pierre. Were they there to save me from myself? Undoubtedly they were there to give me the tools I needed to get to know the one man who hadn't been able to provide me with a past. Instead, he'd provided me with a ticket to ride. In a crazy just-before-you-drop-off-to-sleep epiphany, the thought occurred to me to avail myself of one of his employee pass tickets before the General Assembly started and go track down the steady, solid rock of a man who quietly cared for his own parent in a vastly different sort of way on the other side of the Atlantic. How did Pierre take care of his mother? With grace? Nobility? Strained resentment? Sacrificial self-righteousness? Stout-heartedness? There was only one way to find out.

❦

THE NEXT DAY I called the U.N. Would I like to take a three-month appointment with the Department of Information and Reception for this year's General Assembly?

I would. I was to come in the following day to begin the identification and intake process that accompanied becoming an international civil servant.

"It's only a temporary position," I told Sanja worriedly over the phone.

"Not to worry. We'll start networking as soon as we get there and find a way to stay. Sanja had been assigned to the Fourth Committee on Decolonization. Neither one of us had any idea what that meant.

"Do you know what you have to do?" I asked her.

"No. It doesn't matter. We'll make friends in the right places." She nodded confidently, her fluffy blonde hair a halo framing her vividly alive, perfectly oval face. I could imagine how eagerly African male diplomats at the U.N. would wish to make friends with her. She would manage.

We met at the staffing office the following day, where we presented passports, were fingerprinted and received only the haziest idea of what our assignments were. The office buzzed with new hires, mostly of an international ilk. I felt much more stimulated than I ever had at the downtown brokerage firm where I'd been temping. The U.N. was in my DNA, unlike finance.

Something inside saluted my fellow international mongrels, each with a deep and complex story, many of them far more poignant than my own. Sanja was there to avoid going back to her own country which was breaking up into small, angry pieces; Serbia the angriest of them all.

"Let's celebrate your appointment," my father said enthusiastically when I returned to his apartment. Zsolt Fodor was always up for a party. But was his heart up for one?

"Shall we go to the café on the corner?" I suggested, knowing how much my father liked cafés. He'd pretty much lived in various ones in Budapest during his twenties and thirties.

"*Schön.* Let's go," he agreed, using the German for "beautiful," meaning "great idea." My father accessed any one of at least four different languages to get himself across. Hungarian, German, French, and English all served indiscriminately to help him make his points.

He tossed a light sweater on his far less bulky post-heart attack torso, and we haltingly made our way to the end of the street. It was an exercise in patience, my father walking slower than before, stopping frequently to gesture and look around. Even when he'd been perfectly healthy, he'd had the habit of stopping on the sidewalk whenever he made a point. Now the whole process took twice as long, his points seemingly twice as laborious. But they usually led to something interesting if I harnessed my impatience and took the time to listen and absorb.

My instinct to run laps around him wasn't a good one. At age thirty, I had the energy of an untrained puppy, perhaps an inheritance from my extremely active grandmother. She could never sit still and neither could I. The only person I knew, in fact, who could match my father's sudden stoppages on the sidewalks of Manhattan was my mother—the Kabuki Princess herself. They were well-matched in the weirdest of ways, none of which I shared.

When Tünde was with us, just like me, she'd try to pull my father along.

"Okay, Zsolti, let's go. *Igan igan*—yes, yes, *nem* (&*^(@$#%*$*&^," she'd sputter in Hungarian, chiding him to hurry it up. In that regard alone, Tünde and I were kindred spirits—impatient souls both, unlike my mother and father, for whom time together stood still, frozen back in Unreality Land, when love was young, fresh, and untrammeled by bills and children.

"Okay Papa, let's just get to the café. You can explain it to me there," I said, realizing I sounded exactly like Tünde, Public Enemy Number One. I didn't dislike her because she was my father' s girlfriend. It was her unabashedly insensitive and ferocious personality which drove me up the wall.

My mother's zen-like spirit of non-communicativeness (why bother communicating when you can just watch TV?) had clearly driven my father into the arms of his present girlfriend, the virago incarnate. Tünde loved him, but all the *sturm und drang* that went along with her was too much for me. I wasn't exactly a Buddhist monk in my calm serenity, but I enjoyed relating to people who actually paused long enough to—well—relate. It escaped me to understand how Tünde related to anyone—other than my father. She basically just threw herself at people until they gave up and agreed with whatever she was saying, or else got away from her as soon as possible.

We made it to the café where we ordered a rosé spritzer for my father and a margarita for me. The good thing about cafés in New York is that, unlike in Paris, they're largely ecumenical. A little something for everyone, with condemnation for none. A rosé spritzer and a mango margarita? Fine. Some guacamole and chips with your cappuccino? No problem. Unlike exacting Paris, New York offered the fresh air of food choice freedom.

"So how do we celebrate your new job?" my father asked.

"I have an idea," I began.

"If I had the world, I'd give it to you, Évika...." my father began to sing. Other customers looked round, but fortunately we sat outside on the terrace and mostly, they looked amused.

"That's the point, Papa. You do have the world."

"You want to fly somewhere before you start work. Where?"

"France." He'd caught my drift immediately.

"Paris?"

"No. The south."

"Nice? St. Tropez?"

No. Carcassonne. In the southwest." I'd never been there, but I'd heard it was a medieval walled city. Pierre had been raised there. What aspects of its history had rubbed off on him?

"You have a reason, yes? Who is he?"

I colored. I hadn't told my father much about Pierre. I'd tried to keep the two men in my life separate. Plus my father jumped to conclusions quickly about men I mentioned. Part of him, deep down inside, was eager to see his daughter married off. It could be ticklish bringing a male friend with me to visit him. If my father was in the throes of one of his moments, he was inclined to embarrass me highly.

"Who is this Mister? Is he your fiancé?"

"No, Papa. He's someone from church," I'd sputter, rolling my eyes at a friend I'd brought along after a Sunday service.

He'd peer at the man beside me and let loose with some sort of untoward comment:

"Mister, do you have enough money to be her husband?"

"Papa," I'd cringe. "I told you he's just a friend. He's not in the husband stakes," I'd cut him off, begging my friend's forgiveness with my eyes. Usually whichever friend had accompanied me, would find the scene humorous and highly forgivable. My father certainly provided entertainment, with a dash of deep down truths for seasoning. It was only me who died a thousand deaths at those moments.

Afterward I'd wonder what part of my father's psyche was being accessed when the dementia took over. In normal moments, my father could give a fig about money, social status or career paths. But when the dementia came on, suddenly he'd go on about Misters who were rich, Important People, those who had power, those who didn't. A hidden *haute bourgeosie* value system took over, impelling him to make comments everyone thought about but nobody stated aloud. I could only bring along male friends from church with highly refined senses of humor or compassion. Fortunately there were a few of them in the congregation, eager to do a good turn for a friend at low cost to them on a Sunday afternoon.

"Someone I met in France. A friend."

"The one you told me was a *kutyaszar* bastard?"

Had I mentioned my ex to him? "No, Papa. Not that one." I cleared my throat. "Another one. His friend, actually." Pierre and Arnaud had been childhood schoolmates.

"That's a good way to take revenge on the #%$) (*&%^&*^%."

Zsolt had a point. "Pierre is my friend. I'd like to visit him before I start work. But ...."

"Don't worry about me. Tünde can look after me."

"Are you sure, Papa?"

"And I have my girlfriend down the street."

"Judy?"

"Yes." He referred to Judy Radwany, the neighborhood social worker for senior citizens whom he had gotten to know in the past few years. She had been the one to make sure my father received the Senior Citizen's Rent Increase Exemption or SCRIE that he was entitled to. His landlords hated him for filing for the exemption but that was too bad. It had stabilized his rent at $400 a month and who could argue with that? Judy had helped him out enormously over the years. I'd met her once and for perhaps the first time in my life, I realized the enormous importance of the job my mother had done—looking after low-income senior citizens in New York City. As usual, it had taken appreciating someone else for me to recognize anything at all of value that my parents had done. I had worn the blinders of bitterness, resentment, and contempt for their parenting skills for many years. All true, all true, all true, the mantra of my indignation resounded through my head. But where were the blinders from this kind of truth going to get me? Bogged down like a workhorse, unable to roam free because I was still harnessed to a heavy wagonload of smoldering anger against them? There were moments I found myself deeply irritating. It was tough not having anyone to blame for my negative attitude other than myself.

I looked at my father, weighing the possibility of cutting out for France for a week or two. How would he manage? Fine, probably. And if he didn't, why should I worry about it? Had he spent any time worrying about how I had managed as a child? Would my unkind thoughts ever go away? It occurred to me it didn't really matter. What mattered was actions. Actions spoke louder than words: spoken and unspoken ones.

I could ask my mother if she'd spend an afternoon with him. God knew no cooking would ensue, but the conversation would flow. She could bring cold cuts, her favorite food group, and they could have a ball talking about esoteric cultural stuff. What had that 'I see nothing, I say nothing' comment been about anyway?

Then there was Sanja. Maybe I could enlist Sanja to spend a Saturday or Sunday afternoon with him. What was in it for her? I shrugged off the thought. Not everyone was such a philistine as myself. Many people in my life actually did things for others without thought of what it might benefit them. In fact, those were the kind of people I was attracted to. If only I could become one.

❧

THE FOLLOWING WEEK, my father and I cabbed it to the Pan Am employees' office in the Pan Am building that rose over Grand Central Station.

"Papa, are you going to be okay while I'm gone?' I asked on the escalator up, standing one step behind to make sure he didn't fall. My mother had agreed to visit him once or twice while I was gone. It was a big commitment for her since she rarely left her apartment now that she'd taken early retirement from her City social worker job.

"Sure, sure, Ava. Go and find your *kutyaszar* man and tell him your father says to come back here and marry you."

I prayed we weren't going into one of his spells. This wasn't the time nor place for it.

"It's not that simple, Papa. He's got commitments of his own."

"Who is she?" My father was good at guessing gender, especially when the conversation turned personal.

"Well—to be honest—his mother."

"His mother? Where's his father?"

"They split up a long time ago."

"And his mother can't take care of herself?"

"She's got—she's got MS."

"What? What's that?"

"Multiple sclerosis. She can't walk very well." Or at all. I didn't know where she was in her unwelcome duet with the debilitating affliction.

My father stared at me.

"What? What are you thinking?"

"*Én anyám*," he mumbled.

I dug around in my mental Hungarian dictionary. It was very slim. "Your mother? My grandmother? Eva?'

"*Igan*—yes." His eyes clouded over. Had she needed him? He hadn't been able to return home to visit his mother again after he'd escaped from Hungary by walking across the border through the forest to Austria. I remembered my mother telling me that when he'd gotten news that she'd died, four years after he'd come to the U.S., he'd cried like a baby, something she'd never seen him do before nor after.

"What did she die of, Papa?"

"*Kutyaszar*#$%^(*#%^)()(@#$%&&*%," he muttered angrily.

It seemed unlikely she'd died of a string of swear words slung together like yellow paprikash peppers hung out to dry.

"Come on, Papa. I need to know. For my own future. Was it cancer? Did she die of something?"

"No. She died of old age. And..."

"And what?"

"@#$(*$!#!) I don't know what," he barked.

"Do you wish you could have taken care of her?" Her husband, my grandfather Árpád, had died when my father had been a boy. She'd never remarried. Her older son had emigrated to the U.S. in 1939, my father in 1957. She had been alone.

My father flinched. In that split second, I saw the hurt on his face.

"I wish a lot of things. It didn't happen," he brushed away angrily. Suddenly I saw how much the thought of his mother affected him. He was wracked with regrets. All I could do for him was lay a hand on his arm and decide not to have similar ones.

"Okay, Papa. That didn't happen. But this is happening now," I encouraged him. I'd led him to a bad place with my cruelly thoughtless question. Of course he wished he had taken care of her.

"What's happening now?" he asked, still smarting from my question and the memories it had stirred for him.

"You're taking care of me." I couldn't believe I'd just said that. It went against my entire *politique* with my parents. I'd cast them in the role of villains. But here we were, my father about to hand me a plane ticket to Paris, my mother ready to step in and look after him so I could go. Something was beginning to smell fishy about my world view. It needed rearrangement.

"I am?" He still looked stung.

I wracked my brain for something to distract him from the bad path my thoughtless remarks had led him down.

"Yes. You are." I grabbed his arm and hustled him toward the elevator banks. As we walked, the lingering fragment of an unfinished puzzle I'd been mulling came to me. "Listen, Papa, what was that 'I say nothing see nothing' thing all about?"

"What?" His blue-green eyes looked puzzled.

"The thing you said to mom when we were all together last time." I wouldn't mention where, since he hadn't had a good feeling about the nursing home.

"What did I say?" As always, his expression turned tender when mention of my mother came up. It was a lot better than seeing the hurt expression he'd worn a minute earlier.

"You said some weird thing. Like "I say nothing, I see nothing."

"I see nothing, I say nothing."

"Right. You said it to mom. Why?"

"It's something another Elizabeth said."

"What do you mean?" Which Elizabeth?"

"A famous one." My father's eyes sparkled.

"Who?"

"Guess." We waited at the elevator bank that would take us up to the Pan Am employees' benefits office above Grand Central Station.

"Umm. Elizabeth Taylor?" It didn't sound like something my father's favorite American cultural icon along with Jackie Onassis would have said.

"No."

"Umm, could you give me a clue?"

"European."

"Ohhh." I wracked my European intellectual history database. Compared with my father's it came up woefully short. Then it hit me. I'd bet it was that Elisabeth they called Sissi in Hungary. The one with a seventeen-

inch waist who rode horses; she had been the wife of the
Austro-Hungarian Hapsburg emperor Franz Joseph.

"Sissi!"

"No. Not Sissi! She would never have said such a thing."

"Why not?" I still hadn't gotten my arms around the
famous Sissi, other than what I'd gleaned from the Romy
Schneider movies about her, which had characterized her
as a spirited, impetuous woman magnificently unsuited to
being the consort of a head of state.

"Sissi loved life. She talked, she noticed things. That's
why she got into so much trouble," my father admonished.

"Then who?"

"Queen Elizabeth," he said grandly.

"You're kidding. Queen Elizabeth? You mean Charles'
mother?"

"No. The first one."

"The first Queen Elizabeth?"

"*Genau so,*" he said inexplicably in German, meaning
'exactly so.' "Elizabeth the First."

"Why did she say that? In what context?"

"It was her motto."

"Sort of a weird motto for a head of state, no?" I asked.

"Not at all. She played her cards close to her breasts."

"I think you mean 'chest,' Papa."

"Yes. Exactly."

"So why did you say that to Mom?"

"Why do you think I said it to her?"

"Because she's just like that too," I answered. Why had
I even asked?"

"*Genau so.*" My father put the thumb and forefinger
of his right hand together and kissed it with a flourish.
"Superb. *Magnifique.*" He smiled as if the sun had just

come out, and so it had. What a wonderful tidbit to treasure forever. For one of the first times I'd heard a story about my parents that warmed my heart as well as tickled my intellect.

On this late August day my father and I were in the midst of creating our own story together. The story of how my father sent me off to France as congratulations on landing my U.N. appointment. Okay so it was just a temp job as a greeter with the information and reception unit. Still. We weren't able to go to France together, but my father was the vehicle through whom I was able to go. He was the instrument of my adult life experiences, the one who had encouraged me to backpack in Guatemala at age eighteen, see Christ on Corcovado Mountain in Rio de Janeiro, go to Paris the following year, teach English in Japan a few years after that, follow adventure wherever it took me, and not fear for lack of money or connections. Highly immature, I had been too young to worry and too full of fresh-faced innocence for anyone to mess with me. That, or God's protection.

He hadn't given me what I thought I'd needed—childhood memories, financial support; but he was giving me now what was making me into who I was. The plane tickets he supplied me with plus the encouragement to use them to visit strange, exotic places without much money, no connections and wits alone to guide me had landed me in —well—a lot of adventure and fun.

What my father did do was to open the door to the world for me to walk through again and again—and I had. Partially because I was a crazy, adventure-hound of a half-Hungarian. But partially because of my father's encouragement.

"You haven't been to Rio?" he'd asked in a conversation when I'd been at Yale, trying to figure out where to go, what to do during spring break when they closed the residential colleges.

"No, Papa. You know I haven't."

"You have to go."

"But isn't it dangerous there? I don't know anyone."

My father hummed *The girl from Ipanema* under his breath. "You haven't lived if you haven't been to Rio."

"Are you crazy? I can't just go all by myself, not knowing anyone with no money..."

"Why not?"

So I went.

My father's encouragement was scary, unconventional and exactly the opposite of what a protective father might advise his daughter; but it was also electrifying. I couldn't argue with it. This crazy, unconventional man had given me the keys to discover myself. I grabbed them along with the plane ticket the clerk across the counter handed me with a smile.

"Pierre?"

"Ava! How are you?"

"I got the U.N. job," I said.

"Oh... I'm so happy for you." Something in his voice told me he was a little sad too.

"I don't start until mid-September."

"You don't?"

"So I thought..."

"You thought?"

"I thought maybe I could take some time off before I begin."

"What about your temp job?"

"That's the great thing about temping. I can just tell them I'm not available."

"Are you available?" What was he asking?

"I—uh—can be. If you want me to be," I said hesitantly. Something in his voice sounded distant.

"I can't really get away right now, Ava. I'm down here with my mother for the next two weeks. Then I'll return to Paris for the *Rentrée*. He referred to France's mid-September return from vacation. It was the moment when work, school and the cultural life of all of France's cities began again.

"Oh. Okay." I took a deep breath. I wasn't good at putting myself on the line. "Do you want me to come visit?"

"What? Do you mean it?" A tiny uptick in his voice gave me hope.

"Yes. Do you?"

"Yes. I mean, if you don't mind hanging around Carcassonne with me." His voice sounded hesitant. There was something damping him down, curbing his enthusiasm for my idea. I had been rash to think he'd jump all over it.

"And your mother," I added.

"*Maman* can't go out much now. We spend time in the garden," he said quietly.

"Pierre, I'd love to see your garden," I said, excitedly. I envisioned him there with his mother, a darling, sweet, frail lady surrounded by flowers, sitting in a garden reading together. Chantal was her name; it sounded like a perfume or a song.

"It's just a little patch of land behind our house," he continued.

"It sounds perfect."

"It's not perfect, Ava. It is what it is." He didn't sound upset. Just a tiny bit weary.

"Can I help you with what it is, then?" Whatever Pierre's life was now, it didn't sound like Disneyland.

"Don't you want to take a vacation before you start your new job?"

"Yes. I mean it would be a vacation to come visit you. What are you talking about?"

"It won't be much of a vacation for you." Pierre's voice sounded muffled.

"Why don't you let me decide that?" I asked, wondering if I was doing the right thing. Was I pushing myself on him?

"I just don't want you to come all the way here and not have fun," he continued.

"Pierre—could you let me decide what fun is?" Why was he going on about having fun? What was he—an American?

"I'm not at a fun moment right now."

"Neither am I," I said truthfully.

"Then we can commiserate." A note of relief had crept into his voice. He'd used the first person plural. It was a good sign.

"Let's do that."

We were off to the races, enjoying each other again just by having a conversation. It wasn't the sharp-edged, challenging sort of conversations I'd had with Arnaud. But that sort of fun had worn thin for me after a few months. Instead, it was another kind of fun; a quieter, deeper one that continually reconnected me to Pierre. Our conversations weren't based on one-upmanship. Pierre wasn't the type who always needed to win a verbal point. He also wasn't the type to pass judgment. Instead, he set an example. I wanted to see what he was actually up to in the day to day care of his mother. Whatever it was, I knew I couldn't match it. But that was the reassuring thing about Pierre. He wasn't asking me to be a hero. Nor was he asking me to shine like a star the way Arnaud had. He was simply asking me to be myself.

CHAPTER EIGHT

VISIT TO CARCASSONNE

"*C*ould you close that window behind you, dear?" Pierre's mother called out. "No, not that far. Like that. A little less. Not completely, just so the draft doesn't come in," she instructed.

Pierre fiddled with the handles to the double French windows that opened out onto the garden.

"Too much. No. No. Okay, stop. That's good," she cued him.

He looked strained when he finally turned around.

"How's that?"

"It's as good as you'll get it," his mother replied. *Mon Dieu.* My grandmother's shadow passed before my eyes. Pierre's mother clearly belonged to the same high standards club that I wasn't in. Pierre didn't appear to be a member either.

I'd expected Chantal Castel to be a regular pussycat because of her weakened situation. Instead, she was a tiger, made more ferocious perhaps by the rigors her condition put her through. God only knew what was happening to her body on a daily basis. The fine lines and creases running from the flanges of each nostril to the sides of her mouth told me pain was a close companion.

"Madame, could I bring you a wrap?" I asked, gesturing to the cashmere shawl thrown over the back of the couch.

" My son will get it for me," she sniffed, glancing at me briefly, then back to Pierre.

"Here, *Maman*. Let me wrap it around you," he said, gently draping the shawl across her finely-cut, narrow shoulders. Everything about her was like a china doll. Except for her personality.

"I'll do it. Just get my drink."

"Of course, *Maman*. What are you having?"

"The tisane, what else? And my aperitif."

I followed Pierre out to the kitchen.

"Your *maman* is a regular kitten," I fibbed.

"With claws," he added.

"I see," I said.

"I told you this wouldn't be a vacation," he said, smiling wearily.

"It's fun." It wasn't exactly, but at least Madame Castel didn't know me well enough to get under my skin. Mostly, she had just ignored me for the seventy-two hours I'd been there.

I reached out and stroked Pierre's cheek.

"Stay out of the firing line," he advised.

"How do I do that?"

He shook his head, wryly. "Don't ask me. I've been try-ing for years and it hasn't worked."

"But you've survived." It hadn't worked for me either with my grandmother. No matter what I did, it had always been wrong. Whatever my grandfather did had always been wrong too, but he hadn't seemed to let it ruffle his feathers. Somehow, my grandmother had always ruffled mine. I prayed that Pierre's mother and I would continue our *entente* of conscious non-recognition.

"Love conquers all," he quipped, his words brighter than his worn expression.

"*Bravo*, Pierre." Did it? After all those years of criticism and making me feel like I couldn't put a right foot for-ward, I still felt love and admiration when I thought of my grandmother. This may have been largely due to the fact that she now inhabited a place somewhere beyond the gates of immortality, where she could no longer nag me every five seconds or drop lines every other sentence let-ting me know what a colossal disappointment I had been.

As I picked up the tea cup with the tisane in it, he leaned over and kissed me. "*Courage*," he whispered, then led the way back to the salon where Chantal the ferocious kitty cat sat and sharpened her claws, waiting to take her next swipe.

༄

"Shall we sit in the garden?" Pierre asked after return-ing from the direction of his mother's bedroom. Twenty minutes earlier she had curtly bade us goodnight and wheeled herself out of the room. She was in a wheelchair sporadically, Pierre had told me. Since I'd arrived, three days earlier, she'd been in it the entire time. I wondered if my being there had something to do with it. Had the presence of a second female weakened the dominant female of the house? If it had, I was sorry. Clearly it was making her cranky, although I didn't know what her usual level of discontent was. I longed to support her, but she was too fierce.

"Let's take a walk first," I suggested. Carcassonne's narrow cobble-stoned streets and back passageways beckoned to me. I wanted to explore every inch. I also wanted to get away from Madame Castel. Spending time with her reminded me all too well of visiting my grandmother in the last few years of her life. I couldn't put a right step forward. My only consolation was that Pierre didn't seem able to either.

"Good. Get your sweater." It was the beginning of September, but the night air was cool, hinting of the fall to come.

Quickly, we exited the house and latched the gate carefully behind us. It was amusing to see Pierre attend to every detail around his mother. He hadn't struck me before as such a detail-oriented kind of guy. Was he, really? Or was it just that he didn't want the wrath of his mother to descend on him for whatever he hadn't done in a way up to her standards? The list appeared to be long.

The second we turned the corner from the house, he took my hand.

I laughed, perhaps out of nervous relief. Night had fallen, the air was perfumed, and there was something about the ancient, walled town of Carcassonne that hummed to me. After seven months of separation from Pierre, there was something about him humming to me too. But I was slow off the starting gate. Always had been. I needed time to reacquaint myself not only with Pierre, but with the way I felt when I was with him. Tentatively, I squeezed his hand.

"What's so funny?" he asked, looking at me tenderly. The crinkles at the corners of his eyes looked a bit more crinkly this evening. I put a finger on one side and traced their path.

"You. This. It wasn't what I expected at all."

"*Maman.* I know."

"Has she always been like this?" Then I checked myself. Best to tread lightly when discussing a man's mother with him.

He sighed. "No. It's gotten worse. She used to be— shall we say—rigorous, but now she's frustrated by not being able to move around."

"I can understand." I couldn't really, but being an active type, it would have driven me crazy not to be able to walk, to run, to dance. No wander Madame Castel was grumpy. "What was she like when you were a boy?"

His eyes softened. "Lively, gay. She would chase me around the house, and outside. She'd chase my father too. When she caught him, she'd jump on his back and he'd piggyback her all around the garden then toss her into the bushes. She'd laugh and laugh and—" he trailed off, staring into space.

"And now she doesn't laugh like that anymore."

He shook his head. As I stared, his face began to break up, his mouth working to formulate words, but words not coming.

I backed him into a dark corner. No words could help the pain he felt now. What he needed was release. I hugged him hard, not wanting to disturb the private thoughts chasing themselves across his face. Little by little the weariness in his body seeped out of him. In a minute, his long, lean body began to respond to my touch. My desire to comfort him turned to desire alone. It had been a long separation.

"You're your mother's hero, Pierre."

"I'm a tired one," he mumbled.

"I'm here to make you less tired."

He squeezed me. Deliciously hard. "That you do, Ava."

I put my hand on his thigh and felt it tighten under my grip like taut steel. Suddenly nothing about him seemed tired at all.

It was his turn to press me up against the cool, stone wall of the ancient building. It must have stood there for at least four hundred years. The thought thrilled me, almost as much as Pierre's touch, urgent now in its intensity.

For the next few minutes we kissed in passionate silence, the cares of the day dropping off us like a melted watch in a Dali painting. They slid down onto the cobble-stoned street then disappeared between the cracks. I bid good riddance to each and every one of them.

"*Ma chère*, this isn't for you," he whispered into my hair.

"Don't talk. Just be," I whispered back, smoothing down his dark, thick, unmanageable hair. Love conquers all, I thought but didn't say. But did it? Still stuck in an old Testament way of thinking, the child inside me longed for justice. I hadn't yet conquered the demons of resentment and past hurts that threatened to spoil moments of enjoying my father's company. Would love conquer all? And was it in any way up to me? Maybe love wasn't a feeling. Perhaps it was a decision.

"Do you know what I really like about you?" I asked.

He shook his shaggy hair in my hands. "No. What?"

"You have worse hair than me." Now I was on surer ground—light, teasing.

Pierre laughed from the deepest part of his belly. I hadn't heard him laugh like that since my arrival three days earlier.

"Ava. My Ava," he said, running his fingers down the sides of both of my arms.

I was happy to have helped lift his spirits.The rest was still a puzzle to me, but it didn't matter. We gave each other good gifts. Whether they were ultimately meant to be used with each other, I wasn't entirely sure.

The dark moment past, we continued along the narrow street until it came out into the main square of the town.

"How big is this town?" I asked, looking from one outdoor cafe to the other. There were four occupying each corner of the square, each filled with tourists. It was the first week of September, the final week of France's annual vacation season, when the entire country shuts down for rest and relaxation.

"About 43,000 or so," Pierre said. "Not so large."

"And Paris?"

"About two and a half million," he said, then threw up his hands. "They don't belong in the same sentence."

"There's something about this place that speaks to me," I said wonderingly, looking around at the fortified walls of the buildings on the square.

"It speaks to you? Are you sure?'

"It's like a feeling that I've been here before," I said hesitantly, drinking in the ancient cobbled square. I pointed down a street to our right. "What's down there?"

"That leads to the castle."

"Can we go?"

"Why not?" He took my hand and led me down the narrow side street. About five hundred meters beyond the town square, it began to climb. As we followed the switch-back curve of the street, a feeling of moving toward some-where familiar grew inside me. We passed tourist shops, a few restaurants, a cafe; then suddenly we were in a dark, residential area, the silence of the evening heavy around us. A dog barked somewhere in the distance.

In a minute we came out on a square. It was smallish, with benches along two sides, a fountain in the middle and the rampart wall of the castle bordering it on the other side. Behind us the castle itself stood: solid, monolithic, and dark.

"I've been here before," I said.

"What? What are you talking about?"

I held my hand up to silence him. The limpid, watery sounds of a harp floated toward us. Did Pierre hear them too? As I followed the sound, a vision as sharp as a recent memory came to me. In my mind's eye, a nun sat in the middle of the square, playing the harp as the sun set behind her. Townspeople lounged on the benches, some listening, others quietly talking. A few couples leaned over the walls of the rampart, watching the sun set. Children played nearby. A vendor in one corner sold something that smelled delicious.

I looked at the nun and saw she was blind. I looked closer and saw she was me.

"Ava! Are you all right?" Pierre rushed to me as I sank to the ground. Firmly, the déja vu took hold of me and wouldn't let go. I couldn't stop staring at the fountain in the middle of the square. I'd seen it before. I'd drunk from it. Never before in my life had I been so sure of anything.

Before Pierre could say anything more, I put my hands on his lips. Swallowed up by the moment, I couldn't speak.

∼

"WHAT ARE YOU in the mood for?" Pierre whispered to me as we made our way down the path from the castle grounds. "A drink? A bite?"

"Something else," I answered. With my finger I beckoned him to come closer.

Leaning toward me, he looked expectant, his eyes lit up like a wolf ready to hunt.

I kissed him. Then I bit his lower lip.

The effect was electrifying. We hurried home, then rummaged in the kitchen for thick slices of coarse, country paté on torn off pieces of baguette. Madame Castel was asleep in the back bedroom. Pierre checked and returned to report that she was snoring gently.

Quietly, we crept up the stairs and into Pierre's room. An antidote to my vision of being a nun in Carcassonne in the Middle Ages was in order, right away. The memory of Pierre's thigh nudging mine in the passageway before we'd climbed to the castle grounds had provoked me. His mother's endless carping provoked me more. It all added up to one thing—fireworks.

Wordlessly, Pierre threw me back on his bed. It was narrow but springy, the mattress soft.

"Make me comfortable," I said, bouncing again on his bed.

"Comfortable now?" he asked, his hand on my leg as he leaned over me

"Not yet." I stretched my leg and pushed his thigh with my foot.

He grabbed my ankle. Then he ran his hand up my calf and squeezed.

"Now?"

"Closer." The touch of his warm hand felt good. The intensity of his squeeze was fierce. I raised my leg and rubbed the underside of his chin with my toes. His day-old beard on my skin tickled.

"And now?" His hand moved further up my leg and around to my hip. He squeezed again, harder.

"Watch it," I hissed, scrambling back on his bed.

"I am," he responded, throwing himself onto the bed next to me. "Very closely."

"I see," I said, taking his chin in my hand and squeezing it. My mood was ever so slightly violent, a reaction to the constraints of dealing with Madame Castel over the past four days. I could only imagine how much pent up tension Pierre was dealing with. It would be beyond pleasant to help relieve him of the day's worries, caress by caress.

He looked down at me as his hand traced my torso, from shoulder to hip then back again. Finally, he squeezed the side of my neck.

I shivered. The moment was nigh for us to re-find each other, without constant attentiveness to his mother's needs hanging over our every interaction.

Suddenly he sat up.

"What?"

Head cocked, he listened intently.

I did too. then I heard it. The faint sound of a bell tinkling came from the direction of the stairs.

"What's that noise?" I asked.

"*Maman.* It's her bell." He shot up and quickly tucked his shirt back into his pants."I'll be right back," he promised, slipping out the bedroom door with an expletive.

"*Merde. Merde de bordel.*"

"Holy shit," was right. Somehow we couldn't get away from Madame Castel. I prayed she wasn't having a heart attack or something. Then I thought of my father back in New York, and prayed that he wasn't either.

Rising from Pierre's bed, I went over to the double windows across the room, throwing them wide open. Then I leaned out the sill. A crescent moon hung midway up the sky. Was its scimitar shape a warning from Pierre's mother to me? Had she fallen out of bed, downstairs? Or had she simply discovered that I wasn't in my room and wanted to distract her son from whatever might be going on in his? It was hard ruminating on what was going on with parents who were in fragile health. My emotions ran the gamut from seriously concerned to seriously irritated, mostly the latter. Staring out into the vast, empty sky over Pierre's garden, I prayed she was okay. Then I prayed to be forgiven for having all the wrong motives for praying for her health. Namely, I wanted to spend time with Pierre without her around. Then, for all I cared, she could drop dead. Throwing myself at Christ's imaginary cross in the sky, I thanked Him for being very understanding about all these unkind thoughts. He knew that I knew I didn't want to have them. It's just that I did.

The ink black sky beckoned, cool and fragrant. *Come outside. Come out and play.* I whirled around and grabbed the duvet off the foot of Pierre's bed. For good measure, I took the soft wool blanket folded neatly at the top of the wardrobe too. Then I tiptoed downstairs and quietly let myself out the side door next to the kitchen on the opposite side from where Madame Castel's room was located. To let Pierre know where I was, I unwound the silk scarf from my waist and draped the length of it from the bottom stair out the side door, leaving it slightly ajar. Pierre would know what it meant. If Madame Castel found it first, she would simply think I'd carelessly left my scarf lying around and would probably run over it with her wheelchair before retrieving it and complaining to her son how totally the opposite of *exigeant* or exacting I was.

But I wasn't. I was coming up with an extremely exacting plan. If Madame Castel didn't get in the way of it, the night ahead would provoke a strong response from her son. One that would make him forget all about his stress.

Outside, it was still warm, yet with a hint of coolness in the air. I spread the blanket over the lush grass of the garden, in the corner farthest from Madame Castel's bedroom window. Through the closed shutters, I could see the light was still on. Curious, I slipped over to the bushes near her window and melted into them. The low murmur of Pierre's and his mother's voices wafted out the open window, into my non-comprehending ears. All I could pick up was what I already knew—that French was an exceptionally beautiful language, utterly dissimilar to the rhythms and intonations of English. I couldn't make out what she was saying, but her tone was soft, gentle—unlike her daytime tone of voice. Was this the voice of the *chère Maman* who had put Pierre to bed as a young boy? Dulcet and gentle, murmuring soft, sweet things to him in a language created for intimacy? I wanted that intimacy too. With him. With her son. Confusion swept over me.

Had my grandmother ever whispered to me like that? My first thought was no. But as I lay on my back and unfolded Pierre's duvet cover over me, checking which night stars had already come out, a memory floated into my head.

Second grade—the year of unending earaches. I'd had so many, I'd missed forty days of school. There had been only one comfort against the pain. Not the nasty, orange-flavored penicillin nor the chewable St. Joseph's children's aspirin my grandmother had dosed me with.

I'd found solace nestled against my grandmother herself. The warmth, smell and softness of her generous, squishy chest had relieved my pain. I'd burrowed my head into her soft warmth to relieve the jagged ache in my ear.

Those moments of rocking in her rocking chair, snuggled against her, had elicited soft, soothing words from her; she had crooned lullabies and whispered sweet endearments. Her tenderness to me hadn't lasted long, but that year of mid-childhood, it had been alive and warm, surrounding my sharply aching ears with comfort and love. I thanked the stars for the memory of her they'd just showered on me. She had loved me. I had loved her. That was all that mattered. The rest would wash away like so much flotsam and jetsam. All that mattered was the memory of love that remained.

Looking up into the sky, my throat closed. She was up there glittering down at me, a grand constellation, belonging somewhere between Juno and Venus; she had been a powerful figure, perhaps closer to Juno. At rare moments, a soft, squishy, loving mother to me. Idly, I wondered if her Venus side had gotten fully expressed with her first husband; the one who had died of leukemia at age thirty. It had been clear it hadn't with her second, my grandfather, the dry New England doctor. But the lovely and loving Venus side of her had emerged in her relations with young children. I had been lucky to have her in my life when I'd been young. My grandmother had spent hours tending to me when I'd been sick. It was just when I was well that relations between us began to go downhill, starting around seventh grade or so.

"Ava!" I heard a loud whisper behind me.

"Here! Over here," I whispered back, squeezing my eyes shut to hold back the tears. Instead, they rolled down my cheeks and I put my hand to my face to wipe them away before Pierre saw. His devotion to his mother spoke to me of how precious, how unassailable was the love between parent and child. The gentle night air of Carcassonne had just reminded me I'd known that love too. There'd been a lot of stormy weather since those early days of love and playfulness between my grandmother and me. But they had existed and if I could only comprehend a tiny inkling of what existed between Pierre and his mother now with their shared memories of former halcyon days, I could appreciate how sacred their bond was. I had no business interfering with it.

"Were you crying?" he asked, his hand shooting out and stroking my cheek.

"No. How's your mother?" I asked, putting my own hand on his wrist. It was surprisingly broad, but slim.

"She's fine. She dropped her pill container behind the bed and couldn't reach it."

"I'm glad that's all it was."

"You were crying," he said. "What were you thinking about?"

"I saw my grandmother in the stars. That's all," I reassured him.

Pierre looked up at the sky then back at me. "A good kind of cry, *non?*"

"Yes. A good kind of one."

"*Entendu*—understood."

He reached for me and we embarked on a good kind of activity. One that washed away every care of the day, every poignant memory brought on by the night. We surrendered to something else entirely.

"I'm GOING TO get bread before the *boulangerie* closes," Pierre announced, referring to the bakery. In France bread is made daily, without preservatives. Bread bought the day before turns overnight into a hard, rock-like inedible substance. One of the secrets to French people staying trim, despite a diet rich in bread, butter, and cream, is that the French diet is slim in preservatives. Everyone shops for food daily and whatever isn't eaten within a day or two gets thrown out. The French don't ingest preservatives that the body doesn't know how to expel. What they eat washes through them and doesn't stick around inside, cluttering up the body's machinery and glomming onto existing fat cells.

"Make sure you pick up some crème fraîche on the way back," Madame Castel snapped. We planned to make spaghetti carbonara that evening. It was one of my favorite French dishes, although it was actually Italian.

"Yes, *Maman*," Pierre said.

"I'll come with you," I volunteered, jumping up. There was something about the way Pierre answered his mother that made me want to slap someone. Either the image of my grandmother bossing me around as a child or the image of me as a child trying to please her. I needed some fresh air.

Pierre motioned to follow him into the hallway. "Do you mind staying here?" he whispered.

"No—of course not. Why?"

"*Maman* seems under the weather today. I don't want to leave her alone for too long."

"No problem. I'll keep an eye on her till you get back," I said. Madame Castel hadn't struck me as anymore cranky, grumpy or under the weather than she had been the entire time I'd been there, but Pierre would know his mother's baseline better than me.

He leaned over and gave me a quick kiss.

"Be right back."

I stared glumly at his retreating form as he disappeared out the side door. This would mark the first time I was alone with Chantal Castel. I wasn't sure how long I could remain on my best behavior. Fortunately, the bakery was just down the street.

"Pierre?" Her voice rang from the other room. She hadn't spoken my name aloud once, which was fine with me. As Pierre had advised, it was best to stay out of the firing line.

"No, Madame. He's gone to the market. May I help you?" I hurried back into the living room where his mother sat in her wheelchair next to the couch. I sat down at the end nearest her, to be companionable.

"*Merde.* I wanted to tell him to pick up some parsley too," she grumbled. Madame Castel swore here and there but was no match for my father, the Hungarian.

"For the carbonara?"

"Of course. What else?" she snapped. If she kept up the snapping I would snap too. Once a child under my grandmother's thumb, I no longer was. My tolerance for older, exacting females snapping at me was exactly zero.

"Maybe he'll think to do it himself," I said, trying to placate her. Almost immediately, I wanted to kick myself. My placating days were over.

"Of course he won't. He's a man," she sniffed.

She did seem to have a point."Why don't we take bets on whether he does or doesn't?" I suggested, trying to keep the tone light—or at least tolerable.

"Are you suggesting I bet against my son?" She eyeballed me sharply.

"No, Madame," I amended hastily. "Whether he brings it back or not, he's still your son. I know you'd never bet against him." Why was I casting myself in this thankless role? I was nobody's patsy.

"Don't tell me what you know about my relationship with my son," she wheeled her chair away from me toward the window.

Inside, I tried not to take the bait. But this was a zero-sum game. There would be one winner, one loser. I scraped my match against the crusty old tinderbox. The fuse was now lit.

"I'll tell you something else then." The line was short and the flame moved fast. It always did when I lost it. I was good, I was very good, I was the soul of patience— then BLAM—I exploded. A chip off the block; on both my father's and my maternal grandmother's sides. Both had been fastidious housekeepers with explosive tempers. How little they had known how very much they had had in common.

"What's that?" She looked at me as if I were a cobra.

"You poison everything your son tries to give you," I said in French with my best articulation. Calmly, clearly, I was taking no chances on her not understanding my words. The dynamite stick went off.

"How dare you say that to me? Do you have any idea how much I've suffered?" Her hazel eyes bulged in anger. Still, I couldn't help noticing how beautiful their wide set placement was on her elegant face.

No, I didn't have any idea. But I had an idea of how much I had suffered as a child. wondering where my parents were and why they weren't there with me. They weren't dead, they hadn't been denied visas to cross the state line from New York to Connecticut to come visit me, two and a half hours from Manhattan where they lived. Simply put, they had both been scared off by my grandmother's fierce disapprobation. Had they been killed in a car accident, their lack of presence in my life would have been sad but understandable. But they were alive and well—just absent. My outrage as a child had known no bounds.

"Is that a reason to make others suffer around you? Pierre loves you. He's trying to help you!" I screamed at her. I was not letting this older, disapproving lady roll over me. That had happened once before in my life and it wouldn't happen again. Over my dead body.

"Don't tell me what my son does for me. You know nothing about it. What we had we can never have again." Vinegar poured from her mouth. I knew that taste. It was the taste of my grandmother's disappointment in just about anything I said or did. I was fed up.

"Madame—you had it. That's the point." Having something then not having it was a lot better than never having it at all, in my book. At least she knew she'd lost something. I didn't even know what I was missing. All I knew was that something was.

"Don't tell me what the point is," Madame Castel shouted. "What would you know about it?" Neither rage nor pain lines could hide the perfect oval symmetry of her face. My heart ached for the woman she had once been.

"You have beautiful memories together. Hold them tight. Don't throw them away because of the pain you feel now. Pain is trying to destroy you, your relationship with your son. Don't let it!" Was pain trying to destroy my own relationship with my father? Was I letting it?

"What do you know about pain, Mademoiselle?"

"I had another kind of pain, Madame. A very big one." It had been the pain of emptiness, neglect, abandonment. Not sharp, but a dull, aching one.

"You're too young to know what I'm talking about."

"But I do, Madame. I do!" I screamed. Rage bubbled up inside me. It was the rage of then combined with the rage of now. Then to have suffered as a child, now to suffer as an adult the double injustice that no one would ever recognize how terrible my pain had been.

"You are a very forward young woman," she said, sharply.

"I didn't sign up for sainthood," I exploded.

"*Évidemment*—obviously not," Madame Castel sniffed, her command of English acute enough to catch my gist. She angrily put her hands to the wheels on her chair, rolling toward me. She moved fast when she wanted to: say, to intimidate or terrorize someone. I'd seen that trick a million times. My grandmother had used it on me frequently. But I wasn't five years old anymore, so I stood my ground. If Madame Castel wanted to go *mano-a-mano*, hand-to-hand, we would. Bring it on.

The door opened and Pierre came in, back from the market.

"Everything okay?" he asked, looking from his mother back to me.

I turned to face him, speechless.

He cocked his head, trying to read my expression. It must have been difficult, because even I couldn't figure out what I was feeling. His mother had just accused me of being a forward young woman. She was right. Out from beneath my grandmother's dominating thumb and breathing the fresh air of my own freedom, I was undoubtedly a forward young woman. It had been the only way to emerge from the stranglehold my grandmother had held me in as a child. But what was I doing with my forwardness? Was I myself moving forward? Or was I just spinning my wheels, with the pain of my parents past wrongs eating me up inside? Was I in any better a position than Madame Castel?

As Pierre moved toward his mother, I rushed from the living room to the guest bedroom. His mother disliked me. I wasn't cut out to cater to her. It was time to get back to New York and resume my less than perfect care-giving of my father.

As I packed, it came to me that my father wasn't so bad. With a weakened heart and in the clutches of encroaching dementia, he was still able to seize the moment and wring every last drop of joy out of it whenever he could.

I was proud of him. When I got back I wanted to seize those moments with him. That meant tossing my own pain overboard. Spending time with Madame Castel showed me what would happen if I didn't. I'd turn into her. At least Madame Castel had an excuse for being a killjoy. Multiple sclerosis was a pretty good one.

"What are you doing, Ava?"

"I'm packing," I said calmly as Pierre entered the guestroom.

"Please don't do that. *Maman* was just upset. She'll get over it."

"I won't," I said. Once before I'd dealt with a woman similar to Madame Castel. It had taken every ounce of will I possessed to emerge from her shadow. There was no way I was going back to any sort of relationship similar to the torturous one I'd endured as a child.

"What? What happened? What did you say to each other?"

"Some important things, Pierre. All true." I still wasn't sure of the deep down, resoundingly true parts of what we'd exchanged. But I knew both of our positions had had the clarity and solidity of enormous church bells; only they weren't hanging in the same church. I would have time enough on the train back to Paris then the flight home to New York to sort it all out.

"Just drop it, Ava. For my sake. Please. Put that down and come here." He reached for me.

"I'm leaving, Pierre. For your sake," I said, backing up to avoid his touch.

"Why? No, Ava. Don't go. I need you here," he stammered, looking alarmed.

"Your mother needs *you* here. She needs *me* here like she needs a hole in the head. I've got to get back to New York, Pierre. My father needs me there, just the way your mother needs you."

"But what about us?" Pierre said.

"Now is not the time. It's just not." Before I began to cry, I tossed the rest of my clothes into the suitcase and slammed it shut. Then I turned and marched straight past him to the front door. Okay, so I put out my hand and stroked his cheek as I passed.

"Ava. No!" he grabbed my hand as it touched him, but I yanked it away. This wasn't just about him and me anymore. It was about him, me, Madame Castel, and my father. Pierre and I both knew where we needed to be and it wasn't with each other.

"Where are you going?" Pierre's mother asked as I passed her chair in the living room.

"I'm going to leave you alone with your son, Madame. Thank you for your hospitality," I said, not altogether ironically. It had been interesting. It always was, to meet a man's mother.

"What are you doing, Ava? Don't be ridiculous. My son wants you here."

"I'm not being ridiculous, Madame. I'm being practical. Your son's duty is to you. Mine is to my father. I need to get back to him. Goodbye."

A strange look crossed her face; it almost seemed like respect. "Dear, we had some words, it was nothing. Please sit down."

As she spoke, she grabbed both arms of her wheelchair and began to stand up.

"We had some words and it *was* something," I corrected her. "You've helped me see what pain is and how it affects people's relationships," I continued, looking directly at her. With her wide set eyes, she had the face of a noble, ferocious bird; an eagle. As much as I wanted to hate her, I couldn't. I admired her, as I had admired my grandmother. But I'd had to fly the coop to get out from under her so that one day I could become someone admirable in my own right. That day had not yet come but I was working on it.

"Don't let mine affect ours," she said.

"Madame, your relationship is with your son. I feel for your pain. I truly do."

Struggling up, she finally stood, facing me.

My hand on the door handle, I hesitated. She had said my name. She had referred to our relationship. She'd even stood up for the very first time since I'd arrived. Should I relent and stay?

"Ava, please stay. Listen to *Maman*, she wants you to stay," Pierre said, pleadingly.

As I looked at him, a small movement where his mother stood caught the corner of my eye. Pierre and I both turned as she wavered then began to fall backward. Pierre rushed to her, getting there just in time to break the fall.

I should have rushed to her side.

Instead, an unkind thought rushed to mine. His mother was a master manipulator, just as my grandmother had been. She'd said her son wanted me there. She hadn't said she did. Chantal Castel didn't want me there at all. She'd just spoken with actions, not words. Actions were louder.

I turned and fled.

CHAPTER NINE

ESCAPE FROM
CARCASSONNE

*W*hen I got back to Paris, I had a very bad idea. I called Arnaud.

"Ava—What are you doing here?" He sounded excited, animated—as if nothing hurtful had ever passed between us.

"I'm just here for a day. Thought I'd see how you're doing." As I'd mentioned to Madame Castel, I was no saint. Plus, I was having a very unsaintly moment in the wake of our blow up. It was as if I'd had a knock-down fight with my grandmother. It was all mixed up in my head. All I knew was that I hadn't let myself be intimidated or terrorized or pushed around, and now that I'd asserted my teeny tiny, fledgling will, I needed to let off some steam.

"Let's meet. I want to hear all your news," Arnaud said suavely, as if nothing at all had ever passed between us, nothing amazing, nothing terrible. He infuriated me the minute he started talking and I felt myself falling under his spell again. Or maybe it was myself I was mad at for falling for it.

I sighed. There was so much news, much of it groundbreaking, that even I couldn't sort it all out. Most of all, what about Pierre? Maybe it was best to do something that would stop us in our tracks now, so that he could do his duty by his mother without a divided heart.

"I don't know if that's a good idea," I hedged.

"Of course it is. Let's meet at our old place—Café de la Bastille."

Our old place... It hurt to hear that.

"I have some things to do."

"So get them done. Then let's meet—say four? Where are you staying?"

"Okay, four P.M. then. See you later." I ignored his question and hung up. Unsure of where I was staying, I was toying with the idea of going out to Charles de Gaulle airport after meeting Arnaud and camping out there until the next flight to New York went out. Flying on my father's employee pass meant standby status. I'd never taken a flight with a confirmed seat. Once I'd dressed exceptionally well on my way home to New York from Tokyo and gotten bumped up to first class. I'd worn a dress I'd bought on the street in Harajuku's main shopping street that made a razor sharp fashion statement in New York. At the standby counter, the agent looked me up and down approvingly then bumped me up to first class. The thirteen hour flight home had been an extraordinary experience; replete with linen napkins, bottomless drinks, mineral water spritzers for the face, and an unforgettable hand massage by an Asian stewardess whose gorgeousness was largely wasted on me. God had tossed me some lucky curve balls. I was a curvy-enough character to have caught some of them.

Stuffing my suitcase into a locker at *Gare d'Austerlitz*, I hopped on the Metro to Saint Michel, in the heart of the Latin Quarter. I had a little catching up to do with my old friend Paris before I caught up with my other old friend.

"So what brings you to France?" Arnaud asked, two hours later, when we met. Disgustingly handsome as ever, he tossed his leonine, auburn hair back and ran his hand through it. He knew the effect it would have on me. Predictably it did and I steeled myself. I wasn't here for a fashion show featuring male virility. I was here to figure out how I felt about Arnaud. What I felt about him. And why I still felt it.

"I was in Carcassonne."

"Pierre? You were visiting Pierre?" He looked taken aback.

"Yes. Pierre and his mother."

Arnaud laughed. "You met Chantal?'

"Yes."

"Ferocious, *non*?"

"Yes."

"What a woman." He shook his head admiringly.

"I take it you've met."

"She thinks I'm a blackguard."

"And are you?" I couldn't help asking.

"I don't know. Am I?" Arnaud knew exactly what effect his brazen self-confidence had on women. It should have made him eminently slappable. The problem was that after the slap, he was still catnip to most females. It was an annoying problem, made more annoying by the fact that it was so obvious, yet so inescapable.

"Let's get back to Madame Castel."

"It didn't go well, huh?"

I shook my head, speechless at the thought of our last conversation.

"She didn't eat you alive, did she?" Arnaud leaned forward and took my hand.

I removed it slowly. It was hard not to respond to the warm, muscularity of that hand. I knew it well and it knew me. But there was no comfort in its grip. It would be strong, safe, secure for a moment, an hour, a day or two. Then it would release its grip and drop me. I knew that too.

"She tried. So I bit back."

Arnaud threw back his head and roared. "Good. Good for you."

"What are you talking about? It was terrible. She's in a wheelchair, with MS. I screamed at her. We practically fought. She fell just as I left and I left anyway. I'm ashamed of myself." Strangely, it felt good to tell Arnaud all this. It was like catching up with an old colleague at a blackguards convention.

"Was Pierre there to catch her when she fell?" Arnaud asked, astutely. He wasn't a journalist for nothing.

"Yes. He caught her just in time.

"So why worry? That battle axe has been looking for someone to fight back with her all her life."

"She has?" I was surprised.

"She destroyed her husband's good will toward her and now Pierre's."

"What about Pierre?"

"It's been hard on him."

"I can see that."

"So you went all the way to Carcassonne to see Pierre?"

"Yes. I like him."

"I see. But not enough to put up with his mother."

"That's the point, Arnaud. Maybe I shouldn't get in the way of him and his mother. I just don't know." It felt strangely good to confide in my ex-boyfriend about my present one. Each confidence another twist of the knife. At least I hoped. But the expression in Arnaud's amused, twinkling eyes wasn't cooperating with what I wanted him to feel. Not one glimmer of hurt or regrets about the past emanated from his smug, self-satisfied, unfairly attractive countenance. Was he what the British referred to as a bounder, someone who crosses boundaries? Already, with his hand on the table, just inches from mine, he was confusing me. But who was allowing that to happen? Underneath the table, I lifted my heel and stomped it on the floor.

"You have a point, Ava. But Pierre is his own man. He can decide for himself where his loyalties lie."

"Clearly they lie with his mother. She has no one else."

"She has no one else because she's driven everyone else off."

"Pain is her only companion besides Pierre." I felt like crying just thinking about it. Being stuck in a wheelchair when once she'd been a vibrant, active woman? I couldn't imagine my grandmother stuck in a wheelchair. Or my father. Or myself. I prayed that when my father's closing moment came, it would be swift, decisive.

"And you don't see yourself making up a happy threesome." Arnaud had intuited correctly that Pierre and I had made the transition from friendship to more. Or perhaps Pierre had told him. They were childhood friends, after all, even if they'd had a falling out just before I'd left Paris the December before. Over me.

"It's not just that *I* don't. She hated my guts. It's out of the question."

"She hates her life right now. You just happened to be there. Whoever is around her deals with what she's dealing with, that's what I think. I don't think she hates you personally."

"She called me a forward young woman," I said, smarting at the thought of the way she'd spit out the words.

"Knowing her, that was a compliment."

"The way she said it, it wasn't."

"The way she says and does everything is conditioned by pain, Ava. You need to recognize that and not take it personally."

"How do you know all this?"

"Because I've been on the receiving end too. She's just angry at life."

"Why is she so bitchy with Pierre? He waits on her hand and foot."

"He remembers the old days. He's an only child, you know."

"I was raised as an only child too, and I couldn't wait to get away from home."

"I remember. You were escaping your pilgrim culture, your grandmother." He smiled, probably thinking back to one of our first conversations when I'd told him about coming to Paris for the first time as an *au pair* at age nineteen. "But Pierre's story is different. I remember meeting his mother when I was fifteen. She was *vive,* lively—on fire. The first woman I'd pick at a dance."

I winced. He still had the power to hurt me. Why did I care that Arnaud was choosing another woman over me in a fictitious scenario? When we'd been a couple, I'd agonized over the way Arnaud had spoken so highly of a woman from his past—long gone—named Mélanie. There had been a photo of her on the wall of his country house. He was the kind of man who liked to play games with a woman's head as well as her heart. I'd left him soon after his childhood friend Pierre came to Paris while Arnaud had been on assignment in Thailand. He had suggested Pierre catch my performance at the club where I played piano and sang and so I had had the chance to get to know Pierre in Arnaud's absence and discover what a decent, steady man he was. Yet here I was, a moth buzzing too close to the flame. Was I the moth in my father's poem? I hoped not. Nervously, I shifted my legs under the table.

"Was she as exacting then as she is now?" I asked.

"Being exacting is a way of life in France, Ava."

"I know." The French were all about being *exigeant*, exacting. The only one I'd ever met who wasn't was the Frenchman sitting across from me.

"Remember how much you liked that quality when you lived here?"

"I admired it. I still do. But there's a limit."

He wasn't listening. Lost in thought, he seemed to be remembering Madame Castel, twenty years earlier.

"Above all, when it's a woman who is exacting—it's like sniffing a distinct aroma—it's the quality that makes each woman different and each one interesting," he continued.

"It sounds good, Arnaud. But could you live with it?"

"What do you think?'

Resoundingly, no. There was no way I would ask him his status, still single or in a relationship. He'd been available to get together on short notice. That told me he was most likely still single. Footloose, fancy-free and ready to fly off somewhere exotic at a moment's notice or meet an ex-girlfriend in a café. It wasn't the lifestyle of a man I wanted for myself.

"I think you'll be stepping on a plane in less than seventy-two hours," I guessed.

Arnaud glanced at his watch, an enormous Swiss one, with complicated gears and an ultra-slim face. He had probably picked it up in some luxury goods black market in Bangkok.

"Good guess."

"Where to this time?' I secretly smiled, pleased that I'd been the one to mention he'd be traveling soon, not him. It hurt less. Why it hurt at all, I didn't want to think about.

"Mozambique."

"Will you be studying baby elephants?" I joked, referring to a story he'd told me in the presence of his childhood friend Pierre that had driven me straight into Pierre's arms. If he said yes, he'd drive me straight back there. Even if it was just in my imagination.

He looked at me quizzically. "No. Why?' Apparently his anecdote about watching baby elephants in the jungles of Thailand's Golden Triangle had made more of an impression on me than it had on him. For me, the story had once and for all confirmed that Arnaud's stories starred him alone. He'd seen the baby elephants while alone in the jungle. Meanwhile, I'd been back in Paris waiting and longing for him; wondering why he and I weren't knitting together stories of our own. At the moment he shared with us his tale of coming across baby elephants taking a bath in the forests of Thailand, my own story had quietly shifted from one with Arnaud to a new one with Pierre, as the three of us had walked arm in arm through the Parc des

Buttes Chaumont in Paris. It had been a strange moment; as if my heart had quietly crossed the street. Would it cross the street again? And did my will have anything to do with whether it did or not?

I laughed lightly. "So what will you be covering in Mozambique?"

"I'm doing an exposé on conditions in gold mines. For L'Express," he explained, referring to the French weekly news magazine.

"Same old same old," I responded, not very kindly, but I didn't care. All that mattered was that the man across from me was the same old Arnaud. Same old leonine sex appeal, same old killer physicality, same old traveling lifestyle and openness to every type of new experience.

That lifestyle had been mine once too. But it no longer was. Arnaud had been mine once as well, except that Arnaud didn't really belong to anyone. The baby elephants in the jungle could have him. I'd thrown him back, and if I wanted to kid myself for a few brief hours that I could have him back, I could. But it wouldn't make us a couple again and it would hurt the one man I cared about not hurting more than anyone else—even my father.

I couldn't hurt Pierre. Even if he never found out, I would know and it would get in the way.

"So why did you call me then?" Arnaud asked, acutely.

"I had a bad idea," I said quietly.

"Tell me about it."

"It was bad. Like I said."

"I want to hear all about it."

"No, you don't."

"I want to know." He leaned over the table, his face coming close to mine.

"You don't want to know anything about me, Arnaud. You just want what you want."

"So what's wrong with that?"

His philosophical consistency was maddening. There was no changing the man because the man didn't want to change. What I really needed to do was change myself into someone who wasn't attracted to someone who maddened me the way he did. I was taking steps to do that. Tiny baby steps. Perhaps calling him in Paris had been a teensy misstep along the way.

"And I do want to know about you, *cherie,*" he continued. I want to hear all about New York. Maybe I'll even come visit you there."

"Arnaud—how can you be so casual? What's wrong with you?' I leaned back in my chair to get away from him. His light attitude disturbed me. I felt like his favorite saloon-girl every time I was around him, even when we had been in a committed relationship. Had it been possible that I'd once loved him? It was like loving high fructose corn syrup. The taste was so sweet, once you got hooked you couldn't get off the stuff. But I was off it. My junk food days were over.

"What's wrong with *me*? What's wrong with *you*?" He looked completely bewildered, indignant even.

"Nothing's wrong with me! I just don't understand how you can talk about dropping in on your ex, then just pushing off."

"Isn't that what you're doing now? *Voilà,* here I am. Not a problem, Ava!"

"It's a problem for me, okay?" He had a point there. He certainly had a point.

"Let me see if I got this straight. You came all the way to France to see Pierre. Then when you realized that what you saw was way too heavy for you, you ran away. Then you called me and I came right over. So here I am. Lighter than air, but here. What exactly do you want?"

"I don't know, okay? I just don't know, but I don't want lighter than air!" As usual, Arnaud was right. He was always right, except that he was all wrong for me.

"You don't, huh? You sure?" He backed me into the wall we stood next to. Then he put his knee between my legs and bent it, lifting me up. It was daring, obnoxious and erotic. All trademarks of the maddening man I no longer loved.

"Put me down," I spat out.

"That's not what you want," he said, his eyes boring into mine.

"I know what I want," I lied. "Put me down."

"I know you know what you want," he said, his face coming close to mine."I want it too," he purred.

"Stop! Stop it!" I couldn't cry rape. This was France, after all. Arnaud was my ex-boyfriend. If I filed a complaint at the local police station, the gendarmes would laugh at me and offer their services as superior to Arnaud's.

"I've heard you say that before," he whispered. "And I know what you mean."

Thrusting my elbow into his collarbone, I pushed him back, forcing him to put down his knee to balance himself. In that split second, I got away. Quickly, I ran back inside the Café de la Bastille. I'd stay there until it was time to go to the airport if I needed to.

"What's your problem, Ava?" Arnaud called out behind me, following me into the cafe.

"We were together then, we're not now," I hissed."Don't you even understand the difference?"

"I understand that you called me out of the blue. I came to meet you. You came too. Is there something I'm missing?"

"Yes! I just wanted to see you again. To see how you're doing."

"And to see how you felt about seeing me again."

"That's none of your business, okay?" There was nothing worse than listening to Arnaud spell out exactly what I'd been thinking. With his quicksilver intellect he'd be at the end of my own story before I'd even turned the page.

"Okay, it's yours. So how do you feel?"

"Angry."

"With who?"

"You."

"Are you sure? Or is it Madame Castel you're angry with? Or Pierre for not standing up to his mother?" His face loomed closer. "Or is it you you're angry with? That you ran away when something real that wasn't so easy presented itself?"

"I'm angry with you, Arnaud. You're exactly the same as before."

"You're right. I am. Nothing different at all. Still the one you want." His bloody blue-green eyes stared at me serenely, hypnotic and brilliant.

"You're contemptible," I hissed. "You make me sick!"

"No, Ava. I'm just one hundred per cent honest with myself. And any woman I'm with. This is what you get when you're with me. You already know that."

"It wasn't enough."

"So why did you call?"

"To see if you've changed," I blurted out.

"Have I?"

"Not at all."

He laughed. "And have you?"

Aaargh.... He'd hit a nerve.

"No. But..."

"But what, Ava?"

"But I need to."

"If you know that then you're on your way."

I really wanted to kill him. Not only was he contemptible, despicable and a potential seducer of my soul, he was spot-on right. It made me ill. Especially the fact that I'd called him. Then it hit me. This wasn't about what I was feeling. This was about what I was going to do about it.

"Look, Arnaud, I'm sorry I wasted your time. It was a mistake to call you."

"No it wasn't, *Minouche*." He used the pet name he'd had for me when we'd been lovers. It stung like acid on my scars.

"Don't call me *Minouche*," I shot back. "Don't you understand anything about the difference between then and now?"

"I'm not any different now than I was then."

Right. *You're* not. But *we* were a couple. And now we're not. I'm not your *Minouche* anymore."

"Are you Pierre's"

"No. We're not having a "*Minouche*-like" relationship."

"What are you having?"

"Something solid and heavy," I sputtered clumsily, at a loss for words as usual, up against Arnaud's dizzying wit.

"Too heavy for you, Ava. That's not your style."

"Don't tell me what my style is," I snapped.

"As long as you know what it is yourself," he replied calmly.

That was the whole problem. I didn't.

"Come on, let's have a cognac while you figure out what you're doing next," he said, moving from heavy to light without a pause.

"I'm going to the airport and taking the next flight back to New York."

"You sure you don't want to stay for a few days and we can go to the airport together?'

"Arnaud—the idea of doing something like that is about as sleazy and lightweight as..."

"As a foreign correspondent buying a cognac for a lady in a bar?"

I stared at his blank, handsome face. He'd just put his finger on why I'd left him. There was something so weightless and meaningless about the way he lived his life. Even if he was churning out articles for *L'Express*. There was no commitment in him at all. But was there any in me?

I thought of Pierre back in Carcassonne. He knew commitment. He knew sacrifice. I thought of myself back in New York. It was highly arguable whether I knew sacrifice or not, but I was doing something that required it, however lamely I went about it. My method of caring for my father mostly involved bringing my friends over to meet him, all of whom appeared to enjoy his company more than I did. Sometimes I forgot who I was for a minute, my father's burdened and neglected daughter, and put myself in their place. Those were the moments when I too laughed as lightly and effortlessly as my friends at my father's jokes and stories. Was there a way I could turn him into an uncle or non-blood relative? It was something to think about on the flight home.

"No thanks, Arnaud. I have to go now."

"Are you sure?"

"I'm sure that I have to go now. Yes."

"Quite sure?"

"As sure as I've ever been."

"Fine. So let's have a quickie, then go back to my place and have another."

"Goodbye, Arnaud." Had I ever been that lightweight when I'd been with him? Who had he taken me for? I was superficial, I was unsure of myself, of Pierre, of the us of us, but one thing was certain: I wasn't anything like Arnaud and I never wanted to be.

"Where are you going?' He looked startled. Did he actually think I was going to accept his invitation?

Before I did, I stood up and slipped out the door of the café as a man held it open for me. His face bespoke interest, as he stared at me then back at Arnaud. As I passed through the door, I whispered, "Stop him."

Startled, the man met my gaze. I stared back, pleading with my eyes. Then I fled, for the second time in as many days.

I ran straight across Place de la Bastille, Paris's most dangerous traffic circle, throwing caution to the wind, and headed for the taxi stand. There, a cab, with its available light on, was just pulling up to the curb. I lunged for the door handle and hopped in.

"Gare d'Austerlitz," I breathed to the driver. "*Vite*— fast," I hissed. Locking my door, I glanced out the window to see Arnaud just mounting the sidewalk in pursuit.

"Goodbye," I said more to myself than to him, my hand shaking as I rolled down the window.

"Wait, Ava!" he called out.

My heart panged. *It's not a feeling. It's a decision.*

"Goodbye, Arnaud," I called out the window. Goodbye lightweight love, goodbye dazzling City, goodbye lighter-than-air feelings that vanish at the wrong moment then return at even less appropriate ones.

"Wait!" he called.

I couldn't afford to wait. Whether I knew what I really wanted or not, I knew I didn't want Arnaud or the kind of free-wheeling life of total freedom he lived. I'd go back to New York and lead a sacrificial life, however poorly.

Pierre's earnest, not so handsome face popped into my mind and I felt stronger. Maybe I was a semi-scumball, but because of who Pierre was and what he stood for, at least I wasn't a total one. Pierre gave me gifts that lasted, even when I wasn't using them with him. The thought of our time together in Carcassonne would be something that would continue to sustain me, back in New York. Even if I wasn't worthy of him, I'd take the gifts he'd given me and use them with my father instead.

Rolling down the cab window, I did a naughty thing: I tossed the Café de la Bastille matchbook out the window. It was the first naughty thing I'd done that day that I knew was exactly the right thing to do. Besides, this was Paris and cute street cleaners in red uniforms were everywhere, zipping around on motorcycles vacuuming up litter. Too bad there was no vacuum cleaner large enough to scoop up Arnaud. Laughing at the image, the cab turned the corner as I washed that man right out of my hair. Really.

"PLEASE TELL HIM thank you for the gifts." Pierre wasn't home, so I was leaving a message with Madame Castel. It was all I could do to get through the conversation.

"For the gifts?"

"Yes. And thank you for the visit." Strangely enough I meant it.

"What gifts are you referring to?"

"Pierre will know. Thank you so much, Madame." The phone card I'd bought at the airport had only seconds to go.

"And what if he doesn't know? May I tell him?"

"Madame, please tell him he set an example for me. So when I get back to New York, I'll take care of my father better. Although not as well as Pierre takes care of you."

"What do you mean? He's constantly screwing things up."

"Madame, you have no idea how much more he could screw things up. You should come visit us in New York and see how badly I look after my father."

"Is your cooking bad?" Being French, she instantly thought of food as an example.

"It's non-existent."

"Then what do you eat?"

"Take-out."

"Take-out? *Affreux*—frightful."

"That's why I want to thank your son. He showed me so much. Even how to make spaghetti carbonara."

"You didn't stay long enough to taste it."

"Did he bring back the parsley?"

"The what?"

"Do you remember our bet? I bet you he would remember to bring back the parsley then we had our—uh—discussion. Did he?"

"Yes. He did." A gruff laugh rumbled through the telephone line before electronic beeps announced my phone card time was about to expire.

"You have a wonderful son, Madame," I managed to say.

"Go home and learn how to cook." The line went dead. Pierre's mother's final words had been harsh, but they'd been in line with my expectations of her. She'd been honest with me and I'd been honest with her. It pleased me, along with the thought that Pierre had brought home the parsley, without being prompted. It was something. A lot more than having a foreign correspondent buy me a drink in a Paris café.

One day I could use a son like Pierre. But how to get there remained problematic. I would have liked to think the obstacles in my way were mostly creeps like Arnaud, but more likely I was making poor progress because I numbered among the large group of women who were attracted to them. I was desperate to get out of that particular club.

Sighing, I went to buy a *Paris Match* and headed for the departure gate for my flight back to New York. As I did, an image of Arnaud being swept up by a giant vacuum cleaner on the back of the motorcycle of a Parisian street cleaner in a red uniform popped into my head. This time I realized he was really gone. Still in my head, but no longer in my heart. I had crossed the street to the man waiting on the other side. I just didn't know yet whether he was my father or Pierre.

CHAPTER TEN

PEACEMAKING VERSUS PEACEKEEPING

"*I*talian. With tassles. The leather was like butter," the voice purred over the hum of the United Nations Information and Reception Unit. I glanced at my boss to see if she was listening. Madame LaForge's cat green eyes stared at her computer screen, scanning something intently. Online solitaire? Her bank account? Who cared? I was being paid $500 per week and my glamorous Haitian boss was kind, not terribly strict but terribly stylish, with superb posture. She reminded me of how I wished to remember my grandmother

"No, French ... Yes. Geneva ... I don't know. July maybe?" the silky, whispering voice continued. The new hire other than me was the source. This didn't sound like a public information call reassuring a worried caller that we weren't going to let Serbs slaughter Bosnians in the Balkans. Actually we were, but no one outside the U.N.

seemed to understand it wasn't our job not to let that happen. The distinction between peacemaking and peace-keeping was something I was beginning to parse after two weeks at the United Nations. U.N. peacekeepers only showed up after slaughter and rampage in some obscure spot was over. That was someone else's job.

I cocked my ears to hear more. Her accent intrigued me. It wasn't like Sanja's Serbo-Croatian one, but more French-sounding. I would make a trip to the restroom to find out more.

Casually, I got up and walked past Madame LaForge's cubicle. Her blue-mascara'd eyes slid over me, approvingly. After two weeks on the job, I sensed she thought of me as a good worker, taking my job seriously and not indulging in too many water cooler breaks. She'd taught me so many things already. It had never occurred to me to wear blue mascara but after studying how vividly it made Madame LaForge's eyes pop, I'd bought some soon after coming to work in her department. The effect was transformational. It made my eyes look even more slanted and Hungarian than usual. I had much to thank her for.

"Like Rimbaud, I mean," the voice of the new hire continued as I passed her cubicle.

Had she really said "Rimbaud?" She'd pronounced the name of the 19th century French bad boy in perfectly-accented French. If she wasn't French, she'd clearly spent time there. My skin pricked to think I was working with someone who referenced either Artur Rimbaud or the French cosmetics line in her phone conversation. Either way, I was interested.

I glanced at her as I walked by. The natural white streak in her silky, chocolate brown hair intrigued me almost as much as her silvery voice. Decidedly, she was not discussing world peace or assuaging the fears of a call-in to the United Nations Public Information Department.

I wanted to know more.

Upon my return from the restroom, where I'd bumped into an African woman whose two-foot tall head thingie matched the pattern of her voluminous print-patterned floor length dress with bustle or perhaps not, I passed the cubicle of the only other American working in my department. She was transferring a caller to another department, most likely to someone's voicemail. After two weeks on the job, I'd noticed that ninety nine percent of the calls that came in got transferred to other departments. Of those transferred calls, perhaps ninety nine per cent went directly to voicemail, where they lingered awhile then died a natural death. Of the one or two conversations I'd overheard where a colleague had actually addressed the concerns of a caller, I'd tried to take a lesson and emulate some sort of informed response. "Thank you for your call and please be assured that I am forwarding your request/opinion/concern to the Secretary-General's office where it will be addressed," was as far as I'd gotten. I sensed perhaps a tiny fib built into my response, but at least I was trying. Whether the newly-appointed Secretary-General and his office were interested, or not, was beyond my purview.

Over the past two weeks I'd learned a few fascinating tidbits about him. To begin with he was referred to as "the SG" or more informally as "the Big Enchilda." He was short, ugly and not terribly gracious in the grand French tradition of entitled arrogance. Although he was Egyptian, not French, he was clearly from the French-schooled half of the U.N. as opposed to the Anglo-schooled other half.

The other piece of information I'd picked up from a stray conversation in the U.N. cafeteria then further strengthened by a mysteriously short article in the New York Post that enjoyed only the most cursory follow up before disappearing, was that a member of his staff had been ushered quickly out of the country after assaulting a chambermaid at the U.N. Plaza Hotel the week before the start of the General Assembly. This was not a reflection upon the Secretary-General, of course, but on the company he kept, or at least the staff he hired. I was learning new bits and pieces about him every day, and although I was somewhat interested, I was more interested in my silver hair-streaked colleague now on the phone.

She glanced up as I passed and shot me a warm smile. Her eyes were startling blue. The last time I'd seen light blue eyes like that they'd belonged to my first French boyfriend Jean-Michel. Who was she, and where was she from?

I smiled in return then hurried back to my desk where the phone was now ringing.

∞

"Ava, *salut!*" A voice cut through the cigarette smoke-filled haze of the U.N. Delegates Lounge.

"Oh, hi! You're here too. How are you?" I replied, elated to see my work colleague walking toward me. She was the only person I recognized in the crowd and my *faux* air of serene confidence had only minutes to go. Sanja had been busy and I didn't know a soul at the U.N. shindig

I'd invited myself to after discreetly copying an invitation that had come in over the Info and Reception Unit's fax machine two days earlier.

"Good. And you?" She looked at me warmly, her left eye blinking, or was it a wink? The more time I spent at the U.N. the more I found the whole place to be one large, gleeful wink. I only hoped the joke wasn't on me, but thus far it had been one big party.

"I'm great. I'm Ava Fodor, by the way."

"I know. I'm Narcisa Petrescu."

"Hi. Where are you from?" My inner American sprang to the surface, digging for facts.

"Where are you from?" A giggle like a silver bird flew out of her mouth.

"I'm from New England—land of the pilgrims," I said one hundred per cent half-accurately.

"No you're not. You're from somewhere else too. Where?" Her ice blue eyes twinkled as they looked me up and down.

"Okay, Hungary. My father's Hungarian," I confessed, much too quickly. I wasn't good at all this coy, U.N. international cocktail party talk. I vowed to improve my skills soon.

"That's it. You've got a Magyar face," Narcisa nodded approvingly.

"Actually, he was Hungarian from Transylvanian," I further clarified. My father had been from the part of Hungary that had been passed back and forth between Hungary and Romania for centuries. After the 1919 Versailles Treaty, the Hungarians had lost it again to the Romanians.

"That's the best kind of Hungarian," Narcisa exclaimed.

"Why?"

"Transylvania is where true Hungarian culture lives. The blond, blue-eyed Hungarians come from there—the Szeklers."

"But it's south of Hungary, isn't it?" I'd heard that term before. It was the name of the one of the eight Magyar tribes that made up the Hungarian people.

"Yes, but in Transylvania the Hungarians mixed with the Germans who came in the thirteenth century."

"They did?" Just hearing her refer to the thirteenth century lit up my synapses. I was passionate about European history, which I'd majored in in college. Had there even been a thirteenth century in the United States? The philosopher George Berkeley would have said no, since no one would have perceived it as such at the time.

"Yes. The Siebenbürger Deutsch."

"Does that mean Seven Towns or something?" I'd dropped my German class at Yale. It had been held at eight A.M., three days a week. In direct conflict with my social schedule, I'd missed two of the first three classes. It had been all downhill from there.

"Yes. The Germans came and settled seven towns across Transylvania in the thirteenth century. They were invited by Geza the Second to help defend the borders."

I'd actually met a Hungarian called Geza at a party on the Upper East Side the winter before. He'd been short, ugly and smart; a math whiz who worked in finance. I'd heard many Hungarians were good at math, although I didn't know why. Perhaps because their own language and culture wasn't from the West like the rest of Europe. It was from the East, from Mongolia. Did they think in symbols over there?

So Geza had been the name of one of Hungary's rulers. An entire history lesson and I still didn't know where Narcisa was from.

"How do you know all this?"

She smiled a tight, bewitching smile.

"I'm from Romania."

"Romania! I knew you were from somewhere like that."

"Like what? What do you know about Romania?" she asked teasingly.

"Um—well—Transylvania is in it, isn't it?" That was about all I knew.

"Now it is, yes."

"I heard the Hungarians and Romanians don't get along there."

"That's not true. They get along great." Her smile became sly.

"How do you know?"

"I have many friends who married Hungarians. They get along fine. Except for being married, of course."

"So all that talk about Romania erasing Hungarian culture isn't true?" I caught myself. Better watch it if I wanted to make a friend out of this particular Romanian.

"Propaganda. That's all. Something to sell newspapers."

"Propaganda?"

"Yes. It's what my country runs on. That and *baksheesh*."

"*Baksheesh?*"

It's Turkish for "doing a favor for a favor."

"You mean bribery?" I regretted my *faux pas* instantly. 'Bribery' was a loaded term. Who knew what it really meant?

"No, not really. It's different. More like exchanging little presents." She gave a tinkling laugh; a little present to me. Nothing in her manner indicated she was at all fazed by such a shocking description of her native land. It was as if she'd just told me "cognac and truffles" were Romanian export items.

"Ladies, would you like a drink?" a male voice interjected. A slim, good-looking thirtyish man smiled at us. Definitely not American, but I couldn't guess what.

"Did you sleep?" Narcisa whispered to me as the owner of the male voice headed toward the nearest silver-tray-carrying waiter to capture two glasses of white wine for us.

"Did I what?"

"Did you sleep?" she asked again.

"Yes. I slept well, thank you" I answered confusedly. Did I look tired to her?

"You don't have to tell me who it was. But tell me—who was it?"

Uh—it was me. I mean *I* slept well. Didn't you?"

"Ohhh no. I didn't sleep. I had friends who helped me," Narcisa whispered back, one eyebrow lifted significantly.

"Ohhh, I see. Uh—no I didn't sleep. I—uh- took the tests last spring and they called me the beginning of August." Startled by the conversational curveball, I stepped back from Narcisa, still intrigued but alerted that I had no idea who I was dealing with. The U.N. was on international territory. American rules no longer applied.

"The tests. Everyone takes the tests. So what? How did you get the job?" she pressed.

"Like I said, I took the tests. That was it. I waited, I gave up hope, then they called." I shrugged in what I hoped was the classic Gallic way, perfected by my recent stay in Paris.

Narcisa studied me as I spoke. It was like taking a lie-detector test. Suddenly I felt as if I'd slept even when I hadn't.

"So you just took the tests and they called you. That was it?"

"Yes," I said, crisply. I tried to look like I wasn't lying, even when I wasn't. It was confusing talking to Narcisa. I wasn't used to not being believed.

"I understand. You don't have to tell me."

"No. You don't understand," I shot back sharply. "I did tell you. I took the tests and they called me. My friend Sanja did too. That's how we got the job." Not only was I defending my own honor, but America's. How did she think we did things over here? Then I remembered I wasn't over here anymore. I was on international territory.

"Sanja? Who's Sanja?" Narcisa's eyebrows knitted together in a tiny scowl.

"Sanja Darkovic. She's in Decolonization." Whatever that was. Something to do with disorganized territories in the South Pacific with exotic names like Tokelau and East Timor. From what Sanja had told me, it was a sleepy department.

"Darkovic? What kind of name is that?" Her eyes flashed.

"It's Yugoslavian."

"That's not a place anymore."

"Okay, it's Serbian."

"Ohhhh..." She looked at me suspiciously, as if I'd mentioned my friend was an ex-con.

"We took the tests on the same day, and we both got hired for the General Assembly."

"Of course you did. I understand completely." She smiled beatifically as if to say "I'll get it out of you some other time when we've gotten to know each other better."

My face flushed as I tried to move past the moment. How ridiculous to be questioned like this. Especially by someone I wanted to get to know. I didn't know whether to laugh or walk away, but her eyes sparkled like ice blue windows to someplace interesting and exotic, inviting me in. I decided to stay.

"Here you are," the man said, handing each of us a glass of white wine.

I sipped while I thanked God that I was from one of those U.N. member countries where we didn't have to "sleep" in order to get a job. At least I thought I didn't. Narcisa's assumption was too much to absorb all at once, so I focused on the man in front of me instead.

His eyes were dark brown and slanted. European, but not entirely. Yet another exotic, interesting U.N. person. The United Nations was an incredible place to work, largely for reasons different from the ones I'd previously assumed before working there. Maybe life was just like that.

Pierre's face came to mind, honest, inquisitive and focused. Spending time with him hadn't been confusing. The air he and I had breathed when we were together had been fresh, pure, unpolluted. Unlike the cigarette-hazed air I was breathing now. But who was I kidding? I liked both. That's why I'd had to walk away from our relationship. I didn't want Pierre to have a divided heart the way I did. His mother needed him. I did too, but I needed other things as well. I turned my attention back to those other things, confusing and mysterious. They fascinated me the way Narcisa's conversation did, her ice blue eyes sparkling and absorbing information as she spoke. She was intelligent, I could see. But what she gleaned from the same set of facts presented, was entirely different from whatever my own conclusions might be. Was life just like that too? I took another sip and relaxed. It was all I could manage for the moment.

∾

PIERRE'S AND MY conclusions from what had taken place in Carcassonne were different too. The day after my return to New York, he'd called. Now it was two weeks later and as I did my laundry, I thought about our exchange.

"I'm glad your mother gave you my message," I said carefully.

"I didn't understand it." His tone was neutral, guarded.

I sighed. "Thank you for letting me come visit."

"I didn't invite you to set an example for you."

"I know. I invited myself because I missed you. Thank you for saying yes."

"You see how it is."

"Yes."

"Like I said before, it's not a life for you."

"Your mother is a very special person," I said, with newly acquired U.N. finesse.

"Yes, Ava. A very difficult person."

"But still your mother."

"Yes." This time, it was Pierre who sighed.

"I—it's—I don't think..."

"What don't you think?"

"I don't see how or where I fit into your life." Ouch. The truth had slipped out. Not the whole truth, but some of it. Once out, the words couldn't be taken back.

"No. And you don't see how I fit into yours." he said slowly, supplying the missing piece to the puzzle.

"No." My voice dropped to a whisper.

"Then what, Ava?"

"I—I want us to be friends." My words were coming out all wrong. I wanted us to be more than friends, but I was scared of whatever that might be. With Pierre, it would be something serious. Something I wasn't sure I was capable of.

Silence.

"We were friends before, Pierre. I don't want to give up our friendship. I need you as my friend."

"I can't talk right now."

"Pierre, can you understand that I need you in my life?"

"I'm not a rock, Ava."

"Pierre—I understand. I just don't totally understand myself. I—"

"Let's leave it at that right now."

"It's just that you're too good for me, " I blurted out.

"Isn't that my line? Except I'm not saying it."

"I don't know how to put it," I stammered.

"Ava—let's do something really smart right now," he said, his voice affectless.

"What? What's that?" I couldn't think of anything smart at all either to say or do.

"Let's hang up."

"Only if you'll promise me we'll talk again soon."

"I'm counting to three then we're both hanging up."

"Promise me, Pierre." I had no ground to walk on and I knew it. Part of me didn't want him to agree. He was a man and I'd hurt him. I wanted him to be manly. Already, my heart ached to think of the implications of our conversation.

"One—two—three." The line went dead.

It wasn't until that night as I fell into a fitful, troubled sleep that it occurred to me what Pierre's name meant in French. A *pierre* was a stone. My Pierre was indeed a rock. But he wasn't mine anymore. I'd shut the door on his heart because my own wasn't ready to receive it. Could any sort of friendship between a man and a woman who had once been lovers survive such a blow?

༄

"Do you want to go for a drink?" Narcisa asked, as we exited the Secretariat Building at half past five one week later.

"I can't. I've got to meet my father."

"The Transylvanian?" she said interestedly.

"The same. We're going for a drink to Cafe Geiger." My father was not a big drinker, with his rosé spritzers, but he loved the institution of the cocktail hour. So did I.

"May I come?"

"You're kidding! You won't meet anyone." Despite Narcisa's allergic reaction to Sanja, they were on the same plan in their free time—researching bankers.

"Yes I will. I'll meet your father. He sounds interesting."

"He is."

"What's his name again?"

"Zsolt. Zsolt Fodor."

"Like a lightning bolt," she joked.

"He is rather," I said cautiously.

"Do you mind?"

"Not at all. As long as you're not expecting someone—well—conventional."

"What do you mean?"

"I mean bourgeois. You know."

"Yes. I know." She wrinkled her nose. "Bourgeois is boring. I can't wait to meet your lightning bolt."

❧

"So what was Carcassonne like?" Narcisa asked. Meanwhile she looked at my father and batted her eyes.

"It was like being in a dream, only stronger," I told them both. I hadn't divulged to my father the full extent of what had happened there. Too much had gone on between Pierre and me that was still tenuous, open to suggestion. I didn't want anyone weighing in on what had happened between us until I had reached some sort of conclusion myself. Our last phone conversation still echoed in my ears. I wasn't ready to share it with anyone, as if speaking about it would solidify the reality that we had broken up.

"What kind of dream?"

"Like a déjà vu. As if I'd been there once before."

"Seriously?" Narcisa looked at me for the first time since we'd all sat down at the table at Cafe Geiger. My father did too, leaning forward on his elbows, one hand under his chin.

"What happened, Évika?" he asked, using the Hungarian diminutive for my name.

"I was in a little square next to the castle there. The sun was setting and all of a sudden, I had an image of a nun playing harp in the town square as the sun set. She was blind." I took a deep breath. "It was as if I not only knew her but..."

"But you were her," my father finished.

He got me. My grandparents would never have finished a sentence for me like that. My grandmother would have told me to get up and clear the table while I cleared my head and my grandfather would have grunted, said "well, how about that...," then gone into the other room to see how the Red Sox were doing.

"Yes. Exactly. I knew I had been her."

"You were." My father nodded approvingly. "Your blood is European, Évika. So is your soul."

"Only half, Papa."

"Your mother's soul is European too. She should have been born Viennese. She would have broken mens' hearts there.

Funny. My mother had gone off on her own in Vienna when she'd been sent on a European Grand Tour when she was twenty two. She'd never told anyone the full extent of what had happened to her during the week she'd spent away from her tour group. I'd sensed she hadn't been entirely on her own, but I'd never know. With oodles of mystique, my mother was good at keeping secrets.

"Were you alone when it happened?" Narcisa asked.

"Uh—no."

"She was with her French friend," my father intuited.

"Oh?" Narcisa's ears perked up. "Friend" was a wondrously vague term in English. It covered quite a spectrum, including both sexes.

"Uh—yes."

"The *kutyaszar* bastard?" My father pointedly pressed.

Narcisa laughed. "Dogshit" appeared to be a Hungarian expletive she was familiar with.

"No! The other one," I scolded him. He'd listened to me more carefully than I'd given him credit for, when I'd told him I'd like to make a quick trip to France in early September before starting my U.N. job.

"Oh yes. The one you're not so in love with."

"I didn't say that! What do you think I am—stupid?"

"No, Évika. Just human. Women always go for the *kutyaszar* bastard when there's a choice."

"What do you mean? No they don't!" I spluttered, outraged to think my father had insight into not only my own perversity, but one shared by my entire sex. I choked on the sip of my drink I'd just taken.

"Of course, " he replied patly, as if pointing out the sky was blue.

"How can you say that?" I demanded, indignant.

"Ava, which one do you think I was?" My father smiled, as sly as a cat after polishing ff a bowl of cream. Light cream, not heavy cream.

The silver tinkle of Narcisa's laugh fluttered in the air until customers at the next table looked over, amused. My father had hit the mother lode. In more ways than one.

Narcisa followed me to the restroom where I fled to compose myself. A few important points had been touched upon in the past few minutes. All needled me in various sore spots.

"Your father's not just interesting, he's fascinating!" she exclaimed at the mirror, reapplying her berry red lipstick.

"He knows a lot about human nature," I admitted.

"I'll bet he knows a lot about women," she added.

I choked again. Was there any way I could mine that kind of information out of my sphinx-like mother? I didn't think so. But it would be fun to try.

"He doesn't know what happened to me in Carcassonne."

"What did happen? Tell me!"

"I can't really talk about it.

Narcisa gave me the hairy eyeball as if to ask, "Who do you think you're talking to?"

"Yet, I mean," I amended.

"Tell me about the non-*kutyaszar* bastard."

"Pierre's not a bastard!"

"His name is Pierre?"

"Let's get back to my father."

"Can I see a photo of him?"

"I'll bring one to work, tomorrow."

"Don't you have one now?"

Psychic interlopers surrounded me that evening. First my father, then Narcisa. "I might have one in my bag..." I admitted. I'd been carrying around a photo of Pierre I'd taken in New York the February before like a holy relic since our last phone conversation. Usually I handled break ups like amputations. It wasn't working out that way with Pierre. Frankly, it hadn't worked out that way with Arnaud either.

"Let's see it."

"Not now. Let's get back to my father," I said, trying to brush past her out the restroom door.

She blocked my way. "Not until you show me the photo."

"Okay, okay." I fished in my handbag until I found it. Handing it to Narcisa, I held my breath.

She studied it carefully then handed it back to me.

"So?" I asked, in spite of myself. I didn't want to be held prisoner to her opinion of Pierre's looks. He was no Apollo. More of a Hephaestus, god of the hearth. A rock.

"He looks like a keeper," she said reverently.

"That's too bad," I said, my heart wincing.

"Why?"

"Because I threw him back."

We exited and returned to Zsolt the Lightning Bolt, former *kutyaszar* bastard.

༄

TWO MONTHS LATER, at the public information booth at the entrance to the U.N. Secretariat Building, my heart hiccupped as Arnaud de Saint Cyr broke out of the long, snaking line of people waiting to get in.

He headed directly toward me.

I steeled myself as his blue-green eyes came into focus, his long, leonine auburn hair attracting the attention of my Dutch colleague, Maryam. Out of the corner of my eye, I saw her female antennae waving as she evaluated my suddenly stiff posture.

"Ava." The timbre of his voice hit me in the usual place, somewhere I didn't want it to. It hadn't been easy to push Pierre away. Caring for my father wasn't easy and I needed support. But there was no way I'd play with Pierre's heart just to find solace. The man heading toward me was more the type to provide a temporary distraction. But thoughts of Pierre tugged at me; not just in the friendship section of my brain, either. I didn't know what I wanted, other than to slap the smile off the face of the man now approaching me.

"Arnaud. How are you?" I coolly addressed him. I hated his guts. Actually, I didn't care about him at all. He was history. Gone and all but forgotten.

"So you *are* working here. What good luck to find you right at the entrance!"

Was that some sort of dis? As if I'd been demoted from budding cabaret star in Paris, where I'd been a singer-pianist when I'd met him, to New York security guard? *Ava, you're over thinking. Take a deep breath and stay cool.*

"What are you doing in New York?" I asked, oozing disinterest and whatever the noun for *blasé* is—blasé-ness?

"Didn't I tell you I might come visit you in New York?"

"Without an invitation?" I asked icily. "What's the other reason?"

"I'm covering the President's address for *Libération*," he said, citing France's largest left-wing newspaper.

"Oh." It took me a moment to realize he was referring to the French president, who was due to speak to the General Assembly that week. Although I was now an international civil servant on international territory at the U.N., I still thought like an American. In fact, that had been the whole reason I'd left Paris to return to New York. You can take the American out of America, but you can't take America out of the American. At least not where I was concerned.

"I'm here till the end of the week. Can we get together?" he asked, his incisive voice damning me in all the wrong places.

I gaped at him. What did he mean by "get together?" And why was I jumping to conclusions? Just because he was a foreign correspondent didn't mean he was all bad, did it?

It did. Or at least I needed it to.

"How's Mélanie?" I asked, referring to the woman he'd carried a torch for during the time we'd been together in Paris. Who knew—maybe now he was carrying a torch for me? Whether he was or not, the one thing he wasn't capable of was carrying on an ongoing relationship. I burned at the memory of the anxiety he'd caused me the five months we'd been together in Paris.

For the briefest flicker of a second, Arnaud looked uncomfortable. Then he was all suave moves again.

"How are you?" he deftly sidestepped.

"Great."

"You look *ravissante.*"

I beamed in spite of myself, then became cognizant of the eyes of my even more ravishing Dutch colleague on the man in front of me.

"Thank you. Do you want a visitor's pass?" I asked, remembering my job.

"No, I've got a press pass." He flashed the dog tag around his neck, his long, muscular fingers grasping it firmly, but with finesse. Ouch.

"You'll still need a visitor's pass to get through security," I explained. As I wrote out the pass, I saw Arnaud's eyes flicker over Maryam, three yards to my left.

"Hello," he said to her.

"Hiya'," Maryam offered back in her adorable Dutch accent. I glanced up to see her cornflower blue eyes taking him in. Quickly, I recovered myself from falling for the *ravissante* line. He was the same old no-attention-span fox. There would always be a Mélanie any girlfriend of Arnaud's would have to compete with. Never again would that be me.

I handed him the pass then turned to the next person in line.

Instead of leaving, Arnaud moved a few steps closer to Maryam's station, asking her some inane question. She merrily responded and they chatted on, ignoring the long line of people waiting to gain admission to the Secretariat Building.

My Puritan work ethic rankled inside. The classic attitude of the international civil servant set at the U.N. made French postal workers look positively service-oriented. Maryam and I were on duty and just because my bloody French ex-boyfriend had shown up didn't mean we needed to shut down Visitors Admissions at the United Nations Secretariat Building for twenty minutes while hundreds of people waited in line for our attention. Or was it simply that Arnaud was flirting with Maryam and I was having trouble remembering that I no longer gave a fig for him anymore?

I turned away so Arnaud couldn't enjoy my pique, even though he was now staring at Maryam's cute, honey-colored Dutch doll face. As I did, a familiar figure floated toward the Security desk from the inner sanctum of the Secretariat Building. It stopped for a word with the security guard on duty then blew him a kiss before moving on. Unbelievable. Narcisa walked toward me, her usual half-flirtatious, half mysterious smile lighting up her face.

Sweating like a woman in the midst of a hot flash, I dashed out of the information booth to cut her off. There was no way I'd introduce her to Arnaud de Saint Cyr. Absolutely not. Maybe Sanja? Never. Then despite myself, I had a crazy inspiration. I'd introduce him to both and get him off my back. Or mind. But not just yet.

"Aren't you on duty?" Narcisa asked, as I tried to pass her.

"I'm going to the restroom. I'll be right back."

"I've got to deliver this package to the desk. I think it's Madame LaForge's eye makeup from France."

"Sure. See you upstairs."

"I'm going to stay here. My shift starts in fifteen minutes, so they sent me down early."

My heart sank to think of her meeting Arnaud. But why? She'd be able to sniff out a snake in less than a minute. Why not trust Narcisa's good instincts to sniff out a bad man?

Maybe he's not all bad. Maybe he's just not for you, a small voice inside said. *Bastard,* a louder voice overruled it.

"I've got to make a phone call. I'll be right back."

"I thought you said you were going to the restroom."

"Be right back. See you," I fudged, then turned and fled through Security into the Secretariat Building. Arnaud now had access to the place where I worked. I myself had written out his visitors pass. What had I been thinking?

෬

"WHAT'S AN EGG nog?" Arnaud studied the specialty drinks menu carefully. As an investigative journalist, he was a sponge for new information.

"It's a Christmas drink. Like milk with egg in it and some brandy." Sadly, I thought back to the February before when Pierre and I had been in a similar cozy Manhattan watering hole, drinking spiked hot chocolates. That had been the evening our friendship had become something else. Something there was no way we could sustain. At least it had been real, unlike what present company offered.

Arnaud's eyes lit up. "Now you're talking."

"And a dash of nutmeg," I added.

"Is that the pilgrims' contribution to the recipe? His eyes twinkled as he teased.

"The nutmeg adds a little spice to the mix."

"So you do—superbly."

I frowned. Arnaud knew I was from Connecticut, the Nutmeg State. I needed to stop him in his tracks before he got even more personal.

Glancing at my watch, I rued Narcisa's absence. As soon as she turned up, she'd be able to return the repartée volley for volley—one for France, one for Romania. I'd been good at that game too, the first few months I'd played it with Arnaud, all jabs and sharp returns. But our dynamic had become exhausting.

Volleying with Pierre had been more fun. He'd been gentle and good-natured. As usual, he'd tossed good things my way, gifts I could walk away with, which retained their value.

My heart ached as I thought of how much I missed him. But I couldn't play with his heart the way Arnaud had played with mine. I was lonely, but it was better to be lonely than to use someone to stave off loneliness. Had that been what Arnaud had done with me in Paris? Our relationship had boiled down to a series of light encounters wedged in between Arnaud's overseas assignments. I felt sick just thinking about it.

The Sauvignon Blanc was crisp with hints of kiwi. No egg nog for me. Way too sweet. It had taken a full ten years, but I'd overcome my sugar addiction. Something in my metabolism had changed. Or perhaps I'd just substituted a penchant for white wine for the attractions to sugar and fats I'd felt in my late teens and early twenties. Whatever the reason, I was thrilled to have left those days behind.

Eyeballing Arnaud distrustfully over the rim of my glass, I congratulated myself on graduating from Chubsville University. I was now getting my postgraduate degree in How to Stay Slinky. My time in Paris had helped. No one would get fat from eating such a satisfying diet as the French one. When you ate well, you didn't need to overeat.

New York, another gastronomic capital, was giving me the chance to apply lessons I'd learned in France. The Big Apple presented enough food choices so that I could choose to eat well. It was more expensive, but worth it. The more U.N. functions serving shrimp appetizers I slipped into, the better I could balance my food budget, I reasoned.

"I'll have half a dozen little necks," I told the waiter. Arnaud had already announced he was expense-accounting our drinks and nibbles. It was no skin off my wallet and besides—he owed me something—five months of my life, to put a fine point on it.

"I'll take an egg nog and an order of calamari," he told the waiter.

The waiter nodded approvingly. At that moment, I loved New York. In the United States you could order any food and drink combination you liked, without judgment, without censure.

Not so in France. In Paris, the waiter would have frowned then walked back to the kitchen where he would have spat on the floor at the thought of the execrable combination of egg nog and calamari.

When they say America is a free country, it's not exactly true, especially when it comes to seeing a doctor. Then you're free to see any doctor you like as long as you're rich enough to pay the bill. But in the sense that you're free to choose what you damn well want to eat and drink together, they're right—you're free to do that without any-one judging you. In France, you'd practically get arrested for making a bad choice of what to eat with what you're drinking, or vice versa. Social censure would be the mini-mum penalty.

While Arnaud checked out the female flora and fauna around us, I pondered which was better—freedom to get fat from bad food choices versus enslavement to culturally approved food and drink guidelines guaranteed to keep you slim. Were those slinky French women really happy? Or were they just slaves to their slinkiness? I liked to think they were, but had a feeling they weren't.

"So what did you decide?" Arnaud finally spoke.

"What?" I asked, startled. Had he read my mind?

"Heavy cream or light? Have you figured out which one you prefer?"

I frowned at him. "Definitely not light cream." Instantly, our conversation at Café de la Bastille in Paris two months earlier came back.

"Why not? It's more you, isn't it?"

"It goes bad sooner."

"I think the heavy cream has gone off too," he observed.

"What do you mean by that?"

"I mean your boy toy is no longer waiting around for you to figure out what you want."

"He's not my boy toy," I snapped. "And we broke it off months ago. What do you mean he's no longer waiting around?" I hadn't meant to divulge all that. What did he mean anyway?

"Good. Because he's seeing someone else now."

"Who told you that?"

"Chantal."

"His mother?"

"The same."

"What did she say?"

"She said her son had found a woman who can cook."

"I don't believe you," I snapped, outraged.

"There's lots of women who cook in France. Willingly, even."

"Not that. It's just that Pierre wouldn't. I mean, he hasn't..." What did I know? He hadn't called the week before. Or the week before that. Wasn't he free to meet a woman if he wanted to? I'd told him I didn't see how things could work between us. Yet I couldn't bear the thought of him moving in another direction.

"You can't just keep a man on the hook, you know."

"Like I told you, we broke it off a few months ago. After I saw you in Paris."

"Ahh, I see. So you did arrive at a conclusion."

"It just didn't make sense. He's there and I'm here."

"I'm here too. How do you like that?"

"I—It doesn't matter if you're here or not. You're leaving in a few days. That doesn't count."

"Works fine for me."

"Not for me."

"Are you sure?"

"Stop it, Arnaud. I told you in September and I'm telling you now, you're not the man for me."

"I'm at the Roosevelt if you change your mind."

"I don't want to know." I covered my ears. "I don't care."

"Every cat needs its cream."

I glared at him, disgusted. How could I have once been in love with this man? He knew nothing about being a couple or building a relationship. All he understood was pleasure taken from episodic assignations with no continuity in between. Even if I'd lost Pierre, I wasn't going back to a man who thought of me as a convenient port of call when he was in town.

"So this is the *kutyaszar* one?" a silvery voice rang out. Narcisa's enormous black cape made her look like a sexy version of the old, evil-looking fat guy in the Toulouse-Lautrec painting—the one with the red scarf.

"No, I mean, yes, but not now," I stammered, raising an eyebrow significantly at Narcisa. How long had she been standing there listening to our conversation? My Romanian friend looked wickedly foxy that evening. She kissed each of us twice, once on either cheek and *voilà*—I was back in Paris.

Arnaud nodded approvingly as she sat with a flourish, arranging her cape around her like a bullfighter. The thought flashed through my brain that I needed to warn her off Arnaud when we went to the ladies room. Except that that might pique her interest even more, if she was anything like pretty much everyone else motivated by perverse human nature.

I glanced at her to check, but it was useless. I could never really tell what she was thinking. Usually I was pretty good at reading my friends' thoughts. But with Narcisa, I never knew. If Arnaud found her as mysterious as I did, he'd be intrigued. It would bother me, although the fact that it did bothered me more.

"So you know each other from Paris?" Narcisa asked.

"Yes. We met there last year. At a party," I quickly said, taking charge of the narrative. No need to get into how well we knew each other. Narcisa would extract it from me soon enough, but now was not the moment.

"Ah yes, Ava from New York. She walked in and flattened the crowd."

My heart panged as I remembered my excitement when Arnaud had uttered those words the moment we met. "So what have we here? Ava from New York?" Why did life have to sour from the first encounter in so many situations? If only Arnaud and I could have stayed frozen in that moment or perhaps only slightly beyond. The whole winding down of our relationship had been one big fizzle of enormous, gaping disappointment on my part. What it had been to him, I couldn't say.

"Tell me about it. What kind of party was it?" The only person I'd ever met who loved parties more than me and possibly Arnaud, was Narcisa. Her entire life appeared to be one big party, including the way she handled her job.

I'd given up months ago on trying to pass Puritan judgment on her version of a work ethic. It was too much fun hanging out with her. Unlike Narcisa, I was a conscientious worker at my job and my boss, Madame LaForge, loved me for it. I was one of the only members of the Information and Reception Unit at the U.N. who actually tried to respond to questions callers asked. That was because I was not only an American, but a New England Puritan. Someone inside my head, such as my grandmother, would lecture me if I didn't. The only way to escape the nagging sound of her voice, "Ava, what are you doing right now?", was to get back to work.

However, I drew the line at making international personal calls while on the job. That was easy to do since the only person I wanted to call internationally was Pierre. And I didn't want anyone listening in on my conversations with him. But it had been a few weeks since his last call. I tried not to think about Arnaud's new information.

"Oh, it was a very good party. First, there was good wine. Then there was Ava." Arnaud looked over at me significantly. If he'd only managed to continue looking at me in the same way during the time we were together, we might not have broken up.

Startled, it occurred to me for the first time since he'd shown up two days earlier that it had been me who had broken up with him. Considering the level of anger and hurt I felt, it made no sense at all that it had been me doing the breaking off. Never before had I experienced such feelings of being dumped when I'd been the dumper. It didn't make sense.

"Then what?" I could feel Narcisa's interest warming up. The waiter approached and she ordered a Brandy Alexander. The Europeans at the table were ordering American-style mixed drinks and the only American there was drinking a French Sauvignon Blanc. Was the grass always greener on the other side?

"I can't remember. I don't remember anything after I met Ava. She swept me off my feet," Arnaud said, smiling coyly. He looked like a fox after eating a hen.

I snorted. The idea of anyone sweeping Arnaud off his feet was ludicrous. But why not? Maybe I needed to readjust my ideas of what I could do to a man.

Straightening up, I channeled my inner Super Model. Immediately, the man at the next table looked over while his female companion rummaged in her purse.

"Well—what was it—a French party, a diplomatic party, or what? "

"An ex-pat party. Our friend Larry threw one every Sunday. If it had been a French party, we wouldn't have met," he joked.

We all laughed. He was so right. French people didn't actually meet new people at French parties, especially Parisian ones. They just squared off into cliques and stayed in their respective corners, eyeballing strangers distrustfully and criticizing everything.

"You're probably right," Narcisa agreed. "When I lived in Paris, my French girlfriends would beg me to take them to parties. They told me they never had any fun at the parties they went to."

"What kind of parties did you go to?" I asked, curious.

"Romanian ones. Spanish or English ones. Scandinavian ones. Any parties except French."

"Australian ones?"

"They were the best of all," Narcisa laughed.

"Agreed," I exclaimed.

"Agreed," Arnaud echoed. We lifted our glasses and toasted the Australian party-throwing faction in Paris. Suddenly I was back at Larry's party in Paris, bantering with hearty Australians and other Anglos until Arnaud walked in and captured my heart.

Now it just hurt.

Once again I reminded myself that it had been me who had broken it off with him.

" Are you a *bancaire*?" Narcisa asked, looking at Arnaud doubtfully. She pronounced it "bahn-CARE."

"Yes," he shot back.

I noted that Narcisa asked Arnaud exactly the question Sanja would have wanted to know the answer to, despite the fact that my two friends disliked and distrusted everything they knew about each other, which was not much, since I'd kept them apart ever since Narcisa hadn't appeared to react well to Sanja's Serbian surname. Sanja was still in the midst of researching bankers at downtown financial district watering holes. After her debacle with Victor, nothing had panned out.

"Do you have a lot of money?" Narcisa followed up.

It was all I could do not to choke on my drink.

"Do you want me to?" A classic Arnaud response. I was back at Larry's party, exchanging delicious repartee with a delicious man. Except that he hadn't been good for me. Once again, I reminded myself I was over my junk food addiction.

"Yes," Narcisa stated happily.

"Then, yes," he answered agreeably.

"Good," she rejoined.

Lord, where was this going? If I warned her off Arnaud, she would resent me. If I let her allow him to move in on her, she would ultimately get hurt then accuse me of not having warned her. Or maybe she wouldn't get hurt but they'd fall madly in love, get married and spend the rest of their lives together in wedded bliss, which would piss me off *in extremis.*

But why? I was the one who'd broken it off with Arnaud. Why did I even care?

Human beings were strange and I was the strangest of them all. Actually, Arnaud was, but I came in a close second. Come to think of it, Narcisa was pretty strange too, but I could definitely see myself in third place, still on the podium.

I tried not to seethe as I sipped my drink.

CHAPTER ELEVEN

SERBIA MEETS ROMANIA

"*What* about *mititei?*" Narcisa asked, as we went over possible dishes she might teach me to make for my father. Arnaud had departed after a few days stay and a few vain attempts to interest both Narcisa and Sanja in having short, meaningless flings with him. Both my girlfriends seemed safely vaccinated against Arnaud-types. They were both looking for serious men and had met enough of the non-serious ones to know a time waster when they met one. I only wished I myself had been as savvy as my smart, Balkan girlfriends the year before when I bumped into Arnaud in Paris, but the heart is a lonely hunter. Fortunately, mine was no longer hunting for a man like him. Instead, it was hiding out under a rock while I went about the business of looking after my father and thinking about another rock—Pierre.

He was too good for me. But Pierre's mother hadn't been. Her final words to me—"learn how to cook"—stuck in my craw. Was Pierre really seeing someone else now? Someone who knew how to cook? That would mean practically anyone in France over the age of twelve, female or male.

I decided to expand my repertoire of culinary dishes from Nicaraguan chicken to one other dish. Since I had no idea what that might be, I'd enlisted Narcisa's help. It was a good excuse to have her over to my father's place and besides—she loved to cook as much as Sanja did. It was good to have friends with mysterious predilections. Who knew? Maybe I'd learn from them how to cook something myself.

"Miti—what?"

"*Mititei.* They're a sort of finger-sized sausages. Only they're made from lamb, beef and pork. With lots of onions."

"You mean like *ćevapčići?*" I asked, remembering the succulent fat-fingered grilled meat Sanja had served at a dinner party she'd held the month before.

"What's that?" Narcisa frowned, looking suspicious. I'd noticed her distinct tendency to distance herself from anything Balkan-sounding that wasn't Romanian. God forbid that I would make the mistake of mentioning Romanian and Balkan in the same breath to her. She would chew off my head with a highly debatable, revisionist history lesson. Apparently Romanians didn't think of themselves as Balkan although almost everyone else did. It didn't do to get into internecine definitions of ethnic identity with people from those parts.

"You know, the Yugoslavian grilled meat thing that sounds exactly like what you just described."

"I'm sure it's not," she sniffed.

"Well, do you think it's something my father would like?"

"He'll love them. I'll bet he ate them in Transylvania."

"Good. Tell me what to get and we'll make it for him for Saturday dinner."

"I have a date on Saturday. What about Sunday, around six?"

"Okay, Sunday, Great. Who's your date with?"

Narcisa's tinkling laugh danced through the receiver. "I'll tell you Sunday. Get half a pound each of chopped lamb, beef, and pork. And three large onions."

Getting off the phone, I had an inspired thought. Why not ask Sanja to join my father and me for dinner Saturday evening? She could show me how to make *ćevapčići*, then my father could let me know after the weekend which he preferred—the Romanian or the Serbian version. I tingled. What was a little competition among friends? My father would love the idea, and I'd learn how to cook two versions of the same dish. *Take that, Chantal Castel.*

⁓

"THAT SMELL IS @#$*#$*! my father sang out from the other room, where he sat reading the Hungarian newspaper his best friend Béla had brought back from Budapest the year before.

I agreed, whatever he'd said in Hungarian. It was the chopped lamb in Sanja's recipe that dazzled my nose buds the most. Grilled lamb was a smell people either loved or hated. My father and I both loved it. Strangely enough, my grandmother had too. Her roasted lamb from my childhood had been one of her all-time best dishes. Now that I was getting to know my father, it was ironic to note how many similarities my mother's mother and he shared. If only she could have gotten over the fact that Zsolt Fodor was foreign and penniless, she would have loved him. But those were both points my New England WASP grandmother would never get over. Surely she was in heaven now, holding it against someone at the next table who spoke with an accent or didn't come from the right sort of stock. If God wanted to play a little joke on her, He might have reincarnated her as a Bulgarian sheepherder.

"Ready in a minute, Dr. Fodor," Sanja answered, her salutation of respect tickling my father's ego. The weekend was shaping up nicely. Already I'd enlisted chefs for Saturday and Sunday dinner, and both were friends whose company I enjoyed.

The phone rang. Putting down the wine bottle I was uncorking, I ran to answer it, praying it wasn't my father's girlfriend calling to grill us on what we were having for dinner and why it would kill my father.

"*Kutyazsar* bastard," the voice began. Female. Tearful. Content-wise, it could have been Tünde, but the silvery, whispery tone wasn't within her even to fake.

"Narcisa?" I asked.

"He stood me up. I've been here an hour and he hasn't come."

"Where are you?"

"I'm on East Eighty First. Butterfields."

"Are you sure he's not coming?" The restaurant was practically around the corner, four blocks from my father's place.

"I don't care if he's coming or not. I waited over an hour and I hate his guts."

"Did you call home and see if he left a message?" I couldn't count the number of times Narcisa had made others wait at least an hour in the three months that I'd known her. She made French people look like Germans. Even Sanja seemed punctual next to Narcisa.

"Yes. Nothing. I hate the bahn-CARES."

"Don't lump them altogether just because of one," I said, although personally I thought Narcisa with a banker was about as unlikely a combination as eggnog with calamari. But in New York, anything goes. It was one of the reasons I was relieved to be back. In Paris only one thing ever went with one other thing. If you didn't agree, you were wrong. It was a place my grandmother would have highly approved of. Except that it was foreign.

"Can I come over?" Narcisa asked, her voice as small as a four-year olds.'

"Of course. We're just about to eat. My father will cheer you up," I said without thinking. I wanted to hear the whole story of the *kutyazsar* banker. It would jazz up the evening and my father could advise. I was sure he'd tell her to drop the idea of pursuing bankers at all and go after someone like himself instead.

"What's the address again?" she asked, her voice brightening.

"323 East Eighty Fifth between First and Second."

"See you in ten minutes."

I hung up and went back to uncorking the wine bottle. Then I froze. What would happen when Narcisa came face to face with Sanja? As usual, I hadn't thought out my invitation; I'd just acted.

"Who was on the phone?" my father asked.

"Narcisa," I told him nervously. Would Romania freeze out Serbia? Would Serbia smack around Romania? Would Hungary get blamed for the fall out?

"Where is she?"

"She's at a restaurant four blocks away."

"With who?'

"That's the problem. She had a date with a man, but he didn't show up."

"*Kutyaszar* bastard," my father roared. Already, he was in Saturday evening party mode.

"Exactly what she said," I agreed.

"You asked her over, of course."

"Yes, Papa."

"Narcissa—Na-a-r- ci-i-sa," he sang. My father had a song for every female I'd introduced to him. It was like having a woman in every port. Silently, I congratulated myself on resisting Arnaud's entreaties the last time he'd been in town. The scales had fallen from my eyes with my ex. Still, I was grateful he lived on the other side of the Atlantic. Unlike the way I felt when I thought of Pierre so far away. Taking a sip of wine, I silently toasted him and his mother. He was in the right place, doing the right thing. So was I. But I missed him.

Preparing to mediate Romania squaring off with Serbia, I was half horrified and half intrigued. What might happen? Would a dust-up ensue? A chill frost descent over the evening? All anyone had to do was open a newspaper or watch the news on TV to know what happened when Balkan neighbors from different ethnic groups got together. Usually, it wasn't good. Sometimes it was very, very bad.

Nervously, I opened my father's hutch and extracted a second bottle of Bull's Blood. The evening ahead would require fortitude. I went into the kitchen.

"Sanja?"

"Yes?" she answered, her back to me as she slid the first batch of *ćevapčići* from the frying pan onto a serving plate. The smell was divine.

"My friend Narcisa is joining us," I said. Might as well bite the bullet now to give my Serbian friend time to put on her game face.

"Who?" she turned to me and frowned. What was it with Balkan people? As soon as you mentioned a name from a neighboring ethnic group, storm clouds gathered.

"Narcisa. The one I work with in Information and Reception."

"The Romanian one?"

"Yes."

"I didn't know you'd invited her too," she said coolly.

"I didn't. Her plans fell through and she asked if she could come over."

"Sure. Why not?" Sanja said neutrally, although her eyes darkened. She turned back to the stove while I tidied up the cooking dishes in the sink.

"Ladies—where are my ladies?" my father sang out from the other room. We hurried in with the first platter of *ćevapčići* and sat on either side of him as he filled our wineglasses. Before we could pick them up, the buzzer rang.

As I took Narcisa's coat and inhaled a full blast of spicy perfume I'd never smelled on her, I took her in. Dressed to kill, she looked ready to kill, judging by the scowl on her face. I envisioned a badly bruised banker in a gutter somewhere, unconscious.

"Narcissss-a-a-a-a-, Nar-ci-i-i-sa, you broke my heart," my father sang out. He bent over her hand and kissed it dramatically.

"No, Dr. Fodor. Someone else broke mine," she corrected, cracking a smile despite herself.

Turning, she looked at Sanja. Her smile froze.

"Narcisa, do you remember my friend Sanja? She works in Decolonization."

"How do you do," Narcisa said coldly, without putting out her hand.

"Hello," Sanja said, not bothering to stand up. They eyeballed each other like poisonous snakes from rival species.

"What's this about someone breaking your heart? No one can break the heart of someone so beautiful," my father protested, pulling up a chair and motioning Narcisa into it.

I took another wineglass from the hutch and set it before her. Under Narcisa's eyes, raccoon smudges appeared, apparently from weeping. The effect made her look sexy and smoldering. I'd never seen my fey Romanian friend look so glamorous. Definitely, the *kutyaszar* banker's loss, whatever his story.

"I—he—it," she began.

"What happened?" I prompted her.

Narcisa took a generous sip of Bull's Blood, then looked at my father.

"Tell me, beautiful lady. They're all bastards, I know," he encouraged.

She burst into tears.

I ran to get some tissues, Sanja following.

"What happened?" she whispered, out of Narcisa's earshot.

"She had a date and he didn't show up."

"That's terrible! Who was it with?"

"Some banker guy. She was supposed to meet him at a restaurant near here and he didn't show."

"I hate those banker types. Especially the private ones," she said passionately. I was relieved she didn't say "I hate those Romanians." Score one for Serbia.

"You'll have a lot to talk about then." Hadn't Narcisa said the banker she was dating was in private banking too, just like Sanja's Victor had been? We returned to the living room, where my father was murmuring something in Hungarian to Narcisa, as if she were a baby he was lulling to sleep.

"*Kutyaszar* bastard, *kutyaszar, nem nem, ne sìrjàl*—no, no, don't cry," he crooned, stroking her forearm.

Something deep inside me had heard those soothing noises before. Had he lulled me to sleep like that once a lifetime ago? He'd been there the first fourteen months of my life. The soothing noises he made to Narcisa resonated inside.

"He didn't even call," Narcisa choked out. She took another sip of wine.

"Have something to eat," I offered, delicately refraining from referring to the *ćevapčići* by its Serbian name. Different names for different things could be explosive in certain circles; Balkan ones, in particular. I put two fat fingers on a plate and slid it toward her. She pushed it away.

"How long had you been dating?" I asked.

"Not long," she sniffed. "We saw each other after work a few times over the past few weeks."

"Never on the weekends?" I asked.

I watched as Sanja carefully refilled Narcisa's glass. Score two for Serbia. Ever since I'd met Sanja, It had been clear to me they weren't all animals over there. Sanja was about as refined, and civilized as a person could get. Judging by the amount of time and care she'd already lavished on my father since I'd introduced her to him the winter before, she was also big-hearted. I wished I could be like her.

"No. This was the first time we planned something on the weekend," Narcisa said tentatively, noticing Sanja refill her glass.

"Was it your idea to get together Saturday or his?" I probed.

"He'd suggested Friday, but I was busy," Narcisa explained.

Sanja looked at her sympathetically, saying nothing.

"What?" Narcisa asked, returning her gaze.

"He's probably married," Sanja finally said.

"Why do you say that?" Narcisa asked indignantly.

"When they stand you up on the weekends, that's usually what it means," she whispered.

"Isn't that what happened the night of the Super Bowl party" I asked Sanja gently, referring back to the party at Math House we'd gone to with Pierre, when he'd visited in February. I'd never mentioned to her that I'd spotted Victor at the Met with the woman with the cane. It hadn't been necessary, because Sanja had sniffed out that Victor was married shortly after he'd stood her up for their date that weekend.

"Yes. The snake." She looked at me, then at Narcisa, her face filled with empathy. "I've been there," she added.

"I hate the bahn-CARES." Narcisa sniffed, tentatively returning Sanja's commiserating look.

"Me too. I hate their guts," Sanja said vehemently. "Especially the private ones."

"That's what he was," Narcisa choked out, looking surprised. "A private banker."

"The worst types," Sanja agreed. "Spoiled, and playing with other people's money. Mine went to Argentina all the time."

Narcisa's jaw dropped. "Mine went to Argentina too."

"There's a lot of rich people in Argentina, no?" I observed.

"What was your *kutyaszar* banker's name?" My father asked Narcisa practically, if not a tad personally. Hanging around with Tünde for more than sixteen years had rubbed off on him. Plus, he was a New Yorker. He knew how to get to the point when needed.

"Mine? His name?" Narcisa hesitated.

"Papa, never mind what his name is. It doesn't matter—"

"Mine was Victor," Sanja offered.

"What?" Narcisa looked stunned. "No way. Where did he work?"

"At Goldman. Goldman Tax, he told me." Sanja's eyes widened as she stared back at Narcisa.

"Impossible," Narcisa said, her eyes practically popping out of her head. "Victor Friedman?"

"Yes. That's him. Do you know him?" Judging by the rosiness flooding into Sanja's cheeks, I guessed her relationship with Victor had progressed to the beyond friends point before she'd discovered he was married.

"Bastard," Narcisa shouted. "You dated him too? When? When did you go out with him?"

"Last winter. Until I found out he was married."

"He's married? Double shithead $#*@$% bastard," Narcisa said, half in English, half in Romanian.

My father looked impressed.

"But how did you meet him?" Sanja asked.

"How did *you* meet him?" Narcisa countered, eyeballing Sanja.

"I—uh—Ava and I..."

"We went to a bar on Gold Street and he walked in," I explained.

"Which bar?" Narcisa asked.

"The one I told you about—the one I went to when I was temping downtown," I reminded her. "What was it called?"

"Leonardi's," Narcisa cued me.

"Yes! That's it," Sanja said.

"Leonardis? Who is this Leonardis?" my father asked, puzzled.

We ignored him.

"That's where I met him," Narcisa said.

"You're kidding! What does he do, stake out women there?" Sanja asked, her face screwed up in disgust.

Eastern European women, I'd guess, although I didn't say. Everyone had their type. I did too. Frenchmen.

"What were you doing in Leonardi's?" I asked Narcisa incredulously. The last place I'd expect to find Narcisa would be in a Wall Street bar. She was far too feminine for such a testosterone-filled environment.

"You told me about it. Don't you remember? You said you can meet the bahn-CARES there."

"You told me you hate bankers. You said you only like intellectuals," I reminded her, thinking back to one of our first conversations over coffee in the U.N. delegates lounge.

"Only ones with good hands," Narcisa specified.

Sanja perked up. "Yes. The hands are important. Also shoes."

"Also the shoes," Narcisa agreed. "I couldn't find any intellectuals who wore good shoes. The only men who wear the good shoes in New York are the bahn-CARES.

As I tried to determine what it was about Eastern European women's obsession with men's hands and shoes, I saw my father surreptitiously sneak a peek at his foot to the side of the table. It was shod in large, brown loafers. Nicely polished. For his sake, I silently cheered.

"So you went down there by yourself?" I asked.

"I went to meet my friend Maria down there. She is a secretary at the Goldman Sex."

"Huh." Narcisa had a wide circle of friends. That didn't surprise me. But the fact that she hadn't shared her explorations of Wall Street wall-to-wall male banker-papered bars did. "And you met Victor there? Let me guess. Was he sitting at the bar alone?"

"She's a secretary where?" my father asked, leaning forward.

Instead of answering either of us, Narcisa took a long sip of wine. There was nothing more to say anyway. We all knew the rest of her story. We'd all been there. I'd guess even my father. Only not with a Wall Street banker-type. More likely with someone like Maria from Goldman Sex.

"Listen—there's something I meant to tell you about Victor." I cut off my father, directing myself to Sanja.

"Don't tell me you went out with that asshole too," Sanja shot back, daggers leaping from her eyes. Her English vocabulary had improved in the space of the evening.

"No! No way!" Although if Pierre hadn't been in the picture and Sanja hadn't been Victor's clear preference the day we'd bumped into him, I might have, even if he wasn't French. The smart-alecky, Jewish boy style ran a close second for me. "I bumped into him when Pierre and I went to the Met last winter."

"The opera?" my father asked. "What did you see?"

"No. The museum. I was at the Metropolitan Museum with Pierre and I saw Victor there."

"Who was he with?" Sanja asked darkly.

"That's what I wanted to tell you. He was with a woman."

"Triple bastard, *govno jedno*—piece of shit!" Sanja spit out.

"Here, here" my father pounded the table with one hand. With the other he refilled Sanja's wineglass.

"Well, yes and no," I said slowly.

"What do you mean—yes and no? We were dating when your French guy visited. He shouldn't have been anywhere with another woman. I knew there was something funny going on."

"The woman he was with looked ill," I elaborated.

"She looked what?" Sanja, Narcisa and my father all asked together in one form or another.

"She was walking with a cane. Slowly."

"Was it his mother?" Narcisa asked.

"I don't think so. She looked about his age."

"It wasn't, because he told me his mother is dead," Sanja said angrily.

"Her hair was gray. Almost white."

"Maybe his aunt or a family member?" Narcisa suggested, a glimmer of hope in her voice.

"I don't think so. Her face was young. Unlined. Except for big lines—here and here. I slid two fingers vertically down either side of my nose.

"Pain lines," my father said.

"Right."

"Maybe she was in pain from him being a cheating bastard," Sanja suggested.

"No. I mean there was more to it. Her cane..."

"Car accident?"

"No. Pierre said she looked like she had MS."

"What? What's MS?"

"Multiple sclerosis."

"The one your sweetheart's mother in France has?" my father asked.

"Yes," I said, glowering at my father. I'd told my father Pierre was no longer my sweetheart, but my father hadn't bought it.

"What is it again?" Narcisa asked.

"Multiple sclerosis. *La sclerose en plaques.*"

"Oh no. That's terrible," Narcisa said, slowly. She tapped her lower lip with one slender, beautifully groomed finger. Well-kept hands were important for both men and women in her book.

"Yes. Terrible for both of them," I said.

"What do you know about it?" Sanja asked.

"Not much. But when I visited Pierre in France in September, I met his mother."

"Could she walk?" Narcisa asked.

I shook my head. "She was in a wheelchair."

"That doesn't give the bastard a reason to cheat on his wife," Sanja remonstrated.

"I know. But I wanted to tell you there was more to it than just him cheating."

"Right. He's even more of a bastard than just a regular cheating bastard."

"Yes. and no," I said, thinking how hard it was on the caregiver of a person with a debilitating affliction. My jury was out on how to judge someone walking in those shoes. All I could conclude was that I was glad both my friends had gotten disentangled from Victor Friedman and his complicated story.

"What do you say, Papa?" I asked, turning to my father.

"I say a prayer for the bastard and for the bastard's poor wife. As for you ladies, stay away from bankers," he advised, perhaps for different reasons than the ones Sanja, Narcisa and I shared.

My father was anti-moneymen on principle. Most New York women I knew were pro-moneymen. On principle. It was a matter of survival. My grandmother had always said, "Ava, it's just as easy to fall in love with a rich man as it is with a poor one." But rich men who were married were another thing altogether; off limits, no matter how poignant their stories.

I raised my glass. "Then here's to staying away from married bankers," I proposed.

"Here's to !@#$*@#$ the *kutyazsar* bankers!" my father agreed heartily, also holding up his glass. Whatever he'd suggested doing to them, it wasn't nice.

I clinked glasses with him, Sanja, and Narcisa. From that moment on, the ice between Romania and Serbia melted and warm relations ensued, lubricated by massive quantities of Bull's Blood. There was plenty of common ground to walk on, and by the end of the evening, bankers reputations everywhere had been besmirched, married or not.

ॐ

ONE WEEK BEFORE Christmas, toward the close of the General Assembly, Madame LaForge called Narcisa out on the carpet. Apparently, the daily calls to Geneva, Paris, Bucharest and wherever else hadn't warmed the heart of our genial Haitian boss. Even at the U.N., there was a limit to how much goofing off managers allowed on the job. Narcisa had exceeded hers by anyone's standards.

First we'd heard the gentle murmur of Madame La Forge's French Haitian accent as she stood over Narcisa's desk.

"Could I see you for a moment?"

As the two of them exited the Information and Reception Unit, the heads and eyes of my colleagues swiveled in unison, looking toward the door. I hadn't been the only one aware of Narcisa's fascinating and frequent international personal phone calls. The moment had come for the whip to crack. I wondered how our mild-mannered boss would handle it.

For a person from a country where being savvy and practical were survival skills, Narcisa hadn't played her cards as well as she might have during her three month tenure at the General Assembly. With her focus on schmoozing and networking, she had neglected the actual function of doing her job. The General Assembly was now drawing to a close with the end of the year, and with it the temporary contracts of all the new hires from its September were in play.

Most of us were scrambling to find a way to extend our contract with an eye to getting through the two-year period of temporary contracts on our way to a permanent U.N. position and the protection of the Geneva-based International Civil Servants Union. The benefits that came with being a part of this group were almost unimaginable to an American. They offered dental insurance, stipends for aged parents that lived with U.N. employees, six weeks' paid vacation, with an additional one week uncertified sick leave.

To Narcisa, U.N. benefits had seemed reasonable, not even spectacular. If I had correctly understood he stories about life in Bucharest, the whole concept of a "sinecure" position was alive and well in Romania. Over one of our frequent teas at Narcisa's place, she'd informed me that Romanians of higher education automatically received jobs, frequently with the government, that required little or no actual work but were accompanied by generous perks along with high social status. These were sinecure positions. It was a concept that largely didn't exist in the United States.

"Why did you leave Bucharest, if you could have had a job like that?" I asked, knowing she'd received her Masters degree in Philology from the University of Bucharest, but had neglected to mention it on her U.N. application form for a general services job, which required applicants to hold nothing higher than a Bachelors degree.

She shrugged. "I was bored."

"I see," I said, although I didn't. I had been too busy scrambling for a job, an apartment, and a way to pay back my student loans since graduating from college. At least I was too young to worry yet about pensions or health insurance. Every word Narcisa spoke to describe her lifestyle in Bucharest before moving to Paris left me slack-jawed with wonder. Endless social gatherings, dinner parties, afternoons whiled away at various cafés, summer jaunts to the Black Sea, boyfriends, more boyfriends, lazy days spent lazing about doing what young people everywhere should be doing—hanging out. I loved hearing about it. It was like being on vacation just listening to her go on about life in Romania.

Apparently Narcisa had misjudged the good will of the United Nations and understood that she'd been handed a sinecure position in her role as a temporary hire for the General Assembly of that year.

Americans understand the term "temporary" the way they understand the word "baseball." Most of us do everything we can to move through temporaryland to "permanentsville," where health benefits, paid vacation and a pension reside. Even I, in my footloose, fancy-free late twenties, wasn't oblivious to the siren call of basic social rights.

In places like Europe, citizens actually enjoyed these rights without having to do anything to earn them. It was unimaginable, except that I'd spent a lot of time in Paris in my late teens and twenties. I knew what it was like for a doctor to make a house call, charge the equivalent of forty dollars, then waive the fee when you told him you couldn't afford it, because it had happened to me in France. In America, all three of these possibilities lay beyond our wildest dreams. It was almost like not having to pay for your college education then spend the rest of your life in a job you despised just to pay off your student loans. Here, if you couldn't pay your doctor's bill, you received a pink envelope from a collection agency for the rest of your life until your wages were garnished. As with the weather, the climate was harsher, colder, more brilliant in America than it was in Europe, which was why I was taking my U.N. job so seriously. I couldn't afford not to. That and the Puritan work ethic that had been pounded into my brain by my restless grandmother. The only time she'd ever laid off me was when I was doing schoolwork or housework. As a result, I'd developed a ferocious work ethic of my own.

"So I worked for the Commissioner for six months and did all his work for him while he renovated his villa at the Black Sea," Narcisa continued.

"Did he ever come into the office?"

"Oh yes. He saw his mistress on Mondays and Wednesdays, so he'd always come into Bucharest on those days."

"Huh." Narcisa's conversation had the frequent effect of leaving me tongue-tied. We weren't discussing a New England lifestyle here.

"What work did you actually do for him?'

"I wrote papers. Well I didn't actually write them, but I came up with the concepts and had the assistant secretary write them."

"The secretary had an assistant?"

"Yes. I was the Assistant Commissioner, so his secretary was the senior one, and the junior one was assigned to me. Well, not really assigned, but she didn't have anything to do, so I kept her busy."

Wow. No wonder Narcisa felt like she was actually working when she was calling her friends all over the world who had joined her in the Romanian diaspora. At least she hadn't been going out for coffee. The fact that she remained seated at her desk counted for something, right?

Wrong. In the eyes of Madame LaForge, the most forgiving, gentle woman with the most spectacular eye makeup I'd ever seen on a human being in a day job, Narcisa had really blown it.

As the two women re-entered the room, my colleagues and I tried to look busy while we strained our ears to hear any remnants of their hallway conversation.

"Thank you, Madame," Narcisa responded to something Madame LaForge murmured. Was that a curtsey she was making? Wow. I surreptitiously watched her through my eyelashes in case she decided to genuflect or something. Perhaps she'd make a full kowtow to our elegant, fed-up boss.

But Narcisa just returned to her desk and remained spectacularly silent for the rest of the day.

As I suspected, her U.N. career was over.

CHAPTER TWELVE

CHANGES

"*A*va. Your father—. Please call me. It's Béla." As if the tone of voice of my father's closest male friend with his thick Hungarian accent hadn't told me already, I knew something terrible had happened. Bracing myself, I dialed his number.

"Béla?"

"Aaaaeeeeee—va. Aaaaee–va."

"My father?" I knew what the news was.

"He's dead, Aeeeevaaaaa." Béla's voice rose into another wail. The Hungarians knew how to mourn. They were not New Englanders.

"Bélaaaaa. What happened?" I was no longer entirely a New Englander either. Now that my father was gone, the Hungarian mantle in the family had passed to me. I stepped up to the plate.

"It was right after lunch. I was with him at his apartment. He ate, he seemed to have indigestion, then it happened. It was fast, Ava. Évika. I'm so sorry. Your father was a great man."

"Béla, I'm so glad it was fast."

"Just a minute. Pouf. Then he was gone. Aeeevaaaa. My little Évika, I'm sorry."

"Thank you, Béla. I'm so glad you were with him."

Béla Csordás had found my father a job at Pan Am airlines where they'd both worked as accountants. Somehow he'd managed to get Zsolt in the door there, where he'd subsequently worked for fifteen years. As a result I'd been able to fly all over the world on my father's Pan Am employee pass, once I'd gotten to know him at age sixteen. I'd taken my first trip to Guatemala at age eighteen, then flown to Paris the year after to work as an *au pair*.

My father had opened the door to the whole world to me. Béla had provided the key. I had a lot to thank him for. Most of all his enduring friendship with my father, a man not easy to understand.

"The doctor was here and signed the papers. Heart attack."

"I'll be there as soon as I can. Give me thirty minutes."

"No rush, Évika. I'm at home now and your father's been taken over to the funeral home. Do you know about it?"

"I do. Nardi's is on Eighty Seventh Street, right?" I'd prearranged everything with the funeral home. It had been part of the condition of getting him accepted into the assisted living facility we had been in the process of getting him into. It had been gruesome, but my stalwart New England side had helped me move through the arrangements smoothly, my mother offering a surprising amount of help. She'd wisely advised cremation, when I'd stumbled on what kind of coffin my father would want. My father would fall apart every time I broached the subject, for which I could hardly blame him. It had been left to me to make the decisions.

Fortunately, I'd heard my grandparents go through this process. I had channeled their New England practicality and moved through arrangements as matter-of-factly as possible.

"Yes, darling. Call them first. There's no rush. You can go tomorrow."

"Bélaaaa." I was beginning to sound like the half-Hungarian I was.

"Aeeevvaaaa."

We hung up.

"Zsolt?" My mother's voice was full of tenderness. She stood in the hallway, outside the room I was in. It wasn't her habit to eavesdrop, but this was different The way she said his name told me she had guessed the news too.

"He's gone," I said to her quietly.

My mother put her hand out and stroked my arm. "I'm so sorry."

The richly ironic thought that she hadn't cared to be a part of his life for the past twenty-eight years but was now so sorry, was trumped by another one. I could see from the expression on her face, stunned and filled with emotion—New England style of course, meaning she looked a teensy bit upset—that her sorrow was sincere. Now was not the moment for irony. Death stripped us both of conflicted feelings about my father. He had been my mother's great love. I could read it on her face.

"Heart attack."

"Was Béla with him when it happened?"

"Yes."

"I'm so glad."

"Me too." He'd died in his own apartment, in the presence of one of his closest friends. It was a fine, fast end as endings go.

Before it could sink in, I got the worst over. I called Tünde. Predictably, she was hysterical, crying and wailing into the phone. My mother, to her credit, took the phone from me after a time and spent the next thirty minutes on it making sympathetic, monosyllabic responses to whatever Tünde was saying on the other end. I brought a chair in from the other room for my mother along with a glass of rosé wine to buck her up in the face of Tünde's onslaught. Both my parents liked a glass of rosé in the evenings. I wonder if they'd developed that habit together? It would be one of many questions about my father I'd ask my mother in the days to come.

The next day, my mother accompanied me to the funeral home, where I was required to identify Zsolt Fodor's remains, as next of kin. When the moment came, I was nervous. I channeled my grandfather's doctor's manner and told myself this was just like one of those funeral home visits of my childhood, when I'd accompanied him to sign the death certificate of a patient who'd moved into the great beyond.

The funeral parlor director motioned in the direction of the room my father lay in.

I looked and was startled to see the sliding door already semi-open. My first impression of what I saw inside was of the color gold. I moved closer, telling myself this was part of the cycle of life.

His skin was golden, his gray-blond hair still intact on top of his head. Unexpectedly, he was naked from the waist up, the rest of him concealed by the pine casket he lay in. Gray hair sparsely sprinkled his board, firm chest.

I couldn't believe how handsome the remains of the eighty-one year old Zsolt Fodor looked. No sign of the rage of his impending dementia showed on his face. The deep furrows on either side of his mouth, carved down from mid-cheek to jaw looked noble, rather than careworn. Altogether, he wore his final repose well.

I thought about taking his hand, but stopped. It would be cold. There was something unnatural about my father having cold hands. Everything about him had been warm. His glances, his touch, his jokes, his stories, his rages. It wouldn't make sense for our final touch to be a cold one. Instead I rested my eyes on his face and truly admired him. Frankly, his golden skin tone made him look as if someone had treated him with tanning spray. But I hadn't paid for that service, so I knew it couldn't be. I thanked him for dying well and beyond that I couldn't think. It was a good moment.

My mother and I spent the next few days going down the list of what needed to be done: arrange a funeral at his local Hungarian reformed church; give away his clothes, a job I outsourced to Tünde; figure out what to do with his apartment, which my mother and I agreed I should immediately occupy in order to lay claim.

My father had been Protestant, typical for Transylvanian Hungarians who had embraced Reformation ideals under the influence of the Saxon Germans who had settled there from the twelfth century onward. The funeral, therefore, would be more of a memorial service—Protestant style, meaning no dead bodies in caskets on display; no urns containing ashes either. My father hadn't wanted to talk about end-of-life arrangements, so in keeping with tasteful, sterile, "no blood and guts please" Protestant tradition, I'd had him cremated.

When the funeral director handed me the prosaic cardboard container holding Zsolt Fodor's remains, he mentioned several tasteful urn choices I might consider purchasing to display my father's ashes in at whatever service we were arranging for him. After eyeballing the price list, I decided to forego spending several hundred dollars on an object that would end up in the ground along with its contents, and spend what was left in my father's bank account on a trip to Transylvania instead, where I could personally usher my father's ashes into the cemetery grounds of his hometown of Kézdivásárhely, Romania. My mother concurred.

Over the next few weeks, my mother and I organized a tasteful tribute to Zsolt Fodor at the Hungarian Reformed Church in his neighborhood. Tünde came, and graciously refused to speak to me throughout the entire service, most likely blaming me for hastening my father's demise by plying him with forbidden food and copious quantities of wine over the past few months.

It was true—I had. I didn't regret it either. Our best times together had been at the dinner table, usually with Narcisa or Sanja there too, laughing, drinking and having fun. Sanja was there, but Narcisa had returned to Bucharest at the close of the General Assembly. With the end of her U.N. appointment, her G-4 international civil servant visa had run out, so she was temporarily back home, figuring out her next international move. I missed her terribly. I missed Pierre too.

"How are you, Ava?" he'd asked, sounding surprised when I'd called.

"I'm—my father died," I said, unable to say anything else.

"I'm sorry. You'd become close, hadn't you?"

"I—I—" What was the point of a long, complicated response? "Yes." As the "yes" fell out of my mouth, I realized it was true. We had become close. God had given us a short, precious window of time to get to know each other in and we had grabbed it. Largely, I'd liked what I'd gotten to know. It had been nothing short of a miracle.

"I'm so sorry. What can I do?" The sound of his voice soothed me, but also woke up something inside. My heart danced. Even months after we'd broken up, he offered himself.

"I—I don't know. I mean, nothing. I mean..." I didn't mean nothing, but I didn't know what I wanted.

"What do you mean, Ava?" Pierre had always known how to draw me out. He'd loved to parse our conversations, extract the true meaning from whatever incidental things we said to each other. I desperately missed the way we'd talked to each other. Never had I had conversations like that with anyone else. Even my father.

"I mean, I like your question." *It's so giving,* I wanted to say. but I didn't want to ask him to give me anything. It would be too painful, considering I had no idea what I could offer back. All I knew was that I missed him.

"So what can I do?" he repeated.

"Umm.... can you be on standby?" It was an unfair request. I didn't want to play games with him. But talking with him over the phone comforted me. Would I ever see him again?

"I already am," he answered.

A tiny flame shot up from the bottom of my stomach. It's source wasn't gratefulness. Nor was it admiration. It was something else.

"But what about —? I thought of Arnaud's words. Pierre had found someone else, according to him.

"What about what?"

"Are you—aren't you..."

"Am I what?"

Aren't you seeing someone? I wanted to ask. But wasn't it an unfair question? If he was, he had a right to. If he wasn't, what was I going to do about it? Pierre had his mother to take care of, and I was just weeks into my new position at the U.N. and up to my neck in sorting out my father's affairs and moving into his apartment. My life was in New York. Pierre's was in France. A relationship was out of the question.

"I've got to get off the phone now, Pierre."

"What? I thought that was my line?"

My heart panged to think of our conversation in September—the one he'd ended by saying we should hang up. Then he had. It had been a good idea.

This time, it was me who hung up. I had too much on my plate at the moment to be able to think about Pierre and what he meant to me. Yet still I thought about him. And continued to in the weeks that followed.

With a large turnout of Hungarian friends and admirers of his books from the neighborhood, Zsolt Fodor's memorial service featured lots of flowers, his two books prominently on display, a reading of two of his poems by a local Hungarian writer, huge quantities of food and drink, and a large photo album I'd put together, including lots of shots I'd taken over the past year featuring him and me enjoying happy times with Narcisa and Sanja.

"Wow—you've sure got a lot of photos of your father partying," my somewhat dubious upstate New York cousin observed, leafing through the photo album I'd put out on the refreshments table in the fellowship hall. "Who's the cute blonde here?" he asked, pointing to Sanja sitting next to my father at a café, martini glass in hand.

Sanja was a Cosmopolitan drinker. That went along with her being quite a cosmopolitan kind of woman. Not your average babe from Belgrade. Or maybe I just didn't know all there was to know about Serbia's capital. Ever since meeting her, I'd taken almost everything I'd heard about her country with a grain of salt. If Serbia had produced Sanja, there was more to that place than met the eye. Or the eyes of the world press.

"No one who'd talk to you," I said, hoping he wouldn't notice that Sanja was actually now on the other side of the room, chatting up the minister's assistant, who was tall, young and fiercely good looking. He contrasted favorably with the minister, who was equally young, but short and dumpy, with a permanently disgruntled look on his face. My father's friend Barbara, who ran a Hungarian-speaking travel agency in the neighborhood, had whispered to me that he was actually a Communist spy. That was interesting, considering the Soviet Communist regime had collapsed several years earlier, but perhaps he had needed to find a new job.

My unemployed, party-loving cousin had a point. As I leafed through the photo album of shots of my father I'd taken over the past year, I realized practically every one of them showed him with either myself or one of my girlfriends, drinking, laughing and carrying on. So what was the problem with enjoying oneself in the final year of one's life? My father wouldn't have had it any other way.

Maneuvering away from my cousin, who had already offended several of my girlfriends by offering to sleep with them or at least sleep on their couches—for free—while visiting New York City on extended party weekends, I went into the next room, where the service had been held. Approaching the altar, I began straightening up the flower arrangements on either side of it.

A small bouquet of deep red sweetheart roses caught my eye. They looked so sweet and innocent in between the larger, more traditional bouquets of carnations on either side. Going closer, I spotted a white note card tucked amongst the flowers' stems.

"Zsolti" was written on the envelope. The handwriting looked familiar, but I couldn't place it. Probably a note from Tünde. Carefully, I turned it over and saw that the envelope wasn't sealed. Looking around, I spotted only Barbara Molnar in the church sanctuary, sitting in one of the back pews with her head down. The rest of the guests were in the adjoining fellowship hall, their voices and laughter echoing distantly in the sanctuary.

If the note was from Tünde, it would be in Hungarian, but perhaps I could make out a word or two. Quickly I pulled the note card from the envelope.

"*Szeretlek*—Elizabeth" was written on it in careful, schoolgirl script.

My mother had written "I love you" in Hungarian. In my entire life, I'd never heard her refer to my father as "Zsolti." That had been Tünde's nickname for him, the typical Hungarian diminutive for Zsolt. So my father had been my mother's Zsolti. Apparently, he still was.

Carefully, I tucked the note card back into its envelope and put it back amongst the sweetheart roses. Then I inhaled their scent with a dizzying sniff as I pondered what a whole lot of things I didn't know about my father and mother. Above all, how much they had loved each other.

As I walked back into the fellowship hall I eyeballed my mother. She was someone I didn't really know. Someone it would be worthwhile to get to know. My father had loved her and had held fond memories of their time together. I was beginning to warm up to her, too.

❦

IN THE DAYS following my father's memorial service, my mother and I bonded further over cleaning up and sorting out Zsolt Fodor's affairs. Most importantly, we strategized about how I was going to lay claim to his apartment, which I'd spent a great deal of time in over the past year. I hadn't exactly been living there, but the landlords didn't live on the premises, and the superintendent liked me. It was clear that I needed to begin staying there overnight as quickly as possible to lay claim to a successor's lease.

His landlords, a pair of Sicilian brothers who owned a barber shop around the corner, already knew me. I'd gone to see them the week after my father's demise with a plea to stay on under his rent-controlled lease. Carefully, I dressed all in black—if my father was right, it would burst into color for them when I walked in, blonde hair swept up. Still, I was mindful not to wear lipstick. I was in mourning, after all, paying a call on two older men—bachelors from what I'd heard—from deeply conservative Sicily.

"We lost money on your father all these years," the younger one said fiercely, after listening to my carefully thought out argument to keep the rent at the rent-controlled rate of $400 a month.

"Whaddaya think—we're made of money? We no can afforda no renovations on the building with people like your father living there. We need to raise the rent now," his older brother added, smacking the table with the flat of his hand.

"Gentlemen, I want to stay in my father's home, where his spirit is. It's my home too," or at least I wanted it to be. "Please allow me to stay." Here I brought out my coup de grâce—the homemade tart Sanja had brought over the evening before. "I baked this for you," I fibbed slightly. "Thank you for considering my request." Someone had baked it, right?

"We no can let you stay with sucha cheapa rent. You *capisce?*" the younger one railed. Yet his eyes softened at the sight of the chocolate and pistachio tart. The older brother nudged him and they both turned their back to me for a moment.

"Okay, you go away, we talka to you tomorrow, okay? Come back tomorrow afternoon, we tella you what we gonna do," he said.

"Thank you, gentlemen. My father thanks you from the grave for considering his daughter's request," I said, bowing my head and shuffling out backwards. I'd picked up some kow-tow moves from watching diplomats greet each other at the U.N.

The next day I returned, this time with a spinach and cheese quiche that Béla's daughter had brought over. There were advantages to holding *shiva*, Protestant-style, at my father's apartment in the weeks since his death. I hadn't needed to go to the grocery store for days, only the liquor store at the corner. I was sure my father's spirit was thrilled to receive my glamorous girlfriends in his home evening after evening, sitting around regaling his memory with me over a bottle of wine.

The older brother was busy cutting an old man's hair. But the younger one took a look at me, scowled then shuffled off to the back of the shop. He returned in a minute, a long document in his hand.

"Here. This is what we do for you." He thrust it at me.

I took it. It was a new one-year lease, in my name. The rent had been raised to $700. It was a pretty hefty jump from my father's $400 rent, but still it was a pretty good number for a one-bedroom New York City apartment on the Upper East Side. Still, the tiny, nascent, pushy New York side of me couldn't help stepping up to bat.

"Can we make this $650? I've just started a new job and this is a little high for me, " I pleaded, as sweetly as possible.

"We make-a-no more discount for you. You take it or you get out," Salvatore reached for the lease, but I quickly hid it behind my back. With my other hand I picked up the quiche and presented it to him with a deep bow. Further negotiation was clearly out.

"Thank you, gentlemen. My father thanks you too. I appreciate it very much," I said, handing the quiche to him.

"We do you a big favor, you understand?"

"I do. Thank you."

"So you do us a favor."

"What can I do?" Bring over a few more baked goods?

" You no stay too long, like your father did."

"Understood." Moving away from Salvatore, I pulled a pen out and quickly signed the lease, which they had already signed, then ripped off the top copy and stashed it into my bag.

"You get outta there when you get married, *capisce?* We need to renovate then we raise the rent to crazy number like everyone else, okay?"

"I understand, gentlemen." When I get married? This was old world talk. The kind my father would indulge in too at times. It had a sort of ring to it, I had to admit.

"And one-a more thing," Salvatore said.

"Yes?"

"God rest your father's soul. He was a good man." He turned his back to me and grabbed a broom to sweep the floor. In a flash, I remembered that my father's very first job in the United States had been sweeping up at a barber shop. What was wrong with that?

"Thank you." I got out of there fast before I could blow it. Frankly, my new lease was the deal of the year in New York City. I couldn't complain.

LOVE AND DEATH

"*D*o you like this spot? I chose it for your father because he wrote about our country. He should be honored," the minister said. We stood just inside the gateway to the town's largest cemetery.

"This is right at the entrance. I'm surprised you have any places left here," I said, awed. The spot the minister pointed to was on the left side of the main path sweeping into the cemetery from the main gate. It was beyond doubt a place of honor. I turned to Narcisa next to me, who looked impressed. She nodded her assent.

"These spots are reserved for those who played an important role in our town. Your father was one of them. Are you happy with this, or would you prefer him to rest somewhere more—private?"

"No. No. He loved people. He would want to be here right by the entrance where lots of visitors pass by." How ridiculously glad he would be that I hadn't buried him in New York City. Thinking of Calvary Cemetery in Queens, the largest cemetery in the U.S., occupying miles of land along the Brooklyn-Queens Expressway to Kennedy Airport, I couldn't imagine my father there, never known well enough to be forgotten by anyone.

I had brought my father home to rest. For once, I had indubitably made the right decision. Thank God, Narcisa had returned to Bucharest when her U.N. appointment came to a shuddering halt at the end of the General Assembly. Without her, I would have never found my way to Kézdivásárhely, deep in the heart of Transylvania, and smack in the center of Romania. Earlier that day, we'd driven up to my father's hometown together from Bucharest, about one hundred miles further south.

"Then we will put him here." The minister, Reverend Szentgyeorgy, walked two paces ahead and kicked the hard earth with the toe of his boot. He shouted something in Romanian, and within a minute, a coverall-clad man emerged from the shed nearby, holding a shovel. A young girl trailed him. Wearing a dirt-strewn pink jacket, red pants and rubber boots up to her knees, she looked to be about four. Enormous brown eyes framed by long, dark eyelashes peered at us with a mixture of suspicion and curiosity as she hid behind him as he worked. They were an adorable team, not the only father-daughter one in the cemetery that day.

I looked down at the cardboard canister in my hands. It had quietly and surreptitiously made its way through customs, X-ray machines and whatever else security, nestled amongst my clothing in the large black suitcase I'd checked in. I'd had paperwork prepared, translated and notarized into both Hungarian and Romanian, but no one had asked for it. It was the moment for the remains of my father's earthly form, pulverized into fine dust, to be placed into their final resting place.

As the gravedigger broke the first clump of dirt with the point of his spade, my eyes welled. Narcisa's arm went around me, hugging me closely while the minister looked delicately away. A second man was there too, well over age sixty. He had read my father's books. He'd known my father's mother, who'd remained in the town until she died, a few years after my father had come to the United States. Eva Ambrusz Fodor had been a school teacher. I was named after her, albeit with an American spelling.

As the gravedigger's spade hit the dirt, it hit me that these were my final moments with my father's remains. They'd hung out in my closet back in New York for a few weeks, then in my suitcase on my journey to his hometown. I'd gotten used to them. Now it was time to say goodbye.

Inspiration struck. I handed the canister to Narcisa, who carefully took it. My father had liked her as much as he'd liked Sanja. Both my magical, otherworldly Balkan girlfriends had given my father much happiness in the final year of his life. It was time to join them in offering Zsolt Fodor one final, glamorous gesture.

Reaching into my handbag, I found one of two lipsticks in its zippered pocket. It was a luscious red one—Christian Dior. The case was royal blue, with gold trim. Fit for royalty, it encased my evening lipstick, not my daytime one, which was a more muted shade of dusty rose.

I turned my back to the men and pulled out the compact, opening it to use the mirror. Then slowly and carefully I applied the bright red lipstick. It contrasted nicely with the leaden-skied February afternoon. After I finished,

I snapped shut the compact, put down my handbag and turned back to Narcisa.

She looked at me wonderingly as I held out my hand for the canister.

Before the tears came again, I steeled myself to be brave, queenly. I had one final task before handing over the can. Holding it up to my face, I closed my eyes.

"Papa—this one's for you. *Szeretlek*—I love you." Carefully and slowly I kissed the side of the cardboard canister. When done, I surveyed my handiwork. The imprint of my lips was vividly outlined, even gaily. It was what he would have wanted. A final kiss goodbye.

"*Brava*, Ava." Narcisa burst out, laughing. I turned to see the three men scrutinizing me. They looked impressed. The little girl stared at the lipstick imprinted on the canister. Then she lifted her big brown eyes to me, starstruck. It was a good moment.

I handed the canister to the gravedigger, who carefully placed it on the ground next to the hole he had made. The lipstick mark was prominently displayed on its side. A perfect hit.

"I will say a few words," the minister began.

Narcisa took my hand while I bowed my head. The minister's word flowed over us, but I couldn't process them. All I could do was be with my father. This time I didn't feel like crying. My lipsticked kiss had lightened the mood.

Narcisa's hand squeezed mine and I looked up. The minister had paused and was gazing at something over my head. My eyes met Narcisa's, who smiled broadly. Strange.

"Isn't that your friend? The non-*kutyazar* one? she whispered as she nodded toward the entrance to the cemetery.

I turned and looked.

Pierre was walking toward us. *Mon Dieu.* The man I'd first laid eyes on in Père Lachaise, Paris's most famous cemetery, was now heading directly for me in another cemetery, his eyes fixed upon mine.

"Pierre!"

"Ava."

I fell into his arms, love and death swirling together in my jumbled thoughts.

"What are you doing here?" I asked, stunned. We were in an obscure market town in Transylvania, three hours north of Bucharest. Even I would have never found it, if it hadn't been for Narcisa, a native Romanian.

"I called you at your mother's place in New York. She told me what happened."

The minister looked questioningly at Pierre.

"This is Pierre Castel. Ava's boyfriend from France," Narcisa told him, rather presumptuously. Drinking in Pierre's features, I didn't correct her. It was unfathomable that he was there. Despite my mourning, my heart jumped to see him. This time, I knew what was making it leap.

"Ahh," the minister said approvingly. "I'll begin again."

"Thank you," I said. As if dams were bursting inside me, all the strain of the past few months, the entire year, began to crumble, falling off me onto the hard, packed earth.

"Nice souvenir, Ava," Pierre said. He pointed to the lip-stick mark on the canister at the side of the grave.

I laughed and Pierre's laughter echoed mine. Then the minister and his friend began to laugh too. The grave-digger and his daughter joined in, the little girl's giggles like healing music. Narcisa laughed hardest of all.

"You're a good daughter, Ava," the minister said.

It was healing balm poured on the wounds of a lifetime. I had brought my father home. And now I had sent him off in style. It could be counted on the fingers of one hand the moments in a man's life when he knows with certainty that he has done exactly what he should. Unmistakably I was in one of those moments. It was a good feeling, and even though it wouldn't last, the memory of it would last forever.

In a minute the minister concluded his remarks. It was time. Pierre squeezed my hand and I stepped forward. This time, the tears didn't just well. They spilled over as I lifted the canister and handed it to the gravedigger to place in the hole. When the first clumps of dirt hit the metal and cardboard container, I held my hand out to the little girl and smiled at her angelic face.

She gazed up at me then slowly took my hand. In that moment, I knew that the cycle of life would continue and I would be a part of that cycle, memories of time spent with my father sewn into the fabric of my being. My smile turned inward and toward the soul of Zsolt Fodor, wherever he was. He had been a worthy man to have had a hand in fashioning my tastes.

On our way back to Bucharest, we stopped at a mountain lodge where Narcisa was friends with the hotel manager. They'd gone to school together. In Romania, exchanging favors was a national pastime. Ramona had tutored her friend's son when he'd sat for an English language exam for college entrance the month before.

Before we knew it, two room keys materialized and we went upstairs. Ramona and I put our suitcases in one charming, provincial room and Pierre took the other. It had been many months since our difficult phone conversation of the September before. Had Pierre found someone else? If so, why had he traveled halfway across Europe in the middle of winter to see me?

Despite unanswered questions, I was deliriously happy to see him again. It was like being with an old friend after a long absence where we just took up the conversation again. That wasn't all it was like, either. While we talked, I took in his long, lean frame, bushy hair, and attentive brown eyes on mine. Although in mourning, I was still Zsolt Fodor's daughter. A faint tango began inside as I thought about out moments together. Unlike ones with Arnaud, they had retained their value. Was I going to do anything about them?

That night at dinner, we regaled each other with stories of my father. No pretense of seriousness or sadness prevailed, for both Narcisa and I knew my father was there with us in spirit and would have insisted on riotous revelry with frequent invocations of his name.

"What was he like?" Pierre asked Narcisa.

She thought a moment then took a sip of homemade, raw and robust Romanian red wine. "He was crazy, but in a cool sort of way," she finally said.

I laughed so hard, I choked. Zsolt Fodor had certainly been one cool crazy guy. I was proud of him, my crazy, cool father who had dazzled my friends. As we talked, we worked our way through platters of *mititei*, the fat-finger-shaped grilled meat sausages Narcisa had made for us back in New York, washed down by copious quantities of wine.

"These are almost as good as yours," I complimented her, meaning it. Narcisa's were somehow more flavorful, perhaps because she had made them and I knew how flavorful she was. She'd certainly made the final months of my father's life more flavorful.

"I have a confession," Narcisa said.

"You were in love with my father?" I joked.

She giggled. "Yes. I loved Zsolt and I still do. And Sanja's *mititei* were better than mine."

"You're telling me you thought her *ćevapčići* outdid yours?" That was indeed a confession.

"Just don't call them *ćevapčići*. They're *mititei*, okay?" And yes, hers were better. More onions."

"What are you talking about, ladies?" Pierre asked, bewildered.

"Don't talk, just eat." I pointed to the large serving tray of grilled meat in the center of the table.

"I am. These are delicious." He speared another *mititei* finger, while Narcisa and I toasted the memory of eating both Sanja's and her own delicious versions of the same dish with my father back in New York.

I was glad my father's spirit was there to take the pressure off Pierre and me. We had much catching up to do. But our conversation flowed as if we were just resuming the one we'd left off the last time we'd met. As we talked, Pierre's eyes brushed mine and lingered. When he turned to Narcisa, I returned his looks with sweeping gazes of my own until his moved back to my face. It was as if he couldn't look away.

"I'll be right back. I've got to take care of something," Narcisa told us mysteriously, as we asked for the bill. She got up and disappeared from the dining room and as we waited for her return, I looked at Pierre. It was time to find out what he'd been up to in the four months since we'd broken up.

"So did you find a woman who can cook?" I asked, getting straight to the point. Whatever his answer was, I deserved it.

"Did I what?" He studied me, puzzled.

"Arnaud told me in November that your mother told him you'd found a woman who can cook."

"What were you doing with Arnaud in November?" he asked, looking alarmed.

"Avoiding him. He came to New York to cover the French President's U.N. speech, and found me at work."

"You saw him?" He looked upset. Not like a man attached to another woman would look. My heart somersaulted.

"Yes. I introduced him to Sanja and Narcisa and they both had the same reaction."

"Don't tell me they fell for him."

"Just the opposite," I laughed. "They recognized his type right away."

"His type?"

"The opposite of yours."

"Is that good?"

I laughed. "Very good."

"For him or for me?"

"For you. And for women who like serious men everywhere." He certainly didn't act like he had a girlfriend back in France.

"I'm not sure if women do. I can't find any—" He hesitated, looking at me expectantly. His face was wistful, half-hopeful, half-guarded.

"But he told me you'd found someone new," I blurted out.

"No I didn't! What are you talking about?" He looked shocked.

"He said he called you and your mother told him you'd found someone who can cook."

Pierre stared at me.

"I did. I got fed up with *Maman* criticizing my cooking. So I found Mireille last fall. She cooks for us three times a week. Why?"

"That's it? She's your cook?" Had Arnaud deliberately misled me? Or had it been Pierre's mother who'd misled Arnaud?"

"Well—she straightens up the house too. I mean—I'm not much for laundry and cleaning." He shrugged.

"You mean, you didn't find another woman?"

"No, Mireille's enough. I'm not that bad at housework, Ava. I can do a few things." He looked affronted.

"Pierre—are you telling me you don't have a girlfriend?"

"No! I mean yes!"

"You mean what?"

" I mean—I wish I did." He looked at me hard. Except that his eyes weren't. They were soft, shining.

"You do?"

"Are you saying Arnaud led you to believe I'd started seeing someone?"

"Either Arnaud—or—or your mother."

"Not my mother. She's been asking about you."

"Asking if I'm dead or married off?" I shot back, trying to keep the vinegar out of my voice.

"No. She asked me the other day if I'd spoken to you recently."

"Pierre—your mother hated my guts. It was one of the reasons I knew we couldn't be together. Why was she asking about me?"

"There's something you don't understand about *Maman.*"

"There's a lot I don't understand about your *Maman.*"

"She respects you. She likes it when people stand up to her. It's something my father and I never figured out how to do."

So Arnaud had guessed right. Madame Castel had been impressed by our dust-up in Carcassonne the past September.

"But she called me a 'forward young woman,'" I protested.

"That's just what she said the other day. "What happened to that forward young American of yours?"

"Of yours?"

"I told her you were no longer mine." He shook his head sadly.

"Did she stand up in her chair and do a jig?"

"Ava, you don't understand my mother at all," he replied, looking at me with a strange sort of mirth in his eyes.

"You can say that again."

She said, 'That's a shame, because she was exactly the type of woman you need."

"You're kidding!" My heart leapt.

"I told you, she likes you."

"I—I'm so confused," I began.

"I'm sorry I didn't call in the past few months," he cut in. "I couldn't go back to being just friends after we—after—."

"Your receipt, sir." The waiter held a silver tray with a white slip of paper in front of us.

Pierre plucked it off the tray and opened it.

"A smiley face?" He looked up at the waiter, who smiled and put a finger to his lips. Our dinner had been paid for by the hotel manager. There was nothing to settle.

Narcisa had been our host via her friend whose son she had tutored. It was the way business was done, Romanian-style. Who could argue with it?

The second the waiter left, I took both of Pierre's hands in mine.

"I misunderstood," I said, wonderingly.

"I'm not sure I understand."

"Pierre—I thought you'd found someone else."

"No. I couldn't. What about you?"

"I couldn't either."

"So now?" he asked.

"I don't want to be just friends again either." Confusion no longer reigned in my heart. I knew exactly what I wanted. But obstacles remained.

We stared at each other a long moment, pent up electricity flowing between us. Then Pierre got up and put out his hand to me. Slowly, we exited the dining room and climbed the stairs to our rooms upstairs.

A dark, bulky object stood in front of a door at the end of the hallway. As we glided down the hall, arms around each other, I could already guess what it was.

My large, black suitcase stood outside Pierre's hotel room door. I turned to Pierre questioningly. With his hand already around my waist, he tightened his grip.

"Someone's trying to tell us something," he said.

"Narcisa?" My girlfriend was cheeky. She knew how to make a point.

On top of my suitcase, a note fluttered. I picked it up and read by the dim light of the amber sconce on the wall.

Your father's spirit was here when I opened my door." Narcisa was superstitious as well as spiritual, a trait common amongst her countrymen. "He said to tell you your bags are in the wrong room." How well she knew my father. It was exactly something Zsolt might have said.

A lipstick mark concluded the note. Seeing it there made me laugh out loud. Narcisa was a very good friend. One who thought for me when I couldn't think clearly for myself.

Pierre looked at me calmly, his room key already in the door. His eyes gleamed in the dark.

I put my hand on top of his and turned the key in the lock.

☙

BACK IN BUCHAREST, Narcisa handed us the keys to her small apartment then discreetly melted away for a few days, giving us time and privacy in which to reacquaint ourselves. The landscape had changed for both of us.

"You're going to need time to adjust," Pierre said, over coffee two mornings after our fateful reunion night. "I'll leave you alone, if you want me to." His face looked strained, not quite matching his words.

"I'm not going to need as much time as you think." The changes I faced were all good. My father's apartment was now mine. I had a new position at the U.N. with a two-year contract. The ordeal of putting my father in a nursing home no longer faced me. I was free in a way I hadn't been since returning to New York over one year earlier.

"What do you need then, Ava?" he asked, softly.

"I need you to make a plan," I said. There were challenges ahead. It was good to know Pierre's mother actually liked me, but that didn't change the fact that she was difficult and still needed him. Carcassonne was a long way from New York. But something inside me had changed. My heart was no longer unsure.

"I already have." He looked at me calmly.

"What do you mean?"

"I called you at your mother's place last week to tell you about it."

"What's happened?"

Pierre hesitated. Whatever it was, it was important, personal.

I pulled him toward me, taking his arm and wrapping it around my waist.

"I—umm—some changes happened recently."

"Your job?"

"My mother."

"What happened? Is she worse?" My words came out wrong. I meant her condition, not her personality. Okay, I meant both.

"Something surprising happened last month."

"What?" His face announced it was good. Had they found a medication to reverse the multiple sclerosis?

"My father came to visit over Christmas."

"Wow! How did that go?"

"He's still there." He looked quietly happy, his face at peace.

"He's back with her?"

Pierre nodded. "Something like that."

"But what about his girlfriend? Didn't you say he had a *copine*? I used the French word for female companion. It was a word with an alarmingly light weight to it.

"She left him right before the holidays."

"What happened?" I knew from experience, the end-of-the-year holiday season was fraught with sensitivities for less than fully committed relationships.

"She'd been getting fed up for awhile. She would complain that my father was still tied to my mother in certain ways."

"Was he?"

"Well, they never really got divorced."

"What??"

"Yes. His girlfriend had been asking him for years to finalize the divorce. Finally, she gave him a deadline. She asked him to get it done before the end of the year."

"And what did your father do?"

"Nothing."

"So she left him?"

"Yes."

"Well good for her." And good for Chantal too.

Pierre grinned. "He called my mother on Christmas Eve and they started talking."

"Let me guess. He couldn't manage without a female."

Pierre grinned. "He was managing okay. But it was more than that."

Love always was. Even if it was over, I thought of my mother's note to my father, tucked into the sweetheart roses at his memorial service. *Szeretlek* she'd written; "I love you" in Hungarian. I'd thought my parents love for each other had died long ago. Apparently not.

"Not really. Something more. He sort of never left my mother."

"Except that he did."

"Physically, but not psychically. His girlfriend was always complaining that he was still tied to her in certain ways."

"Maybe because he knew she was ill?"

"That's the short answer. But there's a longer one." Pierre's expression was complex.

"I'm sure there is." And I was. I'd finally figured it out myself over the past eight months, when my mother had accompanied me time after time to visit my father. Her visits hadn't been spurred by guilt. They'd been motivated by love.

"My father came to visit Christmas Day and didn't leave. A few weeks ago he told me he planned to stay with her until—until."

"Until when?'

"Until she no longer needs him."

I knew when that would be. Love hangs around forever. Even when it's gone, the memory of it lingers.

"How does your mother feel about it?"

"She's very happy, deep down inside. But she's already complaining about the mess in the car."

"He's leaving his stuff all over the place again?"

"Yes." He laughed. "I told her to negotiate. To tell him to keep his junk in the car and the garage and not complain if he doesn't bring it into the house."

"Is it working?"

"No." He threw up his hands, Gallic-style.

We both laughed.

"I'm so happy for you!" I squeezed his arm. It was incredible news for myriad reasons. Chantal had her husband back to nag and hound. It would provide distraction from the daily challenges fate had served her. And lessen the burden on Pierre.

"There's more."

"What?" Already the horizon had broadened. Pierre would be more free to come visit. I would be freer too to visit him in France, on my vacation. Yet summer was a long way away. I was already on leave from my job in the first months of my new position, now that the General Assembly was over. I wouldn't ask for vacation time anytime soon, not for another six months at least.

"CUNY is interested to have me come teach on a one-year fellowship."

"What? In New York?" A lot could happen in a year. The last one had shown me that.

"You heard me. Yes."

"Pierre!"

"Ava."

"Is it something you want to do?"

"For several reasons, yes."

"What are they?" I asked, putting his other arm around my waist.

"Well, it would be a good career move."

"And?"

"I like those things we ate for breakfast the last time I visited. Bagels?"

"Well, that's strong. Anything else?"

"Yes."

"What?"

"Something else." He smiled at me wickedly.

"What is it?" I asked.

"You." He buried his head in my hair.

"So, what do you think of my plan?" he finally got out, his voice muffled.

"I'm ready for it," I said. This time I was.

ROZSA GASTON studied European intellectual history at Yale, and then received her master's degree in international affairs from Columbia. In between, she worked as a singer/pianist all over the world. She currently lives in Connecticut with her family.

Black is Not a Color continues the saga of Ava's journey to self-discovery, begun in Gaston's debut novel *Paris Adieu*. Her other books include *Running from Love, Dog Sitters,* and *Lyric.* Visit her at www.rozsagaston.com to learn more.